NOBODY

GOES TO

EARTH

ANY MORE

NOBODY
GOES TO
EARTH
ANY MORE

DONALD WARD

COTEAU BOOKS
WWW.COTEAUBOOKS.COM

Edited by Edna Alford.
Book and cover design by Duncan Campbell.
Cover and interior illustrations by Leanne Flaman

Printed and bound in Canada at Marc Veilleux Imprimeur Inc.

National Library of Canada Cataloguing in Publication Data

Ward, Donald B. (Donald Bruce), 1952-
Nobody goes to earth any more / Donald Ward.

Short stories.
ISBN 1-55050-207-7

I. Title.
PS8595.A692N63 2003   C813'.6   C2003-905085-8

1   2   3   4   5   6   7   8   9   10

Available in the US and Canada from:
Fitzhenry & Whiteside

401-2206 Dewdney Ave.   195 Allstate Parkway
Regina, Saskatchewan   Markham, Ontario
Canada   S4R 1H3   Canada   L3R 4T8

The publisher gratefully acknowledges the financial assistance of the Saskatchewan Arts Board, the Canada Council for the Arts, the Government of Canada through the Book Publishing Industry Development Program (BPIDP), and the City of Regina Arts Commission, for its publishing program.

CONTENTS

CRUISE CONTROL

...by way of being an introduction and a dedication....

We buried my father recently. He died in 1990, so it was not before time. His ashes had spent the intervening years in an oak box on a shelf in the house he had grown old in, and then on my brother's piano after my mother remarried. Her wish had been to scatter his ashes on a flower bed behind their summer home at Wakaw. It seemed fitting; it was a place he loved. But somehow it never got done.

He died alone in a hospital bed on a cold night in February. I knew it could not be good news when the telephone rang at 2:00 a.m. My wife got up to answer it. I heard her speak my mother's name. After a brief interval she returned.

"Your father died tonight."

The simple statement, so long expected, still had the power to shock.

"How is Mum?"

"She has a few more calls to make, then she's going back to bed. There's nothing she can't deal with in the morning."

"She's not going to the hospital?"

"They asked her if she wanted to see the body. She said no, that's not my Norman any more."

The soul was the man, and the soul had fled.

I got out of bed and went to my study, where I dusted off the appropriate volume of *The Liturgy of the Hours* and read the Office for the Dead. I was back in bed before 3:00.

In the morning, I informed my children that their grandfather had died – Papa, as they called him, to distinguish him from their other grandfather. We all cried a little, and the elder said, "Papa's chains are made of flowers." It took a moment to sort out what she meant. That Christmas she had seen *A Christmas Carol* for the first time, and the image of Jacob Marley in his punitive chains had left a deep impression. But "Papa's chains are made of flowers" – a fairly subtle observation for a seven-year-old, I thought.

We took our leave of him, tentatively, in the chapel of a funeral home. There were twenty-one of us present: my mother, of course; my father in his much-reduced corporeal state; five of their six children with four of their five spouses; nine of their thirteen grandchildren; and a priest. My sister and I had made the arrangements, attended by a gay mortician who had coincidentally attended high school with my youngest brother. That was the first hint of farce: not that the mortician was gay, but that he was of the nobility. His own father, a belted earl, had left Britain years before to escape that nation's crippling taxes. Nonetheless, he retained his title under British law, and our mortician thus had the right to the courtesy title of Viscount. That he never used it was a tribute, perhaps, to the civilizing influence of the colonies. We all agreed that Dad would have had an interesting perspective on the situation.

Next came a memorial service arranged by the university. This was a sober affair. A brace of old friends and the president of the university paid him eloquent tribute, interspersed with mournful melodies from a string quartet.

A reception followed, held at my father's expense in the house he had frequently declared to be the only happy home he had ever known. It was part of his personal mythology. If it was meant to lend him a tragic air – as I have no doubt it was; my father was not without a taste for melodrama – it was a singular failure, for the simple reason that he laughed too much. One of the last times I saw him he was composing a piece – he never wrote essays or articles, only "pieces" – on humour in suffering. They had given him steroids the night before, for his leukæmia. "There go my chances for an Olympic medal," he remarked. More than once at the reception I started at what sounded like his laughter across the room, or his distinctive voice relating a story.

He once told me about a poet who had experienced beatific visions while going under general anæsthetic prior to surgery. Once the poet had recovered, he asked his doctor if he could undergo the anæsthetic again, only this time with paper and pencil. The doctor assented, and the same thing happened. As the poet felt himself going under, his muse descended in mists of grace. He felt himself in the hands of the angels. But when he came out of it, he found that all he had written was, "Lord, what a stink!"

In my father's mythology, you were never far from the fundamental experiences of life. Bodily functions were at least as important as high culture. He was moved equally by great art and base humour, both could bring him to tears, and frequently did. If Nature might stand up and declare to all the world of Brutus, "This was a man!" it would speak with like affection of Falstaff, who "lards the lean earth as he walks along." My father loved in equal part "the noblest Roman of them all" and "the veriest varlet that ever chewed with a tooth." For virtue was meaningless without vice, tragedy without farce, gravity without humour. It was pointless to be serious if you couldn't laugh.

It was disorienting not to see him among his friends at the reception. It was more than disorienting; my reference points were skewed. The scene before me was years out of date. These people – an eclectic assortment of Canadians ranging from plumbers to professors, artists to administrators – had frequented my parents' home when I was a child. I remembered dinner parties, casual visits, raucous voices echoing up to my bedroom on New Year's Eve. There was always company at Christmas and Thanksgiving, and frequently throughout the rest of the year. But as my father's illnesses diminished him, his world grew smaller. He never stopped laughing that I remember, but he shed friendships like leaves in the fall. He became suspicious of anything he could not control.

Toward the end of his life, my siblings and I contrived an elaborate system of denial to deal with the fact that our father was not entirely the accomplished professional he presented to the world; that he was, in fact, a fallible and sometimes frightened man who knew his days were numbered and was not above using that knowledge to get his own way. His inflexibility on domestic issues, his obsessive need for privacy, his impatience with those who opposed him, his selfishness, and, above all, his utter dependence on my mother; all were explained away in terms of his various illnesses and the obdurate circumstances of a life forged in the crucible of a world-wide depression and a war. And indeed, much can be forgiven a man who has in a relatively short life been afflicted with a congenitally defective heart, a bleeding ulcer, diabetes, and leukæmia, let alone six children, a widowed and abusive mother, and dependent in-laws. It's a wonder that he ever laughed at all.

The French novelist Germain de Staël asserted that "to understand is to forgive." Perhaps it is in France, though I rather doubt it. In my experience, to understand is more often to accuse. I did not truly understand my father until one day I experienced one of those haphazard epiphanies that are occasionally visited upon the second sons of accomplished men. I had recently bought a car, and I was mentioning among my brothers the convenience of cruise control: you didn't have to worry about maintaining an even pressure on the accelerator, or exceeding the speed limit; on long trips you could even sit cross-legged behind the wheel. My father interrupted to say that he would never order cruise control on a car, and would not use it if it came as standard equipment. It seemed a strange kind of eccentricity, even for my father, like not accepting a present simply because it wasn't your birthday. I asked him why, and he replied, "I like to be in total control at all times." It struck me then that he was talking about more than his car. It was the general philosophy on which he based his life: to be in control of all things at all times.

Of course, it failed him. He could not see himself shrinking with his world – or perhaps he did, and didn't care – but in the end there was only his house, his family, and himself, and sometimes not even his family.

The death of a parent is always a shock, however long it has been expected. After the initial period of mourning, of acknowledging cards and answering letters, there is a time of anger. For there is always unfinished business, things you should have said or done, intentions unfulfilled. "Children begin by loving their parents," Oscar Wilde observed. "As they grow older they judge them; sometimes they forgive them." And after they die, childhood memories spring fully formed from what you had thought was a forgiven, if not a forgotten, past: times you had to apologize because he refused to, times you were deliberately misunderstood, times he subsumed his frustrations and his fears in anger and impatience. It shouldn't hurt to be a child, but it always does. Some people never get over it, and their demons pursue them to the grave.

My father was not without his own demons. He didn't take them all with him, but generously left a few behind, orphaned but still potent. One of these took the form of a rather conventional Christian soul who wanted to be buried. It is said that funerals are for the living, but I suspect it is the dead who demand them. They don't want to be left lying about on shelves and pianos, however neatly packaged. They want to be disposed of. They want closure. It was in response to this gentle but relentless prodding that the three of my father's children who remain in the city he loved and died in undertook to fulfil his final wish.

The place was never in question, but the method gave rise to some perplexity. My mother no longer wanted him scattered over the flowerbed behind her summer home; the prospect, once a promise of comfort, was now an occasion of alarm. Similarly, we couldn't see ourselves simply scattering him about the forest, or tossing him into the water. For one thing, we didn't know exactly what we were dealing with. Were the fires of cremation so thorough that there would be no unpleasant surprises when we opened the funeral vessel? None of us was convinced of it. My brother, in fact, confessed to having shaken it and heard something solid rattling about inside. What could it be? Teeth? A bone fragment? His artificial heart valve?

Eventually, we decided on the place: a natural clearing in the forest, halfway up the winding hill that defined the southern shore of Wakaw Lake. We had all played there as children. It was well away from our remarried mother's summer home, but close enough that she could pay her respects if she wished.

I had recently been given two bur oak seedlings, so I suggested that we dig a hole to bury the ashes and plant one of the trees above them. Everyone thought that was a fine idea. My sister, who is not one to leave anything to chance, phoned a tree nursery to inquire whether human remains might be injurious to the seedling. She didn't like the idea of our father inadvertently poisoning the living thing we had chosen to mark his resting place. Neither did I, but I do wonder what went through the mind of the man she spoke with.

"Woman wanted to plant a tree on top of her father," I imagined him saying to his co-workers, stalwart souls in overalls, with dirt under their fingernails.

"Is he dead?"

"He's ashes. She wanted to know if he'd burn the roots of her seedling. It's a bur oak."

There was a pause while each of the assembly visualized the ragged bark and the lobed leaves of this most modest of oak trees, then: "So what did you say?"

"What do I know? I told her to go ahead."

So we went ahead. Having agreed on the place and the manner of interment, all that remained to decide was the time. We couldn't leave it too late or the young tree would not have a chance to establish a root system before the heavy frosts, but mid-September was the earliest we could all get away. My brother and I went up the evening before with the ashes and sufficient beer to get us through the night. But there was a bitter wind off

8

the lake, and our intention of reminiscing in an alcoholic haze by the campfire was soon abandoned in favour of a more civilized retrospective from the comfort of the sleeping cabin, which was itself a sort of monument to my father. Built in the mid-1960s to accommodate an expanding family, there was not a right angle in the place. He had used the minimum of materials and the dullest possible tools, yet the structure was still standing after nearly forty years.

My sister arrived the following afternoon, and we proceeded to the appointed place with a tree, a spade, a screwdriver, and our father's ashes. I began to dig. Immediately, the spade hit something hard and brittle. I turned it up. It was broken glass. An ill omen, I thought – but, on reflection, perhaps not. Of the five summer cottages that made up our stretch of beach, at least two had been home to dedicated recreational drinkers over the years, and the evidence of their hobby was scattered throughout the forest. Only the summer before my wife had unearthed an ancient six-pack which had been hidden in the brush behind our well, its owner gone to his grave probably still trying to remember where he had stashed it.

But it wasn't a beer bottle I had turned up with my spade. It was clear glass, and from the shards that remained it looked as if it had once contained some kind of patent medicine. It was clearly from the period before our tenure at the lake; I had seen such bottles in antique shops, but never in stores.

Another shovelful turned up more glass, then a rusted can. I kept on digging, and exposed more bottles and cans, as well as some twisted bits of metal, their original function obscured by rust. It began to dawn on us why trees had never grown in this part of the forest. It wasn't a natural clearing at all.

"It's a midden!" my sister exclaimed.

"A midden?" I inquired. My familiarity with the word was owing solely to "Prologue," a dramatic poem by W. H. Auden:

"Oh where are you going?" said reader to rider,
"That valley is fatal when furnaces burn,
Yonder's the midden whose odours will madden,
That gap is the grave where the tall return."

Given my knowledge of Auden and his times, his compassion for the dispossessed and his unerring eye for the crimes and weaknesses of humankind, I had always associated the word with Nazi death camps, imagining heaps of bones and ashes and a sickly smell, not so much of death as of the pure evil of the National Socialist agenda. It seemed rather a lurid term to describe what had clearly been a previous owner's garbage dump.

Subsequent research has revealed that the word came to us through Middle English from the Scandinavian *mog*, meaning "muck," and *dynge*, meaning "heap." This pleasant space where my siblings and I had whiled away the halcyon days of youth was in fact a muck heap. We were burying our father in a muck heap. Oddly, it did not occur to us to look for another spot.

My brother fetched a box in which to carry away the cans and bottles and broken glass. Then he took the screwdriver and opened the funeral vessel. Early on, we had decided to proceed with a minimum of ceremony, as that was how our father had directed his life and our upbringing. Nonetheless, there was a hush as my brother slowly removed the four Robertson screws by which the base was attached to the carved oak box. I didn't know what was going through his mind, or my sister's, but all I could think about was the dreadful rattling we had heard when he shook the box, and I was convinced, for some reason, that we were going to find a fragment of jawbone with a couple of molars embedded in it.

As it turned out, the ashes were contained in a sturdy plastic bag, and the rattling was caused by a card on which had been written the name of the deceased, the date of cremation, and the names of the funeral director and the crematorium. I thought it would make a nice remembrance, modestly framed, perhaps hung alongside a photograph of the deceased. I turned the card over, expecting some dignified graphic or a photograph of the funeral chapel.

Baycrest Pantyhose, it said.

We buried it with the ashes.

N one of us knows what happens to us after we die. Speculation and religious faith have offered a million answers, none of them definitive. As the apostle Paul said, we see in a mirror, dimly. It is a striking metaphor, and particularly apt for my father. I sometimes think what killed him was not his abused and worn-out flesh, but the fact that he could no longer dominate, or even much influence, the people and events around him. He was finally on cruise control.

He was whisked away in an ambulance one day, and I didn't have a chance to say good-bye. Thirteen years later, then, I dedicate these stories, in gratitude and love,

To the Memory of my Father
Norman Ward
1918-1990
REQUIESCAT IN PACE

THEOLOGY

William had dyed himself blue and was dancing naked around a bonfire at the bottom of the garden. Dorothy was mortified, but Sonal told her it could have been worse.

"I don't see how."

"He could have an erection."

"Oh my God! What would I tell the neighbours?"

"What have you told them so far?"

"Nothing. They haven't asked. I mean, they can't *not* have noticed, but so far they've been remarkably quiet."

"That one looks rather interested," said Sonal, pointing to a mound of orange hair above a pair of pale eyes peering over the fence down by the compost heap.

"Buried three husbands," said Dorothy, almost wistfully.

It was a bright morning in May. The low sun

13

streamed through the bay window onto the polished oak table and the fluttering black surface of the coffee. Sonal lifted her cup and took a sip, squinting the while into the garden. It was a scene that her hostess had often captured on canvas – *sans* William, of course – for Dorothy was an artist of respectable, if cloying, achievement. Roses and buttercups, hedges and fruit trees, a girl reading verse 'neath a stately elm: these were the devices of her expression. Her paintings appeared more on greeting cards and calendars than in galleries, but that translated into cash, and Sonal had to admire that.

"Ram asked me to have an affair with him once," she said.

"But Ram's your husband."

"Yes," said Sonal, unsurprised.

"Why would he ask you to have an affair with him?"

"Not him, William. Ram asked me to have an affair with William."

"*Your* husband asked you to have an affair with *my* husband?"

"Not exactly. He just said that if I ever felt it necessary to have an affair, he would take it as a personal favour if I had it with William."

"But why?"

Sonal shrugged, her shoulders padded and eloquent. "He looked so hungry."

"It doesn't hurt him to go hungry now and again," said Dorothy, managing in thirteen syllables to impart her entire theology of marriage.

"A starving man will eat anything," Sonal responded, managing in nine syllables to impart William's.

Her attention returned to the garden as William whooped around from the far side of the fire, knees high, belly bouncing. He had a wooden staff in one hand, and might have resembled a drum major had he not been naked and blue and fifty pounds overweight.

"How long has he been out there?"

"He started at sunrise."

"It can't be good for him, four hours of intensive exercise after fifteen years of practising law. Still," Sonal added thoughtfully, "he's probably taken off a bit of weight."

"You always look on the bright side," said Dorothy, but Sonal didn't believe she meant it. Neither did Dorothy. The two women knew each other intimately but not well. Dorothy, if asked, would have suggested that the only thing they had in common was the fact that their husbands shared a law practice. Sonal, unasked, frequently declared that the only thing they had in common was gender, and sometimes even that was uncertain.

"Dorothy," said Sonal, as William disappeared once more behind the flames, "are you orgasmic?"

"Orgasmic?"

"Do you and William ever fall together with lusty cries and redefine the parameters of your relationship?"

"Well, really!"

Dorothy busied herself wiping the spotless table, her long white arms catching the sunlight almost like mirrors. William had once told Ram (who told Sonal, for they kept nothing from one another) that Dorothy was a tiger once you got a couple of drinks into her. Sonal found it hard to credit. "I've never known Dorothy to have even one drink," she told Ram, "let alone two." "According to William," Ram had replied, "that is precisely the problem." Even so, she was a good-looking woman – not beautiful, like Sonal, but that spare, bleached look of the northern European certainly had its admirers.

Dorothy poured herself another cup of coffee. She rarely had more than one, and knew she would regret it.

"I've called the police," she said. "I can't think why they haven't come."

Sonal raised one elegant black eyebrow.

"It's not just that he's naked," said Dorothy defensively. "He's *blue!*"

"I'm brown," said Sonal reasonably.

"Millions of people are brown, Sonal. No one is blue."

"The Lord Shiva is often depicted as blue."

"My husband is Christian Reformed, not Hindu."

And therein, thought Sonal, lay at least part of the problem, though in point of fact she knew that William was not so much Christian Reformed as simply reformed, for he had been a fairly dedicated pursuer of chemical visions until he met Dorothy.

"The Picts dyed themselves with woad and pranced about a good deal. Perhaps William is rediscovering his ancestral roots."

"Who were the Picts?"

"A tribe of ancient Britons."

"William's ancestry is Irish."

"You were all Indo-Europeans to start with," said

Sonal, pouring herself a third cup of coffee. "Do you mind if I smoke?"

Dorothy made a despairing little gesture that Sonal took for assent. She produced a cigarette from a silver case and touched a flame to it with a gold-plated lighter.

"You should take up smoking, Dorothy. It would give you something to do with your lips."

Dorothy had been pursing them. Sonal rounded hers to blow a perfect smoke ring that rolled lazily toward the window and destroyed itself against the glass. The orange-haired neighbour, she noted, was tossing firewood over the fence. One birch log narrowly missed William as he leapt over the blaze with an agility Sonal would not have expected.

"Why don't you paint him?" she suggested. "The bottom of the garden is more or less your *œuvre,* isn't it?"

Dorothy seemed almost to consider it for a moment, but then she shuddered. She would not violate the purity of her æsthetic.

"Have you called the office?" Sonal asked.

"What would I say?"

Sonal took a cellular phone from her purse and punched in her husband's private number. "Hello, Ram? Sorry to bother you at work, darling, but something's come up....Yes, I'm calling from there...I'm looking at him, as a matter of fact....He's dyed himself blue and he's dancing naked around a bonfire at the bottom of the garden....That's *exactly* what I told Dorothy....No, it'll take hours to wash him pink again. I think he's used food colouring....Would you, darling? Thanks, I'll tell Dorothy....Love you, too. Bye."

"What *exactly* did you tell me?" Dorothy demanded.

"That you should have expected something like this."

"Expected it? What do you mean?"

"Don't be shrill, Dorothy." Sonal ground out her cigarette in a saucer and looked at her watch. "I have to show a house. Would you like me to come back afterwards?"

"What did Ram say?"

"He'll have the secretary reschedule William's appointments as far as possible, and he'll handle any other clients himself."

"That's kind of him," said Dorothy through clenched teeth. The sentiment was a result of rigid social training, the clenched teeth a result of the second cup of coffee and her general disapproval of everybody she could think of at the moment.

"It's a partnership, dear. Even lawyers are capable of helping out a friend. Of course, Ram will bill him for it."

Sonal was back before noon. "I could have gone to the office," she explained, "but for all intents and purposes I carry my office in my briefcase these days. Do you mind if I use your telephone?"

"Don't you have a cellular phone?"

"Can't connect a modem to a cellphone, Dorothy." Sonal opened her slim black attaché case and took out a slimmer black laptop computer. "What's been happening?"

Dorothy nodded toward the window. William stood motionless before the fire, his blue belly depending from his torso like an inverted question mark. His eyes were closed, his hands upraised in an attitude of benediction. His lips were moving.

"He's been like that ever since Vicky left," said Dorothy.

"Who's Vicky?"

"The neighbour. She was tossing firewood over the fence."

"Buried three husbands," Sonal recalled, expertly detaching the cord from the telephone and plugging it into the back of her computer. The machine emitted a polite welcoming beep. "I don't see her there now."

"William drove her off."

"What, physically?"

Dorothy looked away.

"You're holding something back, Dorothy."

"I'm so embarrassed!"

Sonal entered a series of codes into her keyboard and watched the responses on the screen. "They've accepted the offer," she said conversationally. "That's...let me see...a commission of nearly nine thousand dollars. Before expenses and tax, of course. Still, it's not bad for three days' work. And Ram says you can't make any money in real estate....Why are you embarrassed, Dorothy?"

"It may be a Pictish custom," said Dorothy, "for able-bodied females to collect wood when the warriors decide to prance around a bonfire. As long as that was all Vicky was doing, I couldn't see much harm in it. It was revolting, of course, the attention she was paying to William, but Vicky's like that. Shameless. After she'd added her logs to the fire, though, she started to...you know...."

"No," said Sonal, "I don't."

"She started to undress."

Sonal lifted her long, dexterous fingers from the keyboard. "So you called the police again."

"Wouldn't you?"

Sonal smiled, but said nothing.

"It was terrifying," Dorothy went on. "She was *everywhere*. I mean, most people jiggle when they're naked – even you, I'll bet – but Vicky just sort of *erupted* in every direction at once, like a frenzied sack of jelly. I'd never seen anything like it. William took one look at her and stopped dead."

There was a pause.

"And then?" Sonal prompted.

Dorothy took a deep breath. "He went into a crouch. Then he sort of...*growled*...and he started, not exactly hopping, but *bounding* at her. Vicky moved back, but William kept advancing, and finally she just screamed and jumped back over the fence."

"Naked?"

"Down to her eyelashes and wig. Did you know she was wearing a wig?"

"It was fairly obvious," said Sonal.

"It came off when she jumped the fence," said Dorothy. "William burnt it."

Sonal returned her hands to the keyboard and her gaze to the screen, where her attention remained for some time.

"I don't suppose Ram would handle his partner's wife's divorce," said Dorothy.

"Don't be ridiculous," said Sonal. "Ram's a lawyer. He'll do anything for money. But don't you think you're being premature?"

"You can't expect me to go on living with him after this."

"On the contrary, I expect you'll find living with him much more interesting after this."

"I don't see how it could be anything but a constant embarrassment."

"Oh, Dorothy," said Sonal, losing patience at last, "you don't understand the first thing about this male stuff, do you?"

"What do you mean?"

"Men are *primitive*, Dorothy. They only want three things in life: food, sex, and the illusion of a higher purpose. You can't deprive them of any one of those without its showing up some place else. If there's no heat in the marriage bed, you can't blame him for building a fire at the bottom of the garden."

"Must you equate *everything* with sex?"

"I don't," said Sonal. "It just seems that way to someone who equates *nothing* with sex."

"Then why did he drive Vicky away? You said it yourself: a starving man will eat anything."

"Maybe he loves you," said Sonal, glancing at her watch. "Why don't we do lunch?"

"But..." Dorothy gestured toward her husband.

"William will keep," said Sonal, closing the lid of her computer. She took her friend by the arm and led her out to the silver Volvo Ram had bought her when she passed her real estate exams.

They went to a restaurant near the university and sat upstairs by a wall of windows that overlooked a green expanse of playing field where young men and women could be seen disporting themselves in aerobic activity. A strict vegetarian, Sonal ordered the vegetable stir-fry with a small glass of beer. Dorothy was a meat eater and a tea-totaller, but Sonal persuaded her to have a virgin cæsar with her steak sandwich. It would be interesting, she thought, to slip some vodka into it while Dorothy was in the ladies' room. She always had two or three miniatures in her purse. In real estate one never knew when a drink, celebratory or compensatory, might be necessary.

"It's so absurd," Dorothy was saying.

"Absurdity is a large part of a man's life, Dorothy. I should have thought that would be obvious to anyone married to William."

"Well, of course," Dorothy conceded, "William is absurd. But that's just William."

Sonal shook her head. "It's men, Dorothy. Fat or thin, ugly or handsome, clever or dull, cultured or coarse, strong, weak, sensitive, crude – in the end they're all ruled by that insatiable tube of witless flesh between their legs."

"Can't they do something to work it off?"

"They can, and frequently do."

"I mean something *wholesome.*"

"What, like dancing naked at the bottom of the garden?" Sonal was lighting a postprandial cigarette. She allowed herself six a day, and this was her third.

"Add a fire and take off their clothes..." she said, indicating the young people in the playing field across the way, but Dorothy was having none of it.

"After thousands of years of evolution," she said, "I can't believe that things are still so primitive between men and women."

"Men may have changed in appearance since *homo erectus,*" said Sonal, "but they're quite different from us, you know."

"That's what William says. He says they can't help it. He says they're not wrong, they're just different. Men."

"But you don't believe him."

"This is good," said Dorothy, polishing off her cæsar. "D'you think I could have another?"

"Certainly," said Sonal.

.

Dorothy took her friend by the arm as they left the restaurant, not so much out of affection as out of sudden and inexplicable necessity.

They found William kneeling in supplication before the fire as they sat once again at the kitchen table. It seemed to Sonal that Dorothy's gaze was less censorious than before. One could almost imagine she was viewing her husband with a certain tenderness. The illusion was soon shattered.

"Here come the police," said Sonal.

"About time," said Dorothy.

The roof lights of the cruiser were just visible above the fence. They came to a halt at the end of the yard, and a man in blue got out. He watched William for some time. William watched the fire. The policeman shook his head slowly and got back into his vehicle. The lights moved on down the alley.

"Is that all he's going to do, shake his head and leave? D'you know, I wrote City Hall during their pay dispute last year. I told them we couldn't expect to have a competent police force if we weren't prepared to pay them adequately. And this is the thanks I get!"

"I'm sure the officer is unaware of the zeal with which you defended his interests," said Sonal. "But you might wait a second before you condemn him. He probably wanted to assess the situation before he did anything."

Dorothy rolled her eyes. She was of strict Calvinist stock and granted no one a second chance willingly. Then the front doorbell rang. Dorothy went through and opened it. A large and alarmingly young police constable inquired if she was the woman who had complained about a man dancing naked around a bonfire at the bottom of her garden.

"I am," she said.

"Do you know who he is?"

"He's my husband."

"I see." The policeman frowned. "Has he offered you violence?"

"You saw him," said Dorothy.

"What I saw," said the officer, "was a naked blue man kneeling by a fire at the bottom of what turns out to be his own garden."

"He was dancing before you came," said Dorothy.

"Dancing," said the policeman, writing in his notebook.

"Violence is inherent in the situation," said Dorothy.

"Violence is inherent in *every* situation," said the policeman, with the air of one who had seen more than Dorothy could imagine. "Unless and until violence is committed, there's not much I can do."

"But surely it's illegal, what he's doing!"

The officer considered. "He might run into trouble with an open fire, but it's not untended, and none of the neighbours has complained."

"But he's naked!" Dorothy protested. "He's blue!"

"It's peculiar," the officer allowed, "but I doubt if it's illegal. He's on private property, and as long as he's not offering offence to the public, he's probably within his rights."

They had moved through the house to the kitchen. William had resumed dancing. The party were treated to a flash of plump blue buttock as he high-stepped around to the far side of the fire.

"I call that indecent exposure," said Dorothy.

The policeman shook his head. "On the street, maybe, or in a public park. But in order to be offended by him, you've got to walk up to the fence and look over it. If we arrested all the people who went naked in their own back yards, the cells would be full and the hot tubs would be empty."

"Are you telling me there's nothing you can do?"

"There might be grounds for having him committed," the officer allowed. "Is he irrational?"

"*Look* at him!"

"I mean, has he been uttering disconnected sentences, or talking to people who aren't there?"

"I wouldn't know," said Dorothy. "I haven't spoken to him."

"You haven't –"

"She's been distraught," Sonal interrupted. "Surely you can understand that."

"And you are...?"

Sonal handed him a business card. "Do you own your own house?"

"Yes."

"A two-bedroom bungalow in College Park, I'll bet. Maybe it's time you considered something larger."

"On a constable's salary? You've got to be kidding."

Sonal shook her head in practised disbelief. "Too many people make that assumption without investigating the possibilities. You'd be surprised what you can afford when you start looking."

"Could we get back to William, please?" asked Dorothy, managing to purse her lips and clench her teeth at the same time.

"Dorothy, you look like a serial killer."

"I look," Dorothy corrected her, "like a woman who has never been able to live up – or should I say, live *down* – to her husband's expectations of her. I look," she said, her voice rising, "like a woman whose husband has wanted her to be someone she isn't every day for the past twelve years. I look," she continued, her voice rising further, "like a woman who has been expected to remain tolerant and forgiving while her husband has attempted to indulge every appetite he could develop. I

26

look," she concluded, her voice reaching a plateau, "like a woman whose husband has humiliated her in a thousand small ways and now expects her to accept with equanimity the fact that he's dyed himself blue and is prancing naked around a bonfire at the bottom of the garden! Well, I've had enough! I want him stopped, I want him arrested, and then I want him shot!"

"I'll go out and talk to him, shall I?" said the policeman.

"You do that," said Dorothy, poking his broad chest with a sharp forefinger, "and don't come back until he's either pink and clothed or under arrest!"

"This is a side of you I haven't seen before," said Sonal.

"You shut up!"

Sonal threw her head back, and her body shook as she gave herself uninhibitedly to laughter. "Marvellous!" she said. "Marvellous!"

"I told you to shut up!"

"Oh, Dorothy! Don't you see, it's working!"

"What do you mean!"

"William," said Sonal, catching her breath with a smoothly delicate hand on her breast, "has finally managed to arouse your passion!"

But he hadn't aroused her passion, he had made her lose control, and she wasn't sure she could forgive him that. All her life she had been the good one, the obedient one; she had done everything according to the rules, rationing her pleasures lest they become clamorous, lest she overbalance and plunge into that deep well of wickedness she felt seething sometimes just beneath her skin, in the very muscles of her unforgiven flesh. She had saved William's soul for him, and perhaps his body, too, for he had been well on the way to death by self-indulgence when they met, and in return what had she been offered? Oblations to appetite, insults to dignity, and without even the compensation of children.

Well if William couldn't help it, thought Dorothy, neither could she.

"I'm going to kill him," she said, but when Sonal went off into peals of laughter again Dorothy stopped, as if struck. For a tenth of a second, perhaps less, she saw her friend clearly, as she had never seen her before. It was as if a great darkness had been drawn aside. It was an epiphany, of sorts. She saw that Sonal was not really laughing, but crying, and she understood that she couldn't help it, either. None of them could.

At the bottom of the garden, William and the policeman were deep in conversation. One might have expected the constable to be talking and William to be nodding his head, but it was the other way around. A half-hour later they were still at it. By the time Dorothy had set up her easel and primed a canvas, William was dancing around the fire again, and the constable was marking time with two sticks.

The painting was like nothing she had done before. William and the constable were down by the fire, the flames licking the darkening sky. Orange-haired Vicky was slinking behind the fence. Sonal dominated the foreground, her mouth opened wide to reveal perfect white teeth, head thrown back in laughter. In the midst of them stood Dorothy, thin and pale, exhaustion apparent in every line of her body.

The painting was never exhibited, although now and again Dorothy brought it out and they looked at it together. It was a year later that fat blue trolls began appearing in her pastoral scenes. The unimaginative called them cute, sometimes sad. Others were unsettled by their presence amid the roses and the buttercups, although they couldn't have said why. Their mistake, perhaps, was in focusing on the troll instead of on the girl who sat beneath the stately elm. There was something about her aspect – the tension in her limbs, the hands that held the book – that wasn't quite right. Only those who looked very closely could see that she was probably blind.

Things never really got better between them, William and Dorothy. But they got no worse, and that was something.

THE NAME OF HIS LONGING

T hey met in church, of all places, he alone of his family a believer, or, at least, a penitent. He was always unaccompanied. He had heard her in the Sunday choir and thought her voice pleasant but unremarkable. He had never really looked at her. He supposed she had never really looked at him. He always sat in the gallery on Sundays.

For weekday Masses they followed the older rite, kneeling at the elevation of the Eucharist, eyes downcast in reverence. But instead of contemplating the realms of grace that Tuesday morning, he found his downcast eyes contemplating the curve of her thigh in the pew ahead. Thus contemplating, he was granted a brief epiphany of the beauty of all women, and of this woman in particular. He stared at his hands, willing them not to reach out and caress her. His hands obeyed, but his imagination could not.

The dilemma was not new to him. His confessor had advised him to give thanks at such times: thanks for the radiance of humankind, thanks for the relentless logic of sexuality, thanks for the divine humility that allowed woman and man to come together in joyful imitation of their creator. But he had never felt quite so thankful as this.

At the sign of peace she turned to him with that expression of bland piety which the shy and the cynical alike reserve for such occasions. Then, with a shock of recognition, she grasped his hand in both of hers. "May the peace of Christ be with you," she said, smiling broadly, her dark eyes glowing with the light of gratitude and faith. She meant it, apparently.

He was startled, not so much by the ardour of her greeting as by the realization, distant but unequivocal, that he had expected nothing less. He could offer no cause for it, unless, against all probability, she had felt his thoughts against her flesh and accepted them as an expression of love. Experience and common sense militated against any such interpretation. He was equally startled when her expression turned to one of pain, as if a fleeting grief had touched her with his hand, and then annoyance as she read the confusion on his face.

"Peace be with you," he responded, but it sounded insincere. For the first time in six months he didn't take communion. He sat in the pew staring dumbly at the floor, as if he might read there some clue to a mystery which had not yet named itself. When he looked up, she was gone.

"Are you all right, David?" It was the parish priest, leaning solicitously over the pew.

"I didn't take communion."

"I can give it to you now, if you like."

"No," said David, "thank you." Then, more decisively: "I'm not prepared."

"I'm always here," said the priest. But suddenly no one was there, and David walked home to the empty house as the first heat of the day descended to the street.

He removed his shoes at the door, as his mother had taught him. The children followed their own mother's example, donning and removing their footwear according to whim, although David was always expected to know where they were.

"Daddy, where are my thoos?"

"Your thoos?"

"His shoes, David. You know perfectly well what he means. Have you seen my red pumps? I know I took them off in the kitchen."

"I left my shoes right here. I suppose Dad's been tidying them away again!"

The twins had been more than normally creative with their Cheerios that morning, and David picked up a dozen soggy little Os on the bottoms of his socks between the kitchen doorway and the sink. By the time the dishwasher was on its first cycle, his socks were so sticky that he had to take them off. Then he mopped the floor.

She was a worker, unpampered: that much was obvious from the firmness of her grip and the roughness of her hands. A nurse, perhaps. A teacher. Maybe even a home-maker, he thought, contemplating the roughness of his own hands. But as he wrung out the mop and emptied the bucket into the downstairs toilet, he chided himself for assigning her such a traditional role. His experience of women had been anything but traditional. Journalist, academic, executive: he had grown up believing that these were normal occupations for mothers and aunts, and he had assumed that the preponderance of women in lower-paying, relatively powerless positions was the temporary aberration of an otherwise enlightened society. He was still not entirely convinced to the contrary, for he had a deep need to believe in the essential justice of the human condition. When he went home each morning to make the beds and clear up the breakfast dishes, he comforted himself with the thought that his family was, or should be, the norm. It was the rest of the world that was out of balance.

He went upstairs to make the beds: Morgan's first because he had made Jeremy's first yesterday, and the boys kept careful track of such things. Maria, their precocious ten-year-old, was theoretically old enough to make her own bed, although she rarely did. Like her mother, she would cheerfully have climbed into a truck-load of flannel every night as long as it was clean. David was by nature a fastidious man, but years of living with someone who treated the marriage bed more as a garment depository than a place of quiet repose had led him into sloppy habits. Most mornings he was content simply to arrange the bedclothes in a semblance of order. Today, for some reason, he stretched the sheets over the mattress and layered the blankets and fluffed the pillows as if he were expecting the laundry police. He even picked up Rachael's pyjamas and folded them under the pillow next to his own.

He dressed for work in loose-fitting jeans, a light cotton shirt, and a tri-coloured tie in pastel shades reminiscent of the desert at twilight. It was not very different from what he had worn to Mass, except for the tie. And fresh socks, of course. A summer jacket of expensive shot silk — a gift from Rachael — completed the ensemble. Consulting his image in the cheval-glass at the foot of the bed, he noted with approval that he had achieved that look of casual elegance that impressed some clients and reassured others. Not that he would be seeing any clients today, but it was important to maintain one's image.

Another image rose before him as if he were drawing it on the mirror, obliterating his own features with hers: the strong chin, the spattering of freckles across the nose. Her hair, he recalled, had framed her face in shallow waves, reddish-brown in the refracted light of stained glass. In a moister climate they would tighten into curls, would no longer flatter her features; she would have to grow them out or cut them shorter. There was something about her mouth: it was not full and voluptuous like Rachael's, but he had particularly liked the way her lips moved, forming each syllable as if it were some precious thing escaping with her breath.

There was a familiarity about her. He knew her in some sense that was not immediately accessible. Not the biblical sense, certainly; his memory was not the best, but he felt confident he would have remembered *that*. Rachael would probably tell him (for he would surely tell Rachael; they kept nothing from one another) that they had been lovers in a previous life, but David could not admit the possibility of reincarnation. Once through this Vale of Tears was quite enough, thank you. Perhaps she just looked like somebody else.

That was it. She reminded him of those English heroines who populated the BBC programs he watched on PBS: intelligent women in their mid-thirties with sensible hair and practical clothes, not much makeup but a great deal of character. No one could accuse them of being provocative, but only a fool would think them unattractive. Theirs was a deceptive, unaffected beauty, the more startling when one realized, as he had realized this morning, that it could be intensely erotic. For a moment he imagined the whole of England teeming with men, notoriously indifferent as lovers, who were periodically granted sudden, brief epiphanies of the beauty that walked amongst them. How else, thought David, could one account for a population in excess of sixty million on an island the size of a grapefruit?

Satisfied that his little mystery had been solved, he went down the stairs and slipped back into his shoes. He left by the front door, locking it carefully behind him, went round to the back, and let himself in again. He descended to his studio in the basement just as the air conditioner cut in for the first time that day.

His therapist had advised him to separate his domestic duties from his professional life. "Change your clothes," she told him. "Leave the building. This will create a psychological separation and help alleviate those inevitable feelings of inadequacy and hopelessness that come with being a home-maker." Secretly, he felt that his feelings of inadequacy and hopelessness stemmed not from his domestic arrangements but from the fact that he was inadequate and hopeless, but he dared not challenge the good doctor; she depended so much on client acquiescence for her self-esteem. So each morning he left the house as if he were actually going someplace, and re-entered it as if he were arriving someplace else. It did no harm, and some days it actually helped.

He removed his silk jacket and hung it on the antique coat tree that Rachael had bought him for his thirty-fourth birthday. He gazed at the illustration he had been re-working for three days. He was being paid a minimal fee by a literary publisher for designing the cover of a book that no one would read. He hadn't read it himself, except for the few pages that convinced him the work was aggressively abstruse. Nothing he put on the cover would change that. On the other hand, there was nothing between the covers that would induce people to buy it, so it didn't really matter what it looked like. With sudden resolution, he discarded the brooding desert landscape he had been working on and drew a half-dozen thumbnail sketches of a nude in an armchair.

He had no model he could call upon on short notice, and no money to pay her with in any case. But he did possess a few dozen black-and-white photographs of Rachael in various attitudes of undress. She had insisted he take them when she entered graduate school in

Toronto and could no longer justify the time spent posing for him when she should have been doing research. He had permission to use them as long as she was not recognizable in the finished product.

"A fine fool I'd look in the department," she said, "with all my secrets revealed."

He had never had cause to reveal her secrets, not through five years of graduate school, three children, two countries, three cities, and four academic appointments. Tenured now, she was also twenty pounds heavier, but he remained as jealous of his marital intimacy as he had ever been. At some time during the previous two hours, however, he had crossed an unexpected threshold.

He chose a relatively modest pose and scanned it into his computer, where he enlarged the image, adjusted the contrast, and printed it. He pinned the resultant laser copy to the wall before him and began to render it in colour. It was his only gift, or so he believed: he could reproduce an image as accurately as a camera. He worked in charcoal first, tracing outlines on a prepared ground, then switched to tempera, blocking in colours, then adding detail, gradually refining the portrait until it was so much like Rachael that Rachael wouldn't recognize herself. So engrossed did he become that he didn't notice the time until Maria came home from school and he was late to pick up the twins. He had missed lunch entirely. As he drove with his daughter to the daycare, he was conscious of a minor euphoria, and hardly noticed when the director, in concert with Morgan and Jeremy, scolded him for being late.

For supper he sautéed chicken breasts in olive oil, with a squeeze of lime and a sprinkling of oregano. He served them on a pilaf of rice and diced peppers, with a salad of romaine in a raspberry vinaigrette. Morgan and Jeremy inhaled the lot as if it were nothing but meat loaf, and Maria consumed it with the tolerant amusement she had lately been reserving for her father's culinary efforts. But Rachael lingered over it with a gratifying sensual appreciation, sipping her Chardonnay and only occasionally protesting at how fat she was becoming.

Later, in the cool of the evening when the children were asleep, they repaired to the summer house at the bottom of the garden and made love – quickly, passionately, and silently, so as not to alert the neighbours or be too long out of the house. It was, David reflected, a life that should have satisfied any man, and he was vaguely surprised when he returned to his studio after Rachael was asleep and found that the face he had painted on her body was framed in shallow waves of reddish-brown hair that shone as if it were reflecting sunlight through stained glass.

She wasn't at Mass the next morning, and David took communion with a clear, even a celebratory, conscience. He finished the book cover and took it to the publisher, who confessed himself mystified but appreciative. When the author was called in, David found himself being praised for his insight into the subtlety of his, the author's, vision. "This may come as a surprise to you," he said, "but there have been times when I had no confidence in this book. But if *you* can capture the essence of the work with such conviction, then surely the message of the monologue is not lost in metaphor." All of which was news to David, but he took the cheque to the bank and the rest of the day off.

That evening he served cæsar salad and French bread, with tomato juice for the children and a determined California red for their parents. Rachael looked even better than she had the night before. She believed that hair should be worn with a certain abandon, especially if it were thick and black, and curled like a restless beast along the nape of one's neck. She dressed conservatively for teaching, but no measure of dark jackets and high-necked blouses could conceal the fact that she was a voluptuous and beautiful woman. David stood in awe of his good fortune in being married to her. He said nothing about the book cover or the woman at church, but when they persuaded each other once again into the summer house they made love with such single-minded passion that he was convinced nothing had changed.

On Thursday morning she was there again, but in a distant pew. He could not approach her without arousing comment, so he contented himself with watching her when he thought she wasn't looking. Of course she was aware of his every glance, and let him know it with such certainty that once again he felt constrained not to take communion. This time, though, he had the courage to ask the priest who she was.

"Who, Jamie? She was asking about you yesterday. D'you know, David," he said, "I think the colour of that screen behind the altar is a trifle harsh, don't you?"

"The reredos?" It wasn't harsh, it was gauche. Shocking pink. But David was more interested in the single fact the priest had uttered: *She was asking about you yesterday.*

"She wasn't at Mass yesterday."

"Who?"

"You called her Jamie."

"Yes, odd name for a woman, isn't it? I knew her father, of course." They were walking down the centre aisle. Suddenly the priest stopped, and turned back toward the altar. "I think a soft blue would be nice."

"In what connection," asked David, "was she asking about me?"

"What? Oh, she needs another male voice in the choir – that's the nine o'clock on Sunday. I used to see her at the eleven, but since she took a different shift at the restaurant she's been able to come earlier. Weekdays, too. Perhaps a pale red...."

"That's still pink, Father."

"Mm, yes. I see what you mean. Whatever could my predecessor have been thinking of when he mounted that monstrosity?"

"I think he was aiming at a metaphor for the desert," said David. "He asked my advice, as an artist...." The sentence trailed off to a shrug.

"Oh, I'm sorry, David, I didn't mean to insult your taste."

"He *asked* my advice," said David. "He didn't *take* it."

"A pity." The priest shook his head sadly. They proceeded out of the nave and into the foyer. "We were taking communion to the nearly-dead at Sunset Villas." The priest prided himself on his disregard, even contempt, for human mortality; he was not in demand as a funeral celebrant. "Jamie always helps me on Wednesdays. She thought she'd heard you singing one morning this week and wondered if she should get in touch with you. I gave her your name. I hope you don't mind..."

"Not at all. But I can't sing."

"I didn't think you could," said the priest. "Well, I must be off. Parish Council meeting tonight and I've a million things to do. What did you call that thing behind the altar?"

"The reredos," said David, and spelled it out.

"I'll use that," said the priest. "The chairman – pardon me, the chair*person* – is impressed by technical terms. You'd think I could just have the thing painted, wouldn't you? Twenty years ago I would have, but now it's all sharing and caring and if I do anything without the knowledge and consent of the laity I'm being clerical. I'm a cleric, for God's sake! You'd recommend a pale blue, would you?"

"Well..." David began.

"I must be off. Remember, if Jamie Torschyk calls you, it's about the choir."

She didn't call, but she was at Mass the next morning, and at the sign of peace David strode boldly across the nave to take her hand. They took communion one after another, then left before the final blessing, each by a different door.

But Torschyk was not such a common name that she couldn't be found. There were only two in the phone book, and they were both listed at the same address. It was a modest bungalow at the end of a quiet crescent. He almost gave himself away when Jamie herself came out. He could have nodded and smiled and said, "What a surprise – or perhaps it's fortuitous," but instead he ducked behind the neighbour's fence, where he found himself sharing a carefully raked gravel bed with a display of flowering cacti.

"Oh, shut up!" she was saying to someone in the house. "For once in your life, just shut up!"

A voice of indeterminate gender responded. She slammed the door on it. David heard purposeful footsteps on the sidewalk. A car door opened and closed. The starter grated alarmingly, then the transaxle *thunked* as she slammed it into gear and drove off.

David invoked her guardian angel as he became aware of something poking into his back. Thinking it was a cactus, he moved aside. But it persisted. Gradually, he became aware that a human agent was responsible. Turning, he saw a pair of heavy thighs sheathed in Spandex. He also saw a vicious-looking garden implement, the cause of his present discomfort.

"Doing a bit of lurking, are we?" inquired a friendly voice.

"I didn't...*aahhh!*" He had stood too quickly, and the implement raked along his back, drawing blood.

"It's called a Weed Weasel," said the woman, in the same friendly tone. "Pulls 'em up by the roots."

"It does wonders for the skin, too," said David, arching his back to separate the wound from the thin cotton of his shirt. "I'm sorry if I startled you."

"You didn't. I startled you, lurking behind my fence."

"I wasn't lurking. I just didn't want Jamie to see me."

"I call that lurking."

"Well, I couldn't go up to the door and knock, could I? You heard them arguing."

It was the first thing that came into his mind. He was surprised at how reasonable it sounded.

"Ah," said the woman, knowingly, "you must be one of *his* friends."

David smiled and nodded.

"You shouldn't let her bully you," the woman continued. "I mean, it's not as if no one *knows*, especially since the old man died."

"No, of course not," said David. He spoke softly, hoping to convey a sort of conspiratorial agreement. He hadn't a notion what conclusions the woman was drawing beneath her pin curls, but he didn't want her describing this mystifying and entirely ridiculous episode to Jamie when she came home.

"You're right," he added, and began to move away. She took a step toward him, as though she would follow. He did not doubt his ability to outrun the woman, but he hoped it wouldn't come to that. "I think I'll be moving along."

"You march right up to that door and knock" – she gestured with her Weed Weasel – "whether Jamie's there or not. You have every right."

"I think I'll give it a miss today."

"Suit yourself." She arched one eloquent brow. "But *I* wouldn't run *my* life by someone *else's* comings and goings."

The encounter was perplexing, but David didn't waste much thought on it. It was simply one more mystery in what seemed to be an expanding cloud. He went home and had a shower, then spent an uncomfortable few minutes trying to apply disinfectant to the ragged scrape along his back. What would he tell Rachael? "A stout woman in pin curls and Spandex tights assaulted me with a Weed Weasel." Somehow the statement lacked that ring of truth that would preclude further questioning.

As it happened, he didn't have to tell Rachael anything, for she came home, late and furious, from a faculty meeting, and demanded that he sympathize with her: she was one of three women in her department, and the other two might as well sprout testicles for all the good they did. Feminist pedagogy was viewed at best with suspicion, at worst with outright hostility. Could David understand that? David could, but it took him until midnight to explain the mysterious insecurities of the male psyche, for he was challenged at every turn. By the time he finally fell into bed, two bottles of Zinfandel had been consumed and Rachael had been asleep for fifteen minutes.

The next day David went to the noon Mass, always well attended on Saturdays, but Jamie wasn't there. For the remainder of the day, he and the children worked and played in the garden while Rachael confined herself to her study. Maria knew her mother was brilliant, but the twins were not yet convinced of it and had continually to be removed from her presence.

"Can't you keep them away just for a *minute,* David?"

David kept them away for some three hundred minutes before Rachael grudgingly submitted to a meal of chili and corn bread and the company of her family. She refused wine, claiming she would have to work late into the night if she were to get anything done at all. In the event, she worked for another five hours, emerging in exhausted triumph for a snack and a shower shortly after midnight. As she finally crawled into bed, David decided to tell her about the book cover. He soon found himself telling her about Jamie as well, and how the one had sort of transmogrified into the other, and it wasn't until he had finished that he noticed Rachael was fast asleep and he didn't know how much she had heard or understood.

The next morning it was apparent that she had heard little and understood less. He went to early Mass, then prepared a breakfast of crêpes and fresh strawberries while she regaled him with a dream she'd had about a man named James who kept taking away the pages of her article as she wrote them and folding them into origami butterflies, which then took flight and disappeared.

"What do you think it means, David?"

David shrugged, a faint guilt nudging his conscience. "Even Freud said that a cigar is sometimes only a cigar."

"You're right, of course. You're always right." She nodded, smiling. "Can you take the children for the day? I'm sorry to be so boring..."

David demurred. "You should take some time to relax. All work and no play...."

"I know, I know. But you know how it is when your mind is in gear: if you once shift to neutral, you'll be lucky to get into first again, much less fourth or overdrive."

"At least my clichés are comfortably trite, Rae. You seem to make yours up as you go along."

She smiled again. "Would you mind, dear?"

It wasn't that he resented spending the time with his children – although Maria, of late, had seemed to be dedicating herself to making him feel inadequate – but he felt they were missing their mother. Fathers were all well and good, but in the larger scheme of things children needed laps and hips and smiling lips and soft breasts to weep on if they weren't to turn into total assholes. Then he remembered that the scrape along his back was still noticeable enough to demand explanation, and with every appearance of good grace he allowed her to work again until midnight.

On Monday they followed the usual weekday routine, except that David missed Mass for the first time in a year. Later that morning he made a dozen phone calls, looking for a commission, but none of his regular contacts needed anything. Feeling courageous, he made a dozen cold calls to firms he picked at random from the yellow pages. A couple of distant, uninterested voices gave him permission to drop in with his portfolio, but they couldn't promise anything.

He worked in the garden for the rest of the day, in cotton shorts and a loose shirt and a deliberately eccentric straw hat. He had built up a series of raised beds, pleasing to the eye and deeply functional in terms of increased yield and moisture conservation. But they required a good deal of attention. His neighbours were always surprised to see him. "Oh, hi," they would say over the fence, as if it were unusual to find him at home in the afternoon. "No work today?" He yearned to throw the question back into their self-satisfied female (to the north) and retired (to the south) faces, but he usually just nodded and smiled and said that things were slow.

That evening he served fettuccine in a vegetarian sauce of peppers and tomatoes and fresh basil, but Rachael once again refused wine, claiming she had to finish her article while the ideas were fresh. He missed Mass again on Tuesday. He made Greek salad and pita bread for supper, and Rachael marked papers late into the night, for she owed it to her students to hand their assignments back in reasonable time. He missed Mass again on Wednesday, and that evening he prepared a mild chicken curry with pea pilau and ratatouille and a chilled cucumber raïta. Rachael spent the evening revising her article, and was asleep by ten. David finished the Colombard alone.

On Thursday they had dinner with the McClintocks, a frightful couple whom Rachael found amusing. Darlene was a lawyer and Ian sold bits of the desert to frozen Canadians. Darlene felt it would be a nice gesture if all men apologized, just for being men, and she habitually attacked David for his adherence to an outmoded philosophy based on the teachings of a first-century illusionist whose sole contribution to Western civilization had been the principle that power should be concentrated in the hands of the few for the exploitation of the many. He might have defended himself honourably were it not for the fact that Rachael always took Darlene's side – it did David no harm to defend his beliefs on occasion, she felt; Lord knows, *she* never challenged him – and he usually ended up confirming their worst expectations by reducing it all to the level of personalities. Not even Ian could deny that Darlene was a self-satisfied, upper-middle-class professional with no more concern for her fellow females than a bitch dog in heat, but they all thought it was rather tacky of David to point it out.

By Friday morning, David was like an addict in need of a fix. He dropped the boys off at the daycare and fairly sped to Mass. He and Jamie acknowledged one another with curt nods, like old acquaintances who had never had enough in common to become friends. Afterward, curiously unrelieved, he went home to the usual routine.

He had been revising his portfolio, discarding older work and replacing it with examples of recent commissions. He spent a desultory forty minutes at it, then called his therapist to see if he could move his appointment up by a few days. She was away at a conference. He played solitaire on his computer, and lost twice. He called up a drawing program and in forty minutes managed to produce a sketch he could have executed in ten minutes by hand. Then he went for a walk. He was not surprised to find himself passing Jamie's house. Neither was she surprised to see him.

"I've been expecting you," she said, and suggested they go for a walk.

Within half a block he found himself being interrogated.

"What do you think of the papacy?" she demanded.

He thought for a moment, then said, "I remember when Paul VI issued *Humanae vitae*, my mother said that no pope was going to keep her from the sacraments."

"Meaning?"

"Meaning, I suppose, that the church has survived nearly two thousand years despite the papacy, not because of it."

"What about the priesthood?"

"I think a celibate male priesthood is essential to the church's self-identity, but the idea that all priests have to be celibate and male makes no more sense than insisting that they all be Jesuits or Franciscans."

"Would you be a priest if they were allowed to marry?"

He shook his head. "It still involves a vocation."

"I have a brother who's gay."

He didn't know if she expected sympathy or congratulations, so he said nothing.

"Where do you stand on homosexuality?" she demanded.

"I'm not in a position to stand anywhere," he said, "or even to express an informed opinion."

"So express an uninformed opinion."

"I am not sympathetic to the lifestyle," he said, choosing his words carefully. "But, perhaps because of that, I generally find them interesting to talk to. Their experience is so different from mine, you see. And there is a gentleness about them – about the ones I've known, anyway – that I admire. I am not unaware of the teaching of the church, but in the end it's not the church's judgement that counts, but God's."

"Are you always so pedantic when you're expressing an opinion?"

"Only when I'm being forced to formulate it and express it at the same time."

She grunted. "My brother's a pompous little shit."

They walked in silence for a time, then she said, "I'm not sympathetic to the lifestyle either, but I don't find them at all interesting to talk to. Maybe that's more because of my brother than because of his sexual preference. I won't let him bring his lovers to the house."

"You live together?"

She nodded. "My father left the house to both of us, and we can't decide what to do with it. So we live together like a couple of middle-aged spinsters. Pathetic, isn't it?"

"Who is the elder?"

"Oh, I am. That's why my name is Jamie. He wanted a boy" – she laughed – "and got two girls instead."

"What did your mother want?"

"A normal life, I expect." She changed the subject:

"What do you think of artificial contraception?"

"I think God gave us common sense as well as sexuality."

"That's not an answer."

"Yes, it is," he said. "Now, why all the questions?"

"I have to know if we would have been compatible."

A curious choice of words, he thought: *would have been compatible,* as if they should have met long ago, but some aberration in the pattern of the universe had prevented it. On reflection, though, the words seemed less curious than ominous.

"Why didn't you wait for me?" she demanded, suddenly.

He drew back, not in confusion but in alarm. "Life goes on," he said, lamely, "despite our best efforts."

"But you *knew,* David!"

"No, I didn't *know!*" His anger surprised him, it was so unusual. But it was too late for them, too late for her, too late to start trusting his feelings. He was angry because he was finally having to justify the happiness he shared with Rachael and his children when he had known all along that he didn't deserve it. "I had a *sense,* that was all. A *sense* that you were in the world somewhere, that we were meant to be together, to have children, to grow old in quiet contentment. I *waited,* and if you want to know the truth, Rachael waited, too. She waited till I nearly lost her."

"And then you married her," said Jamie, as if he had attempted to deny it. "I felt your wedding band when I took your hand at the sign of peace. I could hardly believe it."

"I married her because I loved her. I still love her."

"Then why are you here? Why are we talking?"

"I suppose because myth and mystery are as powerful as love. Or nearly as powerful," he amended, for that was a line he had not crossed.

"Don't you love me, David? You're supposed to *love* me!"

"I don't even know you."

"No," she said, shaking her head. She was crying now. David thought she had no right to cry. "You can say that to anyone else, even Rachael. But not to me. You can't say you don't know me. You've known me all your life."

A dozen retorts sprang to mind, to no purpose. However much he might convince himself it was impossible, irrational, illogical, in the deepest part of him he knew she was right. Had he built his life on supernatural faith only to disavow its first unambiguous manifestation? She was the name of his longing. He could not deny it.

Despite their best intentions, it was inevitable that they would find ways to be together. The following Tuesday was the soonest they could manage it without feeling it had been deliberately planned. They went for coffee after Mass, ostensibly to discuss his joining the Sunday choir. Three hours later he realized that he had told her more of himself than he had ever told his therapist. Unlike his therapist, though, Jamie had responded in kind. By the time they parted, he was convinced they should never see each other again. The past made one so vulnerable.

On Wednesday and Thursday they met again, each day resisting the temptation to hold hands under the coffee-shop table while they were verbally intimate above it. They spoke of art and music, literature, feminism, politics and religion, philosophy, drama, all the accepted topics of educated conversation. They also spoke of the past as preparation for the future and, obversely, the future as preparation for the past – like love, a not entirely graspable concept. On Friday they decided they would go to confession, each to a different priest (not that they had done anything wrong, mind you), and then they would never see each other again. Jamie would find a different church for daily Mass, and even leave the choir as soon as she could find a replacement.

And so for a time they shared a mutual sanctity, secure in the knowledge that they had done the right thing, the best thing. It lasted nearly a week.

She called him the following Thursday. If Rachael or Maria had answered, or one of the twins, she would have taken it as a sign. But David answered, and she took that as a sign. Her brother was away for a week, up north at some art show. Had she not told him her brother was an artist? No matter, she had the house to herself. David required no more explicit invitation. Clearly, they were in the grip of a power greater than themselves. The next morning they met with the express intention of committing adultery.

She greeted him at the door, barely clothed in a thin

kimono. She led him to the bedroom. He stood in obedient need as she stripped him, then she opened her
garment and let it fall, and they fell upon one another
like ravening beasts, entirely consumed by instinct and
desire. But it was over so quickly, the body spends itself
so quickly, and afterward they felt worse than they
could have believed possible. Jamie cried, it was so
unfair. David cried, too, but in grief at the passing of an
illusion. She was not as slim as he had thought, her
belly not quite so flat − clothes can be so deceptive −
and certainly she was less beautiful than Rachael. But
she was attentive and generous where Rachael was
often distracted, self-absorbed. Everyone knew Rachael
was brilliant.

They tried it once more, not believing it could not be
beautiful. But once again it was deceiving and ugly. She
had skill and experience, that was clear. She was used to
being touched in the way he touched her − used, apparently, to being dissatisfied, to being abandoned at the
very instant she should have been most cherished. But
what was he to do? The body spends itself so quickly.

Of a sudden, he realized that he had allowed his
body to become a creature separate from himself, a
demon that had temporarily taken his emotions
hostage. Tamed now, he clothed it in shame and left the
object of his brief possession weeping on her bed. He
would tell Rachael when she got home. Confession was
good for the soul. And she would forgive him. She had
to, after that incident with her supervisor at
Concordia...what, ten years ago now? He thought he
had forgotten it.

But when Rachael came home, late and furious from another faculty meeting, she began immediately to pack for a conference he had forgotten she was committed to attend.

"Do you have to go?" he asked.

"Of course I have to go," she said. "My head of department was trying to get a motion passed about withdrawing my funding – oh, not my funding in particular, he was careful not to mention *my* funding. But he really doesn't like the idea of a woman representing the department at an international conference. The only way he can stop me is by stopping everybody. He calls it *fiscal responsibility.*"

David was conciliatory. "He feels threatened, Rae. You've published more in the past year than he has since he got tenure."

"He's published *nothing* since he got tenure!"

"Do you have to go?" he asked again.

"I'm delivering a paper," she replied, and that was the end of it.

He drove her to the airport. The children kissed her good-bye, and he took them home to the emptiest house he had ever known. He felt betrayed, somehow, as if a cherished belief had suddenly been rendered a tissue of lies. He wanted to blame Rachael. That was absurd, he knew, and blatantly self-serving, but there is a level of the mind that embraces absurdity and mutates it into truth. David was trying to suppress it when he announced to his incomplete family that they were going out for supper.

Jeremy wanted to go to Berber King. Morgan preferred Macdonnudth. Maria rolled her eyes and asked her father if he had any idea how much saturated fat there was in a single order of french fries. Knowing that any reply was potentially dangerous, David simply herded them into the Cherokee and headed down to the strip. He'd a vague notion that he wanted to try something new. Mexican, Indian, Italian, and Greek were all too familiar, and he knew if they went Chinese the twins would be up all night with gas. Japanese and Thai were a trifle exotic for the children, and Maria was allergic to peanuts, so Vietnamese was out, too. Spanish was a possibility, he thought, until he had images of Morgan and Jeremy gagging on the mussels in their paella, or winging a waiter with the shells. He was beginning to think that Berber King or Macdonnudth were the only possibilities, after all, when he saw a sign that proclaimed, simply, BEEF. Presumably the restaurant had a name, and he might have learned it if he had bothered to read the neon script above that single, carnivorous noun. But he realized suddenly that he didn't want something new. He wanted something old-fashioned and comforting, something that might clog his arteries but would make him think of birthday dinners and family celebrations.

He told himself later that he'd had no idea, it was pure coincidence. But he could never explain to himself why he felt so little surprise when Jamie Torschyk approached him with four menus and asked him if he preferred smoking or non-smoking.

"Non-smoking," said Maria firmly, as if her father had been about to say something different, and Jamie led them to a table near a window where they could watch the muscle cars cruising the strip. Maria surveyed the scene with disgust. "They're insecure about the size of their dicks," she announced.

"I beg your pardon?" asked Jamie, distributing the menus.

"Their dicks," Maria explained. "Morgan and Jeremy have tinkles, but they'll turn into dicks when they get older, and then they'll drive cars like that."

"Where do you learn things like that?" asked David.

"Mummy told me."

"The waitress will take your order," said Jamie, in tones of careful formality. "In the meantime, would you care for something from the bar?"

David wanted a large glass of something very high in alcoholic content, but he settled for a light beer. He had wanted a steak, char-broiled, medium rare, but he settled for a hamburger, as did the twins, while Maria had a chef's salad and a glass of mineral water.

Later, they drove out along the desert road, ostensibly to watch the sunset, but when they stopped in a lay-by he felt Maria's hand on his arm, gentle as a whisper.

"Daddy, are you crying?"

He shook his head – "Just some sand in my eyes" – but he knew she wasn't fooled. Might as well try to hide from God as put one over on Maria. He wondered if John the Baptist, poised like this on the edge of the wilderness, had been as certain of purpose and grace as the evangelists supposed. When the earth curved away to a limitless horizon, when there was nothing but space and wind and rocks and sand, how could a man be sure of anything? Yet John had been sure. John had a commission. *Behold, I send my messenger before thy face, who shall prepare thy way; the voice of one crying in the wilderness: Prepare the way of the Lord, make his paths straight.*

David envied the prophet his certainty, his humility. Even his death. Without looking back, he started the car and drove his children home.

THE END OF THE WORLD

I realized it could not be Moira the instant she walked through the door. The evidence against, marshalled in the split second between startled recognition and rational denial, was simply too overwhelming. True, everything about her was perfect: the height, the weight, the dark expressive brows, the nut-brown hair; the lips at once full and slightly pursed, as though she were in a constant state of mild disapproval, which in fact she was; the way she held herself, elegant and imperious; the confidence with which she scanned the room, picked out the face she sought – mine – and approached without hesitation.

Yes, it was Moira all right.

Except that it couldn't be.

For one thing, it was thirty below. Moira would not go to the corner for a carton of milk in such weather, much less drive 639 kilometres of icy highway and unchanging landscape to an unplanned rendezvous with a husband she was glad to see the back of four or five times a year. Moira didn't drive on the highway. She rarely drove in Saskatoon. She would categorically refuse to drive here in Calgary, a city four times the size. That left trains, planes, and buses. Train service in western Canada had become so erratic as to be risible. Buses were beneath her; people only travelled by bus when it was too expensive or too late to get where they wanted by any other means, and Moira was neither poor nor tardy.

I had left her and the children in Saskatoon early yesterday morning. But even if she had taken a plane and arrived before me, she could not have known where to go. Of course, she would know where I was staying – I always stay with friends on Georgia Street – but she could have no clue that my afternoon meeting had been cancelled and I had decided to take the rest of the day off, or that I was now sitting in Pepper's Delicatessen on 17th Avenue South West, eating a smoked meat sandwich with strong black coffee and wondering if it was worth a saunter up to Mount Royal Village to see if I could resist buying anything in the Italian kitchen shop. I hadn't known it myself ten minutes ago.

So of course it could not be Moira.

The woman addressed me by name: "Hello, Kevin."

I had been looking out the window, to a shop across the street. Le Chateau, it was called, with a little red *chapeau* over the A. Upstairs and to the left was an establishment called To the Point, which, according to

a large and unambiguous sign in the window, specialized in body piercing. Next to that was a place called
Kittens and Creeps, but there was no indication in the
window what went on inside. The building next door
had an outdoor mezzanine on the north side, with stairs
at the front and back, giving access to a line of shops on
the second storey.

"I said hello, Kevin."

I gazed at her thoughtfully. "Do I know you?"

"Don't be an idiot."

She certainly sounded like Moira.

"What on earth are you doing here?"

"I am here to save the world."

"What, in Calgary?"

"To save the world," she repeated, in italics. I hated it
when Moira spoke in italics. It invariably meant that
she expected something from me.

"How did you get here?"

"By taxi."

"From Saskatoon? It must have cost a fortune."

"It seemed a justifiable expenditure with the fate of
the world hanging in the balance."

"What does that mean, exactly?" I asked, but apparently the information was to be released on a need-to-
know basis, and I did not need to know.

"There's a shop across the street that specializes in
body piercing," she said. "It's called To the Point."

"More to the point," I said – rather cleverly, I
thought – "how did you find me?"

"I told you, I came by taxi."

"Yes, but how did you find me *here?* You couldn't

have known my meeting was cancelled this afternoon, or that I would be on 17th Avenue."

"I don't have time for this, Kevin." She was more impatient than usual. "There's a shop across the street that specializes in body piercing."

"You've said that already."

"It's upstairs," she said, ignoring my repartee. She pointed a long, gloved finger at the establishment in question, as if she were zeroing in on where she would aim the bazooka. Her breath poured visibly from her lips and whirled about her nose and cheekbones as she spoke into the cold air. For we seemed to be on the street now, though I didn't remember getting up from my chair, paying my bill, or leaving the deli. Moira often had that effect on me.

"What do you suppose they do in Kittens and Creeps?" I wondered, but this information, too, seemed to be available only on a need-to-know basis. Almost as an afterthought, I added, "I don't want my body pierced."

"A tasteful diamond stud in the left ear," said Moira. "The children have been after you to do it for years. Now it is a matter of utmost importance."

"Couldn't I get a gold hoop instead?"

"A tasteful diamond stud," she repeated. "The gold hoop is for your eyebrow."

"My what?"

"The proprietor is waiting," said Moira impatiently. "She has complete instructions. After that you're to go next door to The Book and Cranny and –"

"The what?" I interrupted.

"The Book and Cranny," she repeated, slowly, as if she were explaining something to an idiot child. "It's a bookstore. You remember books, don't you, Kevin? Papers bound between covers, with printing on them?"

Moira's sarcasm was fundamental to her personality and not particularly endearing. It went a long way toward explaining why she had so few friends. Indeed, sometimes I thought I was the only one left, and even I had to get away at least four times a year. This was supposed to have been one of those times. But there was something in the urgency of her manner that caused me to withhold my rebuttal and simply reply, "Of course I know what books are. I publish them."

"Nonfiction." The word dropped from her lips like a piece of rancid meat. "I'm talking about literature: poetry, novels, plays, the great works of the human imagination."

"We still call them books, Moira, even if they are only about trifles like how to counsel an abusive parent or treat an ADHD child."

It was a testament to the importance of her mission that she did not pursue the point. Normally the subject would have been good for twenty minutes of fruitless argument, followed by three or four days of icy silence and the complete withdrawal of her affections.

"It's along the mezzanine north of Kittens and Creeps" – she pointed again – "right above the Mystic Sceptre."

"Now there's something to think about," I said.

"Don't be disgusting."

"I wasn't being disgusting, I was being Freudian. And don't tell me they're the same thing."

This, too, would normally have been good for twenty minutes of fruitless argument, but there was a look of genuine fear in her eyes as she glanced toward the sweeping curves of the Saddledome roof, which was visible at the eastern end of the street. She began to speak more quickly.

"Once you've had the body piercing done, you're to go along to the Book and Cranny and buy the last copy of *Doctrine of Signatures* by Anne Szumigalski."

"Doctor who?"

"*Doctrine of Signatures,*" she repeated. "Anne Szumigalski."

"Who's Anne Szumigalski when she's at home?"

There was a brief but gravid pause, then her natural contempt overcame, if only temporarily, whatever urgency she might have felt about saving the world.

"You peasant," she said. "You Philistine. You culture-less oaf. Honestly, Kevin, sometimes I despair of you."

"That may be so," I said, "but you had better tell me who this Jane Shumarabski is or I won't be able to help you."

"*Anne Szumigalski,*" she said, with withering contempt. "She's a poet, a playwright, an essayist, an artist" – she counted them off on her fingers – "not to mention mentor to a dozen prominent writers whose names even *you* might recognize. Good Lord, Kevin, she's won the Governor General's Award for Poetry, the Saskatchewan Book Award for nonfiction, the –"

"Nonfiction?" I interrupted, detecting a flaw in her

praise. "Hardly what you would call literature, is it?"

"Don't be so literal-minded."

"Am I to take it, then, that your sudden, almost mystical presence here is symbolic rather than literal?"

"I am here to save the world."

"Is there any point in my telling you that you've gone insane?"

"None."

"Very well," I sighed. I knew better than to argue with Moira when she was in one of her moods. No doubt the holes in my earlobe and eyebrow would heal in time. Then perhaps I would have her committed. It might do us both a world of good, I reflected, and my heart lightened perceptibly as I crossed the street and ascended the steps to the appointed place.

The body piercing was not as traumatic as I might have thought, though painful enough in its way and not something I would have undergone of my own volition. It's surprising how many nerves a little flap of skin can contain. I departed with a tasteful diamond stud in my left earlobe and a gold hoop in my right eyebrow, looking and feeling like a total idiot. What business, I wondered, had a forty-five-year-old publisher getting his ear pierced, much less his eyebrow? Next thing I would be shaving my head.

I shuddered at the possibility, which had become a probability the instant it entered my mind. I stepped outside onto 17th Avenue and immediately felt the cold against my recent cosmetic injuries. Instinctively, one hand went to my eyebrow, the other to my ear. I was surprised to find them both pierced with metal;

although I had just undergone the procedure in full consciousness, I still couldn't quite believe it.

Moira's directive had been explicit: after I had purchased What's-her-name's book, I was to meet her outside the Mystic Sceptre and she would give me further instructions. I strode confidently around the corner of the building where the Mystic Sceptre was located, and began climbing the outside stairs to the mezzanine. I was halfway up when I stopped, abruptly, my mind a total blank. What was the name of the book I was supposed to buy? Who wrote it? Jane Somebody. Jane...Jane...Jane Osiowy. No, that wasn't it. Jane...Gummy...Jane Gallbladder...Jane Scumbowski. No, it was gone.

I turned and descended the stairs. If I was to meet Moira outside the Mystic Sceptre after I had purchased the book, I reasoned, then she was likely to be in the vicinity now. It would be a simple matter to find out the name of the book and its author and then go back upstairs and buy it. Her scorn would be fathomless, I knew. But really, you can't send a man off to be mutilated and expect him to start reciting the names of Governor General's Award winners right afterward.

Moira, of course, was nowhere near the Mystic Sceptre. She is contrary by nature, and will never be where you expect her to be when it is convenient that she be there. The shop itself was a dark and fascinating place, though. Two suits of armour guarded the door, beyond which exotic cloths and bits of esoteric furniture were scattered about in comfortable disarray. It was the kind of place I would happily have browsed in for an hour had I not suddenly remembered: Anne Szumigalski, poet, playwright, essayist, artist, winner of the Governor General's Award for Poetry and the Saskatchewan Book Award for nonfiction. I was to buy the last copy of *Doctrine of Signatures* from the bookstore upstairs.

I left to do so, but apparently I was too late. The pavement was hot beneath my feet, and getting hotter. The snow was vaporizing. Sheets of steam fled upward between the buildings. I could hear the shattering of glass, the cracks and crashes of concrete and masonry as a great fireball swept westward from the Saddledome, destroying all in its path. Buildings folded in upon themselves and tossed their detritus into the street. Cars and trucks converged in a single speeding blur, careening into pedestrians and buildings and one another as the tires turned to liquid beneath them. I heard the cries of the dying, cries of terror and awe. I saw people rushing toward me, stampeding, hardly human, pushing one another aside, the smaller and the weaker being trampled under feet made swift by panic. I saw bodies sinking into the pavement, bodies crushed beneath melting tires. And overarching all was the wailing of a wind, a roaring, crashing, screaming banshee of a wind that wrenched limbs from torsos and heads from necks. A solitary face, frozen in a rictus of terror, flew by me, its final scream echoing in an empty throat.

I felt a hand on my arm, and turned to see Moira beside me, her face a mask of disappointment and sorrow. She was swept away before she could speak, but I knew what she would have said. It was my fault. This was all happening because I couldn't even remember who Anne Szumigalski was. Then I felt the pavement melting beneath me, and the high demonic wind tossed me backward like a leaf into brief pain and utter blackness....

"Excuse me...." A tentative pull on my sleeve.

"Mmm?"

"Excuse me, sir."

I looked up into a face half puzzled, half annoyed.

"I'm sorry," I said. "I must have dozed off. Do you want me to settle up now?"

She ignored the question. "Is your name Kevin MacNeill?"

I started. "It is."

"You're wanted on the telephone."

"That's impossible. No one knows I'm here."

"She says her name is Moira."

NO MORE THAN HUMAN

*W*onder intruded on consciousness. All things were new: the pale pastel walls, the white tiled ceiling, the attendant's starched uniform, the crisp smell of clean linen. He reached out with the curiosity of the child he seemed to be. A burst of laughter came from somewhere behind him. As he craned his neck to discover its source, he felt his hand ungently slapped away. The sting of skin on skin hurt him. He began to cry.

"Why did you do that?" demanded the voice behind him, a voice of unquestioned authority.

"He shouldn't have touched me like that."

"You speak as if he were something more than human."

A pause. "I suppose I had hopes."

"Well, get on with it." The voice was curt, impatient. "He's got the rest of his life to live."

He experienced a brief, unpleasant vertigo, and then he

was lost, spinning downward through the depthless dark until every trace of who he was fell away and he was nobody and nothing, not human any more, not animal, not even sentient.

It might have been a moment later, or a year. Again, all things were new. He awoke to the comforting noises of a family getting up in the morning: shuffling feet, stifled yawns, childish voices from a distant room, the eager snuffling of a dog at his ear. And something else, something moving above his head. A trembling in the air, warm and soft. Tentatively, he opened one eye, then the other. The breasts that floated above his face, he knew, were related to the shaking of his body, the shuffling of the feet. She was shaking him awake. But it was the breasts that commanded his attention. He reached out, tentative, a deeper level of his mind remembering the words, *You speak as if he were more than human.* And somehow it was necessary, being no more than human, to reach out.

The laughter he heard was merry, flattered.

"Not again, Andrew! Good heavens, you're insatiable!"

He sat up, and the dog fell with a yelp to the carpeted floor. It was a terrier, small and cinnamon and terminally cheerful. It immediately jumped back onto the bed and attempted to climb his torso, the better to lick his face. He lay back again and looked at the woman standing above him. She was not beautiful so much as striking: a square Teutonic face capped with a mass of unruly curls, brown-eyed and freckled, with laugh lines spreading outward from the corners of her eyes. Not young, then, but decidedly not old. Well formed but not extravagant.

"I've had my shower," she said. "Your turn."

He processed the information. Her hair was wet. The towel she flung at him was damp. It was his turn. He began to rise. But suddenly two small girls burst into the room and wrestled him down with cries of "Daddy!" and "Playtime!" and the dog inexplicably attacked one corner of the bedspread, growling ferociously.

The woman turned, her eyes almost disappearing in the creases of her laughter.

"Not now, girls. Mummy and Daddy have to go to work and you have to go to playschool."

But they were having none of it. They jumped on him while the dog growled in idiot delight. They pinned him down and squealed with excitement each time he broke free, upon which they redoubled their efforts. Their aim, apparently, was to render him immobile without in any way hampering his mobility, which set up a peculiar tension between mind and body, intention and act. For while he suspected that he had the authority to silence them with a word, he suspected also that invoking that authority would come as a sudden and painful surprise to them. He supposed, too, that he must have been uttering terms of playful endearment, for they seemed to come naturally to his lips, if not his memory.

But it was over soon enough, and as he rose for air he saw that the woman had put on a brassiere and a pair of bikini panties, which for some reason rendered her almost painfully desirable. She turned.

"Really, Andrew!" she said, no longer amused. She swept the little girls from the room with effortless efficiency. The dog followed. "Get dressed, my loves. Mummy will be there in a few minutes."

"Really, Andrew!" she repeated, closing the door. "It's a good thing they're too young to understand."

He wasn't sure that he understood himself.

She reached behind her back to unfasten the brassiere, smiled in a way that seemed familiar, then advanced like some miraculous predator.

"I suppose there are more important things than getting to work on time," she said.

He responded to the beauty of her body, touching and being touched. He was amazed at the softness of her skin, the way her hair fell through his fingers, the way their bodies moulded each to the other like hands clasped in familiar friendship. But this was less than familiar and more than friendship. Delight rose in him like a wave, building from the depths of his being to define itself in his flesh, where it seemed to join hers and expand, where it became a kind of power, a power at once begging to be released and begging to be withheld. It was magnificent and terrible...and then it was over.

They lay together, limp and helpless. In a moment she rose and said, "Enough of that. Time for work. We can still make it if we hurry."

But he was stuck on her first sentence: *Enough of that.* How could there ever be, he wondered, enough of *that?*

He reached out as she moved away, took her by the hand and pulled her back.

"Andrew! For God's sake!"

It was different this time, less intense but somehow deeper, appeasing a different level of appetite. He thought of friendship and familiarity. *Intimacy.* The word popped into his mind.

"Have I missed something?" the woman asked at last. "Is it Lust Awareness Week or something?"

He silenced her with a kiss and a smile, then rose to have the shower he should have had half an hour before. The rituals seemed to fall into place naturally: the water, the soap, the shampoo. He experienced a brief confusion between the toilet and the bidet, but the cold, vertical surprise of the bidet soon resolved it.

Shaving looked easy enough: there were explanatory graphics on the can of foam. *Menthol!* it proclaimed beneath a beaming masculine face, and he had no trouble recognizing the scraping implement amid the paraphernalia on the vanity. He was interested that the face on the can seemed to be glowing where the foam had been scraped off. And indeed, when he felt how smooth and cool his own cheeks and chin were after passing the razor across them, he lathered up his chest as well, for the object of the exercise was obviously the removal of hair. But the skin below his face was more sensitive to the aggressive freshness of the foam, and something warned him not to proceed any further.

The aftershave was a revelation, cauterizing chest and face alike so that he was forced back into the shower for relief, but then the door opened and a female voice spoke through the steam to the effect that maybe being late didn't matter if you were so secure in your job that you could backhand the dean at faculty meetings and still be assured of a generous income for life, but some people didn't have tenure and really should show up within an hour of when they were supposed to if they wanted to keep their jobs.

Hyperbole, he thought, but something warned him not to say it.

"You'll have to get your coffee at the college," said the woman as he emerged from the shower. "Good God, what have you done to yourself?" Then she got that predatory look again. "It's so smooth," she said, running a hand across his hairless chest. Then, "No!" she said, as if he had asked her a preposterous question, and she turned and strode purposefully away. "We'll be waiting in the car."

He dressed hurriedly and found his way down to the sleek red vehicle in the driveway. The woman was in the front seat, the two girls in the back. His place was in the front beside the woman. He experienced a moment of panic as he realized that he hadn't a notion what to do once he got in. His fears were eased when it became apparent that he was not expected to do anything. The woman pulled levers and pressed buttons and moved her foot against the pedals on the floor and the whole thing started moving.

"Really, Andrew," she said, glancing over at him, "you have the fashion sense of a Maoist. What possessed you to wear camouflage pants with a silk jacket? Are those sandals on your feet?"

He looked down at himself with interest. He decided not to tell her about the sheer panties that had seemed to fit so naturally when he slipped them on.

"I suppose a certain level of eccentricity is expected of a college professor," she said as she turned a corner and accelerated. The word *sarcasm* popped into his mind. "In any case, it's too late to go back and change."

They drove on amid the chattering of the children in the back seat. He was interested to learn that he was a college professor. More words came into his mind as they drove, names mostly: Plato, Augustine, Kant. Then words began to resolve themselves into phrases, at once deeply strange but maddeningly familiar: summa theologiae, phenomenological existentialism, critique of pure reason.

"The triad of the dialectic," he said suddenly, "is immeasurably complicated by the fact that it is not linear."

The woman took her eyes from the road. "What?"

"He called it 'the little death,' you know, Augustine. He said the human orgasm was a little death."

"Andrew, have you gone mad?"

"I may be experiencing a psychotic interlude," he admitted.

She steered the car to the side of the road and brought it to a halt. "Look at me," she ordered.

He looked at her blankly, already receding.

"You're not my husband."

He shook his head in confirmation. "I have never seen you before in my life."

With awful awareness, she drew away from him. She

held up her hands as though she were warding off an assailant, then pressed herself against the car door and screamed.

He was aware, dimly, of the swish of starched linen, connections failing, levels adjusted. He didn't open his eyes.

"What happened?" asked the second voice.

"There must be a glitch in the database."

"Don't get theological on me."

"In layman's terms," said the authoritative voice, "he had no past."

"But he remembered how to make love, and how to play with children."

"They're hardwired for that. In fact, once they get started, it can be difficult to get them to stop. But the rest he learned as he went. Next time he would be more self-conscious. Next time he wouldn't shave his chest. Next time he would dress appropriately. But all he actually remembered were disconnected words and phrases and a few complete sentences uttered entirely out of context."

"But the woman and the children – even the dog – recognized him when he couldn't recognize himself," said the second voice. "It was only when he had an intuition into his own condition that the woman no longer knew who he was."

"They are relational creatures," said the authoritative voice. "Clearly, if he had no past, she could not exist in it. They could interact physically, but at the theoretical level she ceased to be part of his universe, and so logical denial was

the only alternative to self-annihilation."

"I'm lost."

"Imagine how he feels."

"So what do we do?"

"Well, you could run the diagnostics, search for the error. But in the meantime we have to find some way of getting them all back into the same workflow."

The second voice was anxious. "Where do I start?"

"The question is relevant only if time is linear."

"And it's not?"

"That's for you to decide."

The woman was suffering a profound moment of disorientation. She looked about her, fighting down panic. The children were chattering away in the back seat as if nothing had happened. But clearly something *had* happened, otherwise why was she parked at the side of the road? She had no memory of pulling over. Yet here she was.

Blackout, she thought.

But she hadn't had a drink in five years, not since before the twins were born.

She looked into the back seat. "All right, girls?" she asked, forcing a lightness into her voice that she did not feel. The twins were strapped safely in their seats, as usual.

"Why are we stopped?" asked Kathleen, always the inquisitive one. Miriam just smiled, accepting that whatever her mother did was the right thing. The woman forced herself to smile in return. "I just wanted to make sure you were strapped in properly," she said. "You can never be too careful."

And indeed you can't, she thought, remembering Andrew as he was pulled from the wreckage of his Porsche, his face a mask of blood. "If he'd been wearing his seatbelt...." the police officer said, letting the thought trail off. A thousand times she had finished the sentence for him: *he might have survived the crash, he might have been a father to his daughters, he might have lived to make more children, he might not have left me alone and bereft, a suddenly single parent with two infant girls, we might have been lovers until the pair of us grew old....*

But now she was remembering something else. Her body was remembering...no, it couldn't be. She had not been with a man since Andrew. So why did she feel as if she had just made love? Why was memory so cruel?

"Why are we stopped?" asked Kathleen again.

"Mummy's not feeling well," she said.

"Got a tummy ache?" asked Miriam.

"Something like that." The woman looked at her hands. They were shaking.

"We're going to be late."

That was Kathleen again, slightly imperious, slightly disapproving. *Like her father,* the woman remembered. *My God, but he could be maddening sometimes!* The instant the memory rose in her mind, she was assailed by a grief as poignant and intense as she had not felt since she stood by the grave and watched the coffin being lowered. She had grieved not just for herself, but for the children who would never know their father, never be loved by the man whose love had transformed her. She had never wanted a drink so much in her life, she remembered. But that was nothing compared to how much she wanted a drink now.

It would be easy to drop the girls at playschool, call in sick, stop at a liquor store on the way home. A quick drink to steady the nerves, another to ease the pain, one more to bring her to the edge of euphoria, and then a quick slide into oblivion. She might never have to feel pain again.

She was crying as she put the car in gear and pulled away from the kerb. She accelerated rapidly, as if driving were a metaphor for drinking and she could make herself feel better if she could just go fast enough. She did not see the man who stumbled into the road until it was too late, and then there was the hideous thud of unyielding steel against human flesh.

"Mummy!" Kathleen yelled.

Miriam screamed.

The woman slammed on the brakes, and in an instant hope met certainty and was destroyed.

"**B**rilliant," *said the first voice.* "You've killed him twice now, and you've turned her into an alcoholic. Why don't you give her an axe and set her on the kids?"

"He may not be dead," *said the second voice defensively.*

"Well, it hardly matters if he is or if he isn't, does it? If he is, she's just run over and killed a man she buried five years ago. If he isn't, she's just run over and nearly killed a man she buried five years ago. Either way, you've got massive contradictions in space, time, memory, and experience. Does* *the woman even have a name?*

Joanna, thought Andrew, *consciousness briefly surfacing. Her name is Joanna.*

"Her name is Joanna," said the second voice, gaining confidence.

A *drink,* thought Joanna. *All I need is a drink.* But in the meantime she had to get out of the car. She had to face the man she had killed. For she had no doubt he was dead. She had seen death before; it was not easily mistaken for anything else. She had to view the body, as she had viewed her husband's body five years before, and feel again the sorrow and the recrimination and the despair of facing a death that should have been hers but wasn't. There was no logic to it. There was no reason to believe that she should have died instead of Andrew. There was no reason to believe that this man would not have stumbled in front of someone else's car if hers had not been there. Morally, he had been at least partially responsible for his own survival. Clearly, he had not been watching where he was going. But desire supplants reason as reality supplants hope.

I have killed another man, she thought. *I deserve to die.*

She was conscious of the gathering crowd, exclamations of alarm, horns honking, and her children crying in the background as she approached the body on the pavement. He was on his side, a pool of blood spreading outward from a face that was suddenly, appallingly, sickeningly familiar.

"I've called 9-1-1 on my cellphone," she heard someone say.

"Don't move him!" someone else warned.

But she had to move him. She took his head in her hands and looked down into a face she had known and loved and mourned in a thousand dreams.

H e was strangely at peace. He did not try to open his eyes, but lay in the blissful consciousness of hope, remembering what had inexplicably been forbidden him before: love, family, home. It was so simple, really. Why had they made it so confusing?

"Well, you've done it now," said the voice of authority. "He's alive, she's alive, and the whole logic of man, woman, birth, death, and infinity is shot to hell."

"I can't stand it!" said the second voice. "The guilt, the pain, the useless death! I just can't stand it!"

"That's as may be," said the first voice, "but what do you propose to do with our friends here?"

"What can I do?"

There was a moment's pause, and then the voice of authority seemed to relent. "Reboot," it said.

"Is that permissible?"

"Not according to the literature, but sometimes it's necessary."

"I wish we weren't so dependent on the one operating system."

"The other is worse, believe me."

It might have been a moment later, or a year. He awoke to the comforting noises of a family getting up in the morning: shuffling feet, stifled yawns, childish voices from a distant room, the eager snuffling of a dog at his ear. He opened one eye, then the other. He reached out, and a woman's laughter greeted his desire.

"Not again, Andrew! Good heavens, you're insatiable!"

"No." He smiled. "Just human."

THE KING'S HEAD
AND EIGHT BELLS

Twenty years later, untimely widowed, his children all but grown, he returned to London to see if he could find her. The neighbourhood had changed but little. The derelict synagogue on the corner of Elgin Avenue and Morshead Road had finally been torn down, though the debris had yet to be cleared away. The shops across the street had altered in ownership but not in custom. Many of the local restaurants had switched nationalities, but they still exuded the heady aromas of the East. The old couple in Elgin Mansions, noticeably aged, still sat on their balcony when weather permitted. They returned his greeting with a puzzled grace. There was no reason they should remember him. Around the corner, in Paddington Recreation Ground, he found the same mixture of children and sunbathers, dog-walkers and elderly North Londoners basking in the heat of the long afternoon. The sunbathers were probably the children of the couples they had shared the space with two decades before. Nothing changed, really: sunbathers turned inexorably into mothers and fathers and dog-walkers, then into elderly North Londoners soaking up the rare sun of high summer.

And middle-aged widowers returned to the scene of their first happiness to see if life was worth living at all in the summer of 1989.

She wasn't at the address in Shirland Road. He hadn't expected she would be. No one there remembered her except the bishop's daughter, a lean, grey woman who occupied the garden flat.

"Miss Shirley?" she said. "Of course I remember her. They used to sit in the garden, she and her mother, when weather permitted. Days like this, you know." She glanced at the sky. "I don't fancy the heat myself, but the hotter the better for old Mrs. Shirley."

"Do you recall when they moved?"

"People come and go at such a rate these days." She frowned her disapproval of the modern generation. "Mind you, in their case there was reason for it."

He nodded noncommittally. He had no cause to remember Cassandra's mother with fondness.

"The steps became more than old Mrs. Shirley could manage, with her arthritis."

"Do you remember, or did she say, where they moved to?"

"She was not a friendly person," said the bishop's daughter, "and of course I didn't inquire."

"Of course," he agreed.

He thanked her, and the image of her bleak smile of acknowledgement stayed with him as he retraced his steps to the Maida Vale tube station. Everything was familiar: the brick mansions lining the street, the voluptuous plane trees, the smell of diesel exhaust, the omnipresent hum of the city in the background, even the heat. It put such a weight of memory on him that he nearly wept. He could almost hear her voice there beside him. *Of course I'll marry you, Thomas. How could you have thought otherwise?*

He went south, switching to the Circle Line at Paddington Station, which took him to Sloane Square. From there he walked west on the Kings Road, past the Duke of York's Headquarters, past Walpole Street and Wellington Square and Flood Street where Mrs. Thatcher used to live. He stopped outside the Old Town Hall, which housed the Chelsea Library, and gazed up at its unremarkable stone façade.

"How was I to know I would never see you again?" he asked aloud.

An elderly woman stepped aside and walked quickly past, casting fearful glances and hugging her purse. Embarrassed, he shook his head and moved on. At Oakley Street he turned south, toward the river.

In the King's Head and Eight Bells on Cheyne Walk he ordered a pint of bitter. The server asked him to be more specific. "We're a free house," she said. "You've a dozen brands to choose from."

"Surprise me."

"Would you like one of our traditional ales?"

He nodded, but when she placed it before him he

was disappointed to find it at room temperature and nearly flat, hardly the thing he would have asked for on a hot July afternoon if he had thought about it. A fat American with a neck-load of cameras and a dripping brow came in and specified "something cold, real cold, none of your warm traditional piss." The pint glass was sweating satisfactorily as the server placed it before him. The fat man quaffed a third of it before paying.

"Bloody Yank," muttered a singular-looking man at the bar. Louder, he said, "Give us another pint of your warm traditional piss, love."

The server gave him a censorious look, but the Yank took no notice, retiring with his gassy lager to a corner table where he unslung his cameras and lit a very long cigarette.

"I've got that," said Thomas as she drew the pint. He placed a £5 note on the bar.

"Ta," said the man, unsurprised. He had two days' growth of beard on a jaw that looked like a shovel, and a great shock of greying hair arching over his brow. "Who are you, if you don't mind my asking?"

"You were sitting on that same stool when I left here twenty years ago," said Thomas. "I suppose you *have* gone home now and then?"

"Only to fulfil my marital duties."

"So you finally married her, then?"

"Who?"

"Polly."

"Polly-be-damned. Took off with a bloody Finn, didn't she. Steam baths and rolling in the snow, and welcome to it. Who are you?" he repeated.

"A gaggle of geese," said Thomas.

"Come again?"

"A brace of grouse."

"Aye, and a herd of fucking elephants." He addressed the woman behind the bar. "I don't think I've ever had a loony stand me a pint before. Not an American loony, anyway."

"Canadian," Thomas corrected him. "Do you drink at the Cross Keys any more?" It was a pub around the corner in Lawrence Street.

"Only in the evenings," the man said. "They keep the old hours."

"An enormous Scotsman came in with a friend one night and ordered two Grouse."

"Famous Grouse?" A flicker of recollection. "The scotch?"

Thomas nodded. "Someone at the bar said, 'You mean a *brace* of grouse,' and the Scotsman thought that was a great joke and bought him a drink. You couldn't figure out what had happened, but when I tried to explain it to you, you only got more confused. In the end, all you knew for certain was that someone at the bar had got himself a free drink just by using a collective noun, so you tried it yourself."

"A brace of grouse," said the man.

"A gaggle of geese," said Thomas.

"A pride of lions."

"A pack of wolves."

"A school of fish."

"A murder of crows."

"A *what?*"

"A murder of crows."

"Gag me with a breeze block," said the man. "You're Thomas-bloody-Martin!"

"And you're Arthur-bloody-Strongbow."

"Aye, well, I can't help that," he said. "You'll have another?"

Thomas nodded, although he was only halfway through his first.

"Old friends, are you?" the server asked.

"Ye've a fair brace of grouse yourself," said Arthur Strongbow.

"The upturned bellies of breathing fallen sparrows," said Thomas.

"More like turkeys," said Arthur.

"Here, what are you on about?" she demanded.

"Only your tits, love," said Arthur Strongbow. "We're a pair of old poets, aren't we, and there's nothing you can do about it."

"I can stop serving you."

"Aye, and you can stop doing the lad from the brewery, too. But you won't."

"Why, you cheeky sod!"

"Leave it out, love, and pour the beer. That's all anyone cares about." He turned to Thomas. "You've lost a fair bit of hair, Thomas."

"Aye," said Thomas, lapsing into the other's comfortable accent, "and you're still ugly as sin. But I can buy a wig."

"You always were an impudent bugger." Strongbow drank thoughtfully. "Leonard Cohen, wasn't it?"

"What?"

"The upturned bellies of breathing fallen sparrows."

"Oh, yes, from *The Spice-Box of Earth.*"

"It amazed me when the bugger started singing." Strongbow shook his head. "It amazes me more that he can make a living at it. I went up to Abbey Road myself one day, but EMI wasn't interested. Are you still writing?"

Thomas shook his head in turn. "I only had the one book in me, apparently."

"Sometimes it works that way," Strongbow agreed. "Music was more your line, anyway."

"Mm." Noncommittal.

"In fact...in fact...." Strongbow looked at the ceiling, stroking the black stubble under his massive chin. "Yes" – looking at Thomas, pointing – "that's why you left. You had a bloody great contract in New York City. The big time. I kept expecting to see your face on an album cover. Or I suppose it would be a CD cover now."

"It was the year Jimmy Hendrix died," said Thomas. "The world wasn't much interested in folk singers any more."

"So what happened?"

"I recorded an album that sold well over twenty copies, then found myself locked into an eight-year contract with a company that refused to take another chance on me but wouldn't let me record with anybody else."

"Bad management," said Strongbow.

"And naïveté," Thomas agreed. "And hubris. And greed."

"And a fair bit of self-flagellation, by the sound of it."

"Aye." Thomas drank, remembering now how much he enjoyed the taste of warm, bitter beer on a summer afternoon in Chelsea. The earthy smell of the malt, the bitter undertaste of the hops, the minuscule bubbles that bit the tongue and followed it down your throat: it was an experience to be had nowhere else on earth. He drained his pint and started on the second.

"Is that why you never came back? You were embarrassed?"

The acuity of the man had always been maddening. Thomas changed the subject. "I've kept up with you, Arthur Strongbow, winner of the Whitbread Prize, the Manchester Book Award, and the Glasgow Fellowship. Very impressive."

"It pays the rent." He shrugged. "A man can't live on royalties."

"Are you working on anything now?"

"Oh, aye, always working on something. Faber's bringing out a *New and Selected* in the fall."

"Congratulations," said Thomas, then: "Do you remember Cassandra Shirley?" He asked the question almost casually, as if saying her name in the presence of someone who had known them as a couple would not set events in motion that he could not control.

"Of course." He was surprised that Thomas had asked. "Though she doesn't call herself Cassandra any more, not since her mother died."

There was so much information in the statement that Thomas had to pause to collect his thoughts. *Of course,* he'd said, which implied that Strongbow not only remembered her, but that they were still friends. He knew where she lived. And the old woman was dead...finally. And Cassandra had changed her name...in celebration? in defiance? *Cassandra!* He could almost hear the quavering tones from the back bedroom. *Cassandra, are you going to stay up all night? Cassandra, I'm thirsty. Cassandra, don't leave me alone. Cassandra.* She spoke the name like a witch's spell that would keep her daughter forever close, forever guilty, forever obedient. *Cassandra, you* are *going to take me to Harrods' this afternoon, aren't you?* And the unspoken, *I've given up everything for you, Cassandra.*

"I had a dream about her the other night," said Thomas. "Out of the blue, after twenty years. I can't remember it, exactly, but I woke up with a sense of pain and loss that I couldn't shake."

These were half-truths, at best. Dreams didn't come "out of the blue" when a woman has entered your thoughts with regret and affection weekly, if not daily, for two decades. And he remembered very well what had happened in the dream.

"Good God!" said Strongbow. "You're not telling me that's why you've come back after all these years?"

"It was the catalyst," Thomas admitted. "I'd been meaning to come back ever since I left, and after Gwen died there was no longer any reason not to."

"Give us two more, love," Strongbow said to the server, and gestured Thomas to a table in the corner.

They fell easily into the intimacy of shared experience and remembered friends. In less than half an hour, no one listening would have thought that they hadn't seen one another in years. For Thomas, it was as if he had never left. They stayed well into the evening, drinking and talking, remembering, speculating, and finally lurching home as the sun set over Chelsea Reach, Thomas to his room in Flaxman House, Strongbow to the flat in Old Church Street that he shared with Eva, whom he had married, he claimed, for her money. Thomas missed breakfast the next morning, and spent the day in his room recovering from such a hangover as he had not experienced since 1969. He felt obscurely blessed by it.

Two days later, nervous and unready, he arrived at the rendezvous Arthur Strongbow had arranged for him with Cassandra Shirley, now known simply as Sandi, with an *i;* she was particular about that, according to Strongbow. It was early afternoon. They were to meet at the King's Head and Eight Bells. She would be waiting for him. He wasn't to be early.

It took a moment for his eyes to adjust to the interior dimness, but he knew she recognized him the minute he walked in. She was smiling at him. His heart lurched at the sight of her. Twenty years on she had the same fine, black hair, the same pale, oval face, the same girlishly crooked English teeth. She was sitting at a table near a window that faced a small square in which Thomas Carlyle sat in aging bronze, brooding over the Thames. There was a half-pint of untouched bitter before her. It was a familiar pose. He had expected Strongbow to be there, and was almost disappointed that he wasn't. It would have been easier to break the ice a bit at a time rather than all at once.

She did not rise as he approached, and made no

move of welcome other than to hold out her hand. There were only half a dozen drinkers in the pub at this hour, but he felt they were all staring at him as he took her hand self-consciously and shook it as if they were strangers.

"Hello, Thomas."

"Cassandra..."

"No one calls me that any more."

"Yes, I'm sorry. Strongbow told me you were calling yourself Sandi now. With an *i*," he added.

She laughed. "Do you think you can get used to it?"

His heart lurched again. Implicit in the question was the possibility that he would have time to get used to it, that this meeting was not just a courtesy but the beginning of something, a new beginning...But he was getting ahead of himself.

"I was sorry to hear about your mother," he said.

"No, you weren't," and she laughed again, a deeply feminine sound, but with an edge to it, Thomas thought, that hadn't been there twenty years ago. "Mum hated you, and she made sure you knew it. Afraid you were going to take me away from her. I've wondered if she was the reason you never came back."

She was one of the reasons, certainly, a small but extremely toxic reason. But he wasn't prepared to get into that so soon. Instead, he asked, "When did she pass away?"

"She didn't *pass away*, Thomas." There was a bitterness in her tone that she did not try to conceal. "That implies a certain degree of peaceful acceptance. And she certainly didn't *fall asleep* or *join the choir invisible*. She *died* three years ago, after five indignant and implausibly drawn-out years in a wheelchair. It wasn't a real life at all any more, when every movement caused her pain. But she clung to it like the devil."

She had aged, Thomas noticed. The lines around her eyes and mouth were not all from laughter. Yet when she did laugh she was as young as she had ever been. And she had always liked to laugh, even when her mother was hovering over her like a malevolent goddess of judgement. She was laughing now.

"You must think me terrible, talking about my own mother like that."

"On the contrary, I think it's healthy. I sometimes thought you couldn't really see her for what she was."

"Oh, I saw her all right, none clearer."

The hum of traffic along the Embankment grew louder as the door opened. A young couple appeared, holding hands. The stench of diesel and unleaded gasoline followed them in from the street. They took a seat in a corner where they could be private.

"You'd better get yourself a pint," she said. "The barmaid's gazing askance."

"What can I get you?"

She glanced down at her untouched half of bitter. "I'm fine."

"Canadian?" asked the barmaid.

"No," said Thomas, "a pint of traditional bitter."

"I meant you," she said, drawing the pint. She was a different server than the one that had been here the other day, less buxom but more robust, with a compact body and an intelligent face. "You're Canadian."

"Oh," he said, flustered. "Most people mistake me for an American."

"Most people haven't travelled enough to tell Durham from Dorset." She lowered her voice, confiding. "I'm from the north meself."

"Newcastle?"

"You've been there." She nodded approvingly as she placed his pint on the bar. "It's not always a good thing to be from the north down here in the Smoke. The nobs don't like our accent. I don't suppose it makes any difference in Canada?"

"None at all," he lied.

"So you know our Sandi, then," she said, returning his change.

"She's a regular?"

"Regular as bran flakes. She just lives around the corner in –" but she stopped herself. "Maybe I shouldn't be saying so much to a stranger."

"I'm not really a stranger. This was my neighbourhood pub twenty years ago."

"Well then," she said, "welcome home."

He returned to the table with his pint. Cassandra was carefully lighting a cigarette with a wooden Vesta. He was conscious of a brief disappointment, which she was too sharp not to notice. "I suppose you've stopped?" she asked.

"Hardest thing I've ever done," he nodded. "I think it's why Gwen finally left me. She could put up with moodiness and irritability, she said, but insanity wasn't covered in the wedding contract."

"But I thought your wife had died, Thomas." There

was a hint of alarm in her voice. "Arthur told me you were a widower."

"Oh yes, she died. But she left me first."

Cassandra took the first sip of her ale, raising the glass carefully to her lips and just as carefully lowering it. "What was she like, your Gwen?"

"She was...." But what could he say? that she was as close a physical match to Cassandra as he could find in all of Toronto? That she was utterly unlike Cassandra in temperament and patience? That she made love passionately but far too quickly, intent on immediate gratification? That her work was always and forever more important than his, or even him?

"She was a strong and beautiful woman," he told her at last, "and a loving and generous mother. She was a dentist, if you can imagine. You could never hope to meet a woman more passionate about teeth. She had me brushing five times a day until I quit smoking. And then, of course, she left me."

"So you have children." Cassandra had infallibly picked out the most important word in his brief statement: *mother.*

"A girl and two boys." He nodded. "Eighteen, sixteen, and fourteen years old, respectively. Gwen was an obedient Catholic until she found out how exhausting it could be, then she cheerfully sent me for a vasectomy."

"They must miss their mother."

"They do, the boys especially. There was never any question that they would stay with me. Gwen moved out temporarily to give me time to pack and find a place to live, but she would have been back within a month.

It was her house, after all. God knows – and so did Gwen – I could never have afforded a place like that on my own."

"How did she die?"

"A drunk driver ploughed into her on Yonge Street. I thank God none of the kids was with her." He turned his glass in its circle of sweat on the varnished table top. "I suppose I should be grateful that she didn't have time to change her will."

"I don't remember you being so cynical, Thomas."

"The last time you saw me I hadn't been a husband yet, or a father, or a widower. I hadn't failed at two separate careers, or been rejected by my children in favour of their mother. A lot can happen in twenty years."

"I suppose one can build up a fair store of self-pity in that time, too," she said, but there was no condemnation in it. She seemed to be speaking reflectively, almost to herself. "I hear you've been dreaming about me."

"Strongbow told you everything, then."

"No, not everything. He didn't tell me what the dream was about."

"Only because I didn't tell him."

A trio of suits walked in and made for the bar. One of them, casting a speculative eye over the other drinkers, saw Cassandra and nodded briefly. She acknowledged him with a slight movement and half a smile.

"Friend of yours?"

"One of the regulars."

"What is your relationship with him, anyway?"

She looked surprised. "I don't even know his last name."

"No, I mean Strongbow." He was faintly, absurdly, and unjustifiably, jealous. Cassandra saw it, and was amused.

"He has been a dear and compassionate friend. Even when Polly left him, and later when he took up with Eva, he always had time for me. More important, he had time for my mother. Every Sunday he took her for a walk in Paddington Recreation Ground, and later, when we moved, in Battersea Park, then Hyde Park or Kensington Gardens. When she couldn't walk any more he took her in her wheelchair. Sometimes she came back giggling like a schoolgirl."

"An unlikely couple, I'd have thought."

"I didn't think. I was just grateful he gave me my Sunday afternoons."

"Yes, well, with Strongbow you don't have to think, do you? What you see is what you get" – he paused – "though it's sometimes hard to know exactly what you're seeing."

He remembered a cycle of poems, three or four books ago now, about a cripple in a wheelchair. It had always seemed incongruous to think of that great, rough man being capable of such delicacy of expression, such gentle passions. Knowing that he had been writing about Cassandra's impenitent mother made it even more incongruous. For Strongbow, though, everything was grist for the mill. That was an attitude that Thomas had never mastered – had never thought to master, if he was honest with himself.

Someone started playing a fruit machine against the back wall, and someone else must have fed the jukebox, for the plaintive strains of "Stairway to Heaven" suddenly filled the room. Odd choice for a pub song, Thomas thought, mentally going through the chord changes as Robert Plant's voice opened the lyrics: *There's a lady who's sure all that glitters is gold, and she's buying a stairway to heaven....*

"I beg your pardon?" Cassandra had spoken.

"I said, are you going to tell me what the dream was about?"

"Stupid, really." He shook his head, took a drink. "It was the middle of the night, and a train came up my street. It's a quiet residential street in Richmond Hill, just outside Toronto. And it wasn't one of your civilized English passenger trains. It was a huge diesel, thirty cars long, what the railway used to call the Super-continental. I went out to the street in my bathrobe. It stopped in front of the house and you got out. You were wearing cut-off jeans and a tee-shirt. You were weeping uncontrollably, but when I reached out to comfort you, you kept moving away. Or rather, you were moved away by some force so that I could never quite touch you." He took another drink; the level of the liquid was receding slowly. "When I woke up, I had to go to the window to make sure the train wasn't really there. I half expected to see you wandering about the street, lost and crying...."

The pub was filling up as the afternoon progressed. He found the chatter of English voices familiar and comforting. Tobacco smoke was beginning to compete with the traffic smell. Someone nearby lit a cigar. Snatches of conversation intruded on the silence that had risen between them.

"Do you remember when Tony Adams died and we all got pissed at the funeral...?"

"*No, love*, I said, *I'm an alcoholic diabetic, not a diabetic alcoholic. Get it right, for God's sake.,..*"

"So when I woke up, I said to the doctor, *I can just about manage a poached egg....*"

"I wouldn't have a dog in the house...."

"Is that it?" she asked.

"It was enough," he said.

"Enough to bring you back after twenty years?"

He nodded.

She lit another cigarette, a Silk Cut. He couldn't recall if that was the brand she had smoked before.

"Well," she said, "I'm sure Jung or Freud would have had an interesting take on it, but I can't say it makes much sense to me."

He couldn't hide his disappointment.

"Thomas," she said, reaching across the table to touch his hand briefly, "I'm touched – and surprised, I must say – that you still think of me after all these years. But it was only a dream. Besides," she added, with just a touch of bitterness, "did you really think I was that pathetic?"

That shocked him. He hadn't thought of her that way at all. But he couldn't bear to pursue it, so he changed the subject: "Did you stay with your mother till the end?"

She stubbed out her cigarette. "How could I not?

She had no one else. I think I might have left at one time, made a life for myself, but...."

With a visible effort, it seemed to Thomas, she suppressed the words he yearned to hear: *I might have had a life if you had returned as you promised, if you had given me the children we both wanted.* He needed to hear the words so that he could stand accused before her and begin to make reparation. He needed to hear them so that he would know that she remembered him, even a little, and in some measure regretted losing him.

"Cassandra, I'm sorry."

"It was twenty years ago, Thomas."

"But we might have been –"

"Happy?" she interrupted him. *"Might have* doesn't mean anything. Let it rest," and she smiled gently. It was clear that she had forgiven him, if he hadn't.

"You don't understand, Cassandra. I'm not sorry for leaving as much as for not being worthy of you."

She was stunned. "Worthy of me?"

"Half the time I was a penniless poet, and the other half I was a penniless musician. Your mother lost no chance to bring that to your attention. Or mine, for that matter. I had to have something more than that to offer you. So I went to New York, hoping to return with something. But I couldn't seem to manage it. My album failed and I'd locked myself into a ludicrous contract, so that was the end of that. I've been a session man in Toronto for eighteen years. In a good week I work three full days, and if you look closely you'll find my name in a few liner notes as backup guitar and vocalist. I couldn't bring that back to you. You deserved better."

There was a long silence. The afternoon sun poured through the southern windows, highlighting the motes of dust and the wisps of tobacco smoke that hung in the air. On his plinth outside, Carlyle seemed to have changed positions, his implacable bronze face following the sun.

When Cassandra finally spoke, it was in the unmistakable, hollow tones of defeat: "What you're saying, then, is that you destroyed my happiness — our happiness — because you found you couldn't satisfy your ego?"

He felt the accusation as a blow to the solar plexus, a physical pain that nearly doubled him over. It had never crossed his mind that there was anything *selfish* in the decisions he'd made. But she wasn't finished.

"You lived an entire other life as a failure without me, when all you needed to be a success was *me*. That's what we were about, Thomas. Not fame. Not money. Maybe not even happiness. Maybe just coping — coping with my mother, coping with what you call your failure, coping with children and taxes and overdraughts. But coping *together*. That would have been our success. Everything else is jam."

He stared at the table, unable to meet her eyes. "I...I'm sorry," was all he could say.

"So am I, more than you can imagine. For a long time I wondered why you stopped writing, not just to me but to the world. Your poetry was beautiful, I thought, even heroic. I always thought that the printed page was the only place you could say what you really meant. I kept looking for your name in bookstores. That was where you belonged, not on some concert stage but between the covers of a book. But I couldn't find you on the stage, either, or in the music stores. I should have known enough to drop it then. It was twenty years ago. You went to New York and I went home to my mother. End of story."

"Except that I haven't lived in New York for eighteen years, and you no longer live with your mother."

"That's right," she said. "I've my own life now, my own flat, my own toilet. You can't imagine what a luxury that is."

It was clear to him now, clear as ice, frozen and unyielding. Even the heat of a summer afternoon in Chelsea could not melt it. *I've my own life now.* Clearly, there was no room in it for him.

He stood. "There's no hope for us, then."

"I didn't say that."

"You didn't have to." He shook his head, as close to tears as he had been in two decades. "I understand."

Minutes after he left, Arthur Strongbow came into the pub. He looked about uncertainly, then made for Cassandra's table.

"He's gone?"

She nodded.

"It didn't go well."

"No."

"Are you all right, Sandi?"

She looked at him, tight-lipped. "Just take me home, Arthur."

He nodded and strode away. He was back in a moment with the wheelchair he had stowed behind the bar for her earlier. He unfolded the contraption and helped her into it, then held the door open as she wheeled herself out.

THE PHILOSOPHER

Zelda arrived home later than usual, for she had been visiting her brother at the home. There was an insane man by the door as she got off the elevator. She thought it was Professor Anderson at first, for he looked remarkably like her employer: small, weary, red-eyed, moist-lipped, limp yellowish-grey hair combed back from a high forehead, a sagging tweed jacket, baggy corduroys, and Oxford shoes that should have been given to the Salvation Army years ago. But it was the eyes that placed him among the élite circle of the unbalanced. They regarded her with a kind of pathetic lust. Pitiful, she thought. But hungry, too. Hungry could be dangerous. Zelda knew about such things. It made her uneasy.

"I'm your Fullway representative," he said, lifting one of the grip bags he held in either hand. It was made of artificial leather, and frayed at the seams.

"I'm not interested," she said as she tried to fit her key into the lock. Her fingernails were beyond anything that could be called stylish – Tibetan, Professor Anderson called them; she meant to ask him what he meant by it one day – and it took her longer than most people to perform simple tasks. She typed with a sort of flat-handed scurrying, her fingers moving crab-like across the keyboard. She was neither fast nor accurate, but Professor Anderson was fond of quoting Samuel Johnson. Watching Zelda type, he would say to his colleagues, "is like watching a dog walking on its hind legs; it is not done well, but one is surprised to find it done at all." His colleagues suspected that Professor Anderson was more enamoured of her black tights and short skirts, her delirious blond hair and her extravagant bust than of her secretarial eccentricities, but they were philosophers too, so of course they said nothing to the point.

"We have a nice line in spices," said the man.

"I'm not interested," Zelda repeated. She had been using her whole body to fit the key into the lock, bending at the knees and swaying from the hips. Even her tongue was involved somehow, curling over her lips and rubbing against her teeth. Now she was trying to turn the key without doing violence to her thumbnail. It really was getting too long, even by her standards. She resolved to file down an eighth of an inch while she watched television tonight.

"Cleaning products," the man continued, "personal grooming items, vitamins, shampoo and conditioner, feminine protection" – this last with a sort of disconso-

late leer – "skin care. I'm sure I could show you something you liked."

"I don't need anything," said Zelda, turning the key,
finally, and pushing the door open.

"Ah, now," said the man, "need is something I can't
help you with. That's not my job. And it's not fair, is it,
telling a man that he has to fulfil a woman's needs. It's
not fair and it's not right. But want is another thing.
When it comes to *want*, I'm your man."

"I don't *want* anything," said Zelda. In fact, she
wanted to close the door in his face, but now she couldn't
get the key out of the lock.

"Allow me to congratulate you, then," said the man
lugubriously, "for you are unique among the 5.7 billion
inhabitants of planet earth."

"What are you, Tibetan or something?" Zelda
thought that was pretty good, as rejoinders go, though
she had no idea what she meant by it.

"I'm your Fullway representative," he repeated, and
once more lifted a battered grip for her inspection. He
was in the front hall now, the door was shut, and Zelda
had her key in her hand. She had no clear idea how any
of this had come about.

"This is a security building," she said. "How did you
get in?"

"I can usually get into a building if I want to." His
tone suggested that this was not a point of pride, but
rather a cross he bore with fortitude.

"I'm calling security," said Zelda, and she picked up
the telephone. She had one in every room, for she
couldn't bear to miss a call, but she wouldn't have a cell-

phone because it might ring while she was on the toilet and she couldn't bear to answer it, but then she couldn't bear not to answer it if it rang, so it was best not to have one at all. The phone in the hall was a soft yellow, its keypad glowing like translucent ivory in the handle of the receiver.

"Use your knuckle," the insane man suggested after a moment of watching her trying to depress one button at a time with her long-nailed forefinger. She tried it, and was surprised at its efficiency. She wondered if it were a technology she could translate to the keyboard. God knows what Professor Anderson would say.

She held the receiver to her ear and listened to the reassuring clicks and whirrs that told her that her call was going through. At the same time she heard the muffled bleating of a nearby cellular phone, and her heart missed a beat. With an existential sigh, the Fullway representative put down one of his grip bags and reached into an inside pocket of his sagging jacket. He pulled out a cellphone and put the instrument to his ear.

"Security," he said. "How may I help you?"

It did not take Zelda long to realize that the movements of the insane man's lips matched exactly the words she was hearing over the telephone. She hung up.

"Are you going to kill me?" she asked, halfway between blind panic and fatalistic acceptance.

"That depends," he said, replacing the cellphone in his jacket.

"On what?"

"On whether or not you die as a result of my actions." He picked up the grip bag he had put down and held it up for her inspection. It was the third time he had done so. "I'd still like to show you our line of spices, though."

It was the bags that saved him. Zelda was a sturdy young woman, and agile, for she took regular exercise and followed a low-fat diet, but she was no match for those bags. She went first for his crotch. Her skirt was short enough not to hinder her wind-up, but when one high-heeled foot shot forward to unman him, she struck only a barrier of artificial leather. She went for his face then, fingernails poised to rip the tender flesh, but again she was met by artificial leather, battered but impervious.

She kicked off her high-heeled shoes and went into a crouch, swaying with menace, holding her hands karate-style before her. She had never actually kicked anybody in the face, but she thought it was something she could manage with relative ease. And indeed, she would have hit him in the region of the upper chest had it not been for those damn bags. The force of the recoil sent her back against the wall.

There wasn't enough room in the hallway, she decided. She needed to lure him into the front room, where she would have space to defend herself.

She went into a crouch again, moving backward, cat-like, beckoning with her unsheathed claws. "Come on, sucker," she said, trusting that her tone conveyed the appropriate mixture of challenge and contempt. "You want a little action? You've got it!"

The man followed, still holding up his bags. "Perhaps you're not interested in spices," he said. "Fair enough. My mother never used anything but salt and pepper, and rarely even those. But I can't believe you don't want to look at our nail-care products."

"You're pathetic," she said. "You're just a little boy, aren't you? A pathetic little boy."

She had learned from visiting her brother that appealing to the wounded child in a man was often the best way to reach him. By the same reasoning, she thought, berating the wounded child should induce a puerile dread which would establish her dominance long enough to make good her escape.

Admittedly, she did not articulate the thought, but she acted on it nonetheless. She knew how to hurt a man. It was something you learned early if you didn't want to spend most of your leisure time being groped.

"Just a quick demonstration," he said.

"Let's see how you like *this* demonstration!" she responded.

Her intention had been to gain the back of the couch in three quick strides – from the cushion to the arm to the back – and with the momentum thus generated launch herself toward him and capture his neck in a vicious scissor hold. Unfortunately, the couch tipped over before she could launch herself, and she found herself sprawled on the floor, winded.

One of Professor Anderson's colleagues had once remarked that even the destruction of the universe and everything in it could only kill you once. Professor Anderson had argued the point, but Zelda had taken comfort from it, without knowing why. Now she realized that it meant that she could only die once. This man could do whatever he wanted to her, but he could only kill her once. That was a kind of power she held over him. In a sense, she was invincible.

"You've broken a nail," said the man, putting his bags down and sitting cross-legged on the floor beside her. "I've got just the thing for that."

"Go ahead," she said. "Have your will of me. You can dishonour my flesh but you cannot touch my soul!"

The statement was not original with Zelda. She had read it in a romance novel, and, like many of the things she read or heard, it had stayed with her. If Professor Anderson were aware of this rare talent in his secretary, he had yet to exploit it. Zelda experienced a certain dire satisfaction now in being able to exploit it herself.

The insane man opened one of his grip bags and took out an elegant box with the Fullway logo tastefully printed in the lower right corner. He placed it on the floor in front of her. "This is from our *Have Your Will of Me* series. It's quite popular."

"Go ahead!" she repeated. "Do your worst!"

"My dear woman, my worst is a good deal better than you imagine, and my best would spoil you for any other man."

He said this with such doleful sincerity that Zelda straightened her skirt and propped herself on her elbows, regarding him closely. "Are you a philosopher?" she asked.

He didn't respond, but opened his other bag and began taking samples out of it, arranging them in rows on the floor between them.

Another thought struck her: "Do you know my brother?"

He looked up quickly.

"Who, Dick?" He shook his head. "A sad case. So much promise...."

"You're from the home."

Again, he did not respond, but continued taking items out of his bag. Alongside a wide selection of handsomely packaged samples he now placed a stack of clothbound notebooks, a ball-peen hammer, a plumber's wrench, and a length of PVC pipe.

"What do you want?"

"I thought I had made myself clear."

He delivered the statement with a sort of piteous leer. Really, he was not to be taken seriously. If he was a lunatic like her brother Dick, who had without warning one day decided that he was a minor deity, then he was harmless. But if he was a lunatic like the sex offenders they kept in the isolation ward, then, again, he could only kill her once.

"The reason Professor Anderson refers to your nails as Tibetan," said the Fullway representative, "is that certain ascetics of the Eastern tradition have been known to let their fingernails and hair grow as a sign of withdrawal from the world. I've seen lamas with fingernails as long as thirty centimetres. The tradition is not strictly Tibetan, however, and I hardly think it applies to you."

Zelda, whose knowledge of llamas was limited to a high school history course on South America, should have been greatly surprised. But if the ruminant quadrupeds of Peru chose to grow their fingernails to the length of thirty centimetres, it was no concern of hers. She was interested that he knew Professor Anderson, though.

She raised herself to sit cross-legged, mirroring his pose. "Why didn't you tell me you knew Professor Anderson?"

"You didn't ask."

"I didn't ask if you were my Fullway representative, either."

"True," he said, picking up the length of PVC pipe. "Do you know what this is?"

"Looks like the pipes under the sink."

He shook his head unhappily. "It is an aid to meditation."

Zelda shook her head in turn, and absently picked up the first of the boxed items he had placed before her on the floor.

"That's our new line," he said. "Guaranteed," he added as Zelda opened the box. It was filled with foil-wrapped condoms.

"Guaranteed?"

"One hundred percent latex rubber."

"What kind of guarantee is that?"

"The only kind we can legally offer."

Zelda closed the box and put it down. "My husband will be home soon."

"I shall be delighted to meet him."

"From work," said Zelda. "He car-pools with the man across the hall."

"No doubt they are employed in the same building."

"They work outdoors," said Zelda. "Construction,"

she added, lifting her shoulders and scowling by way of illustration.

"But surely what they construct are buildings."

"Sometimes," Zelda allowed.

"So, in fact, they are employed in the same building."

"You know what I mean."

"On the contrary," he said, picking up the ball-peen hammer. "I *don't* know what you mean. What is more, I question whether *you* know what you mean."

"Are you calling me a liar?"

"I am merely suggesting that your perceptions in no way conform to reality." He gestured with the hammer. "In short, you don't know what you're talking about."

She got him in the head this time. It was as neat a trick as she could have imagined. She simply leaned back and, while he was staring up her skirt, straightened her right leg with such force and speed that he had no time to take evasive action before her heel connected with his left eye socket.

"Asshole!" she said.

"Bloody hell!" he responded, one hand over his eye. "The things one does for the love of truth."

"Truth?" she demanded. "What's that supposed to mean?"

"Philosophy." He was rocking back and forth with the pain. "I have a PHD in Hegelian metaphysics."

"It's no wonder you can't find a proper job," said Zelda.

Hegelian metaphysics. Professor Anderson had been arguing with someone over the telephone last week and had raised his voice, a circumstance so singular that

Zelda had unconsciously committed the term to memory. "Hegelian metaphysics!" the professor had thundered. "With Hegelian metaphysics and a dollar you can get yourself a cup of coffee!"

"Hegelian metaphysics?" she asked, with such scorn that the man seemed almost to cower.

"I have a PHD," he repeated.

"And I have a certificate from West End Business College."

"But you have no husband," he accused. "You were lying."

"That's all right," said Zelda. "I don't need one now," and she got up and disarranged his samples with a casual sweep of her foot. "Pack up your things and get out."

There was an anguished pause, during which the insane man gazed alternately at Zelda and at the hammer he still held in one hand. His eye, behind the other hand, had begun to throb.

"I'm afraid I haven't made myself clear," he said, at length. "I probably know more about Hegel than any man alive. I have a PHD in Hegelian metaphysics."

Zelda briefly considered kicking him again, now that they both knew how easy it was, but the inclination was overruled by another.

"Fine," she said, and she turned her back on him and walked into the kitchen. She put the kettle on for tea. She dearly loved her cup of tea when she got home from work. When she turned from the stove, she was annoyed to find that the man had crept up behind her. His eye was ripening into a nice, pale mauve. He was still holding the hammer.

"Or at least, I *would* have a PHD in Hegelian metaphysics – and a proper job, too, probably – if it hadn't been for the labyrinthine functioning of your employer's picayune brain."

"Eh?"

"Seven long, lonely years selling useless articles door-to-door to make ends meet while I write my dissertation, then your Professor Anderson destroys it in an afternoon. My thesis is indefensible, he said. *Indefensible.* Can you imagine?"

Zelda could, in fact. She was not without sympathy for the young men and women whose careers Professor Anderson periodically chose to destroy. She did not pretend to know why such things were important, but the parade of broken lives she had watched pass through her employer's office door had left her in no doubt that some people took it very seriously indeed.

"Who made him head of the department, anyway?" the man demanded.

This was a question Zelda had heard before, and it always amazed her how stupid such smart people could be.

"You should have come to me first," she told him. "You have to get him in the right mood. Look, tell me your name and I'll have a chat with him in the morning."

"I'm afraid it's too late," said the man. He raised the hammer and pointed to a clot of blood on the peen. "I killed him."

"That's impossible," said Zelda. "I saw him just this afternoon at –"

"At three o'clock," the Fullway representative interrupted, "as he left for a committee meeting. *My* committee, as it happened. I took the hammer along just in case. And a good thing, too, because I needed it. You see, Zelda, it can take years to destroy a man – seven years, in my case – but it only takes a moment to kill him."

The kettle was boiling.

"You know my name," she said.

"I also know that he was in love with you."

"That little ferret?" Zelda scoffed as she turned off the kettle and made the tea. "Don't make me laugh!"

"I have the proof in the next room." He pointed with the hammer. "Professor Anderson's private diary: five cloth-bound volumes of crabbed academic script, page after page devoted to his beloved Zelda: Zelda of the Tibetan Fingernails, Zelda of the Miraculous Bosom, Zelda of the Shapely Buttocks, Zelda of the Legs that Just Don't Quit. Callipygian, he called you."

"You're sick," said Zelda.

"Quite possibly," said the man, and Zelda noticed that his eye – the one that was not now swollen shut – had begun almost to glow. "But then, quite possibly we are all sick. It's only a matter of degree, or of how much we manage to conceal from the world. Professor Anderson's fondest fantasy was of the two of you eating linguine with clam sauce and falling together with lusty cries afterward, bellies full and inhibitions abandoned. No, Zelda, he yearned for you 'as the hart panteth after the water brooks.' Sick he was, dead he is. I am not sorry that I killed him."

It occurred to Zelda, with a teapot in one hand and a kettle of boiling water in the other, that she had got the better of him once and it would be a simple enough matter to do so again: brain him with the teapot, then pour scalding water over his head. As he suffered and screamed, she could make it to the door, then to the elevator and down to the lobby where Bernie the doorman would call the police. But the insane man had Bernie's cellphone, and she did not want to ponder the implications of that. Besides, her curiosity was raging. She could deal with this lunatic, she had no doubt, but first she must plumb the depths of his lunacy.

"Did you kill the rest of the committee, too?" she asked.

"I had no choice, did I? I mean, they were all sitting there, watching. I couldn't let them go unpunished."

"Did you use the hammer?"

"Oh no, the hammer was strictly for Professor Anderson. The rest I did with that PVC pipe I showed you earlier. *An aid to meditation* I called it, remember? It did my heart good, I must say, to see all those tenured faculty meditating to such purpose. Beat them senseless, I did, then finished them off with this," and he produced a .38 revolver from the pocket of his baggy tweed jacket.

"And how did you get into this building?"

"I'm afraid I had to kill your doorman as well." He looked almost sheepish. "Tough little fellow. Fought like a tiger."

"And you used the plumber's wrench on him?"

"How did you guess?"

She shook her head. It wasn't important. "I suppose it was my brother Dick who put you up to this?"

"Not at all," said the Fullway representative. "It's true that we bunked together for a few weeks last year, and he may have made a few suggestions in his role as Lord of the Universe. But he certainly didn't command me."

"Lord of the Universe? He's promoted himself."

Zelda put down the tea things and turned away from the man. She directed her gaze upward, as though she were looking for something on the ceiling. Then her eyes focussed.

"There you are," she said, nodding grimly. "Before we go any further, would you mind telling me how you propose to resolve this situation?"

As an author, I generally have a fairly good idea what's going on in the minds of my characters, so I confess this took me by surprise.

"I presume one of us is going to bite it soon," she continued. "I just can't see how you're going to justify it."

"Your brother Dick is still alive," I protested.

She scoffed. It was the second time she had done that in as many pages. "A peripheral character," she said, "a cypher."

"Maybe you're all peripheral characters. Maybe the real protagonist hasn't even arrived yet. I'm the author. I can do what I want."

"Then why don't you give me a name?" asked the man. "Thirty-seven hundred and thirty-six words into the story and people still don't know what to call me."

"On the contrary," I bristled, "you are the Fullway representative. Alternatively, you are the insane man."

"Awkward," said the man, shaking his head. "People find it easier to relate to a person if he has a name, not just a label."

"Very well." I smiled wickedly. "I'll give you a southern accent and call you Billy-Bob-Jim-Bob-Joe. I've always wanted to name a character that."

"Oh, please, no," he said, "I hate that," but already he was speaking like a native of Savannah.

"Rise above it," I said. "And stop picking your nose."

"What's with Professor Anderson and the clam linguine?" Zelda demanded. "Whose idea was that?"

"His, presumably."

"And how am I supposed to do anything with nails like these?" She held them up for my inspection. I had to admit they were longer than I had imagined, and more curved. As for Zelda herself, she seemed to be gaining insights and intelligence I had not meant her to have.

I shrugged. "Cut them if you like."

"Do you mean it?"

"Of course," I said, and tried to mask my expression as I caused a horn to sprout from her forehead. Billy-Bob-Jim-Bob-Joe started visibly. Zelda ran her newly clipped fingers along the smooth arc of the *cornu* from base to point.

"What is a *cornu?*" she asked.

"It's Latin for horn," I said smugly. "I looked it up."

"Remove it," she said. "It's not logical."

I refused. But I did give Billy-Bob-Jim-Bob-Joe his normal accent back. Not being a native of Savannah myself, I could not render in print the myriad nuances of that subtle tongue.

"How am I supposed to have beaten people to death with a pvc pipe?" he demanded. "And what do you know about Hegelian metaphysics?"

"I gave you a .38 revolver, didn't I?" I asked, neatly turning his question aside with another.

"Without bothering to tell me about it. How did it get in my pocket?"

"I put it there."

"Oh, you put it there. That's a good one. Talk about manipulating the plot."

"Face it," said Zelda as Billy-Bob-Jim-Bob-Joe, whom I had just renamed Ken, produced a red cape and flourished it like a bullfighter, "you've lost control of both plot and character."

"I wouldn't say so," I said as she lowered her horn and rushed at the cape. Ken turned the charge aside effortlessly.

"This is pointless and demeaning," he said.

"I'm rather enjoying it."

But he was right. They were both right. Hegel's phenomenology of culture had been a powerful stimulus to the acceleration of intellectual history, but that was long after his metaphysics had fallen into disrepute.

I put down my pen – a Mont Blanc which had beggared me – and leaned back in my chair. They were gazing up at me, the pair of them, as if they had never read a Ken Follett novel. With a sigh, I picked up the sheets of foolscap and tossed them into the recycling bin. I could almost taste that first and most satisfying sip of scotch as I made for the door.

"Thank God he's gone," I heard a voice say behind me.

NOBODY GOES
TO EARTH ANY MORE

An aged man is but a paltry thing,
A tattered coat upon a stick, unless
Soul clap its hands and sing, and louder sing
For every tatter in its mortal dress.
W. B. Yeats
"Sailing to Byzantium"

Years later he told me a story about a woman and a hammer and a black dress. It was his own story, he said. I laughed where it seemed appropriate, but otherwise listened with respect, and marvelled that that withered flesh had ever felt such passion. Perhaps because of that, the story struck me as more mythology than truth, despite his protestations that no word of it was a lie. Not that it was unbelievable, you understand. Rather, it was the echo of ancient superstition that permeated the narrative — love, honour, comradeship, supernatural fear, however comically presented – that touched a chord in me. His story felt *familiar*, somehow.

Now, human existence admits the possibility of pleasure and pain, greed and generosity, prudence and folly, even good and evil, but perhaps we fail ourselves when we assume that myths are simply fictions created in the image of the tribe. Perhaps we unravel the mysteries of the past only to weave a subtler cloth. We do not truly know ourselves, after all. And why should not an old man weave his own myth? Surely the clandestine forays of memory and desire across the battleground of the soul are as worthy of story and song as any tribal fantasy.

I speak in metaphor, you understand. My own mate serves me well enough, and I him, I trust. We were bonded by hormonal injection (what the old man would call "falling in love") at the age of consent, and have led a life of mutual satisfaction ever since. The idea of actually living together, of eating and sleeping together, of sacrificing time and property to one another's welfare, the idea of rutting like beasts to bring forth children: it all seems so ludicrous. Still, there was that in the old man's tale that gives me pause....

The ritual (he told me) was worked out well in advance by whatever mystical agency is responsible for these things. She taught a dance class each evening at five o'clock. I came into possession of this intelligence one day while visiting my friend Murphy who lived in the flat below hers. After that I made it a habit to visit him at the same time every day. I would sit on his doorstep and watch her walking away from me down 3rd Avenue, the ragged sun slanting eastward across her footsteps. Then it was not difficult to arrange casually to be on the steps again to watch her return, her shadow two hours longer, her footsteps that much slower. She usually wore tight pants, which pleased me, although it turned out it was less a concession to style than a gesture of defiance: she refused to buy them larger, preferring to believe she would one day lose weight.

"I like them a little fat," Murphy confided, presumably because it proved they had appetites. He had himself sublimated all æsthetic appreciation to the impulses of the flesh, and fondly imagined that the women who attracted him shared his philosophy.

"That's the type of girl you *should* be seeing," he added, for he disapproved of the lean English version of that gender who had been monopolizing my attention of late. He went so far in support of my current interest as to tell me that she "did it." No doubt he imagined this would elevate her in my esteem, although he had the grace not to suggest that the information had come to him first-hand. Whether she "did it" or not, our relationship had not yet developed to the point where I was comfortable in any role other than observer. For her part, she exhibited no distress at being observed.

Oddly enough, although I was frequently tormented by erotic fantasies, she did not figure in any of them. When she walked away from me along the pavement I did not imagine the smooth naked back above her flexing buttocks, nor when she returned did I envision her bare breasts jogging above the curve of her belly, or the dark fleece at the apex of her thighs. I did not imagine her standing naked above me or lying naked below me. In short, she had every effect on me but the expected one.

So I went home each night and smoked strong Canadian cigarettes and read Leonard Cohen and composed lyric verse and finally slept. I awoke in the morning wondering if she would look any different than she had the day before. She never did, of course, and my friend Murphy was never rewarded by the sounds of shrieking orgies, nor even the squeaking of bedsprings he imagined should be emanating from the floor above. Men went up there. He saw them go up there, sometimes in twos and threes. That they were not "getting it," immediately and exhaustively, was a proposition not to be credited. For she had a lovely shape that did not conceal itself in her movements or her clothes. Clearly, she took pleasure in her body – why else would she dance? – yet every evening she came down the stairs just like a woman who has not spent the previous twenty-two hours devoured by thoughts of "getting it" and "doing it." Every evening I watched her progress down 3rd Avenue, waited a couple of hours, and watched her come back.

Perhaps I did imagine her naked once or twice. One cannot read Leonard Cohen in the small hours and *not* imagine women naked. But it was an intellectual nakedness, unsullied by lust:

Hungry as an archway
through which the troops have passed
I stand in ruins behind you
with your winter clothes
your broken sandal straps
I love to see you naked over there
especially from the back
Oh take this longing from my tongue....

Then one afternoon I was sitting in the Chinese lunch and grocery next door when she came in wearing tight blue jeans – she had tightened them herself; you could see the telltale seam up the back – and a grey T-SHIRT, and through the jeans you could see the outline of her panties, and through the T-SHIRT you could see the outline of the brassiere that would later prove so troublesome, and where the T-SHIRT almost met the waistband of her jeans you could see a thin sliver of swarthy flesh.

She bought hand cream and soap, and paid with a five-dollar bill. She gave me a friendly glance as she waited for change. My friend Murphy, who was eating breaded veal cutlets with chips across the booth from me, watched me watching her, and I could see that the neurons that fired his concupiscence were expectant and alert. He had asked her to pose nude for him. He had asked her to be in his film, nude again. This he told me, smugly, and for all I know he might have asked her to perform the Dance of the Seven Veils in his unswept living room while he and a clutch of like-minded Herods contemplated the beheading of prophets.

He slopped gravy and grease around his plate and into his mouth, no doubt imagining her in his lens. But all I could think of was that she had bought soap, which demonstrated, in some peculiar but irrevocable sense, that she was no longer untouchable.

And so it proved.

It was an evening like any other, a soft summer evening, a lean blue sky hung high with feathered clouds like dusted flour on a baking board. There was a scent of flowers from the landlady's garden, an odour of diesel from the street. She came down the stairs to borrow a hammer.

"I think Marcella has the hammer," said Murphy, referring to an aging artist three doors down who was notorious for seducing young men. She had been known to answer the door unclothed, a prospect that filled me with anxiety.

"*The* hammer?" she asked. In a block of twelve flats, she seemed to be saying, surely there was more than one hammer.

"I can lend you a hammer," I said boldly.

She was no more anxious than I to knock on Marcella's door, and accepted my offer with a gracious smile. Arrangements were made for delivery, and we each went about our business. Murphy, who had made my business his own, dedicated himself to the proposition that I should seize the day. In my innocence, I thought I had. Seize the woman, he meant.

One thing at a time.

I had to find a hammer first.

I thought he was finished then, and turned off the recorder. He tended to ramble – not surprising for a man in his nineties who has twice been awakened from cryogenic sleep. Many of his stories were no more conclusive than this one. In linear time, after all, he was nearly three thousand years old. My predecessor had found him and four others in a cultural ruin she was excavating in the western desert more than a century ago. He was the only one to survive the awakening, but she found his "erratic verbosity" of little use for her research. She had had him refrozen, she recorded, "in deference to tribal memory, and in the hope that his knowledge might prove more useful to future generations."

It was that notation which had led me to reawaken him: "in deference to tribal memory." What could it mean? The old man had been a major poet of a minor clan – "a big fish in a small pond" was how he put it. It is possible that my predecessor traced her bloodline to his tribe. But if that were so, why did she not record the fact? Her case notes are startlingly incomplete. In any case, it was so unusual for sentiment of any kind to impinge on historical research that the mere hint of it was enough to arouse my curiosity.

Interestingly, she availed herself of a kevorkian less than a year later, as was her right, refusing cryogenic intervention. There were the usual petitions from traditionalists, of course: there was no evidence of fatal disease or waning productivity, she should be frozen for her own protection, things might look a little better a century or two down the road. To her credit, she did not

NOBODY GOES TO EARTH ANY MORE

take matters into her own hands but waited until the appeals had been heard before exercising her fundamental right to avoid pain. It is not recorded whether she went by gas or injection.

The old man interested me immediately. He was in his late seventies when I revived him; although 2,892 years had passed since his birth, he had been sentient for only seventy-eight of them. He was adamant that he would not take part in the program. Nor would he be returned to his cryogenic state. Nor, when I invited him, would he avail himself of a kevorkian. He was determined, he told me, to live out what was left of his natural span at the expense of the state, which, in his peculiar idiom, "owed him one."

No amount of cajoling or pleading would change his mind. Lectures on duty were equally ineffective. When one of my graduate students went so far as to threaten him, he broke into such peals of laughter that I feared for his heart. My student felt so humiliated that she visited a kevorkian herself the following day. Fortunately, she did not qualify for treatment even under the present, notoriously permissive, administration, and she was back in my lab the following morning.

Make no mistake: the old man knew he was unique. His favourite riposte when being rebuked was, "If you don't like it, why don't you wake up somebody else?" Oh, he could be maddening! He knew he was our only link to the twenty-first century, the only survivor of their primitive cryogenic techniques. In him alone was deposited the cultural treasures of pre-plague humankind. And what did he offer us? Tantalizing glimpses of social structures and cultural mores, snatches of memorized verse. He was particularly fond of asking me if he dared to eat a peach. "I shall wear white flannel trousers," he told me, "and walk upon the beach." I can only assume he was quoting a verse from some forgotten poet, perhaps even himself. The lines match nothing in our data banks. The single stanza he quoted from Leonard Cohen, who was apparently a hugely popular entertainer in the late twentieth century, is the only surviving example of Cohen's work, and no one knew it had survived until the old man uttered those haunting lines.

In the end, though, he took part in the program almost in spite of himself. He was given everything he wanted, and was observed in everything he did. Often enough, it is true, he did no more than sit quietly, holding up the middle finger of his right hand. This gesture was not recorded in my predecessor's notes, but several of my colleagues have suggested that it is a posture of prayer, or meditation. There is ample evidence to support the theory, but somehow it doesn't seem right. He has assured me that he will tell me what it means one day. To use his own idiom, though, I'm not holding my breath.

My own building (he continued, as I scrambled to turn on the recorder) was across 3rd Avenue on 25th Street, a 1920s vintage block of flats largely occupied by young people starting out and old people finishing up. I slept and ate, smoked and drank, read and wrote in a basement room just large enough to think in, with one corner set aside for cooking and another for sleeping. The only heat, and it was often excessive, came from an insulated pipe that emerged from one wall, ran directly in front of the only window, and plunged through the opposite wall into the laundry room where two ancient sisters spent their Saturday mornings running frilly things through a wringer washer. They knew I was a writer – I had published poems in literary magazines and sold a short story to public radio – and they pointed me out to the other tenants as one points out a rather clever dog. Because I lived directly below them, I suppose they felt they had certain rights of ownership.

Here he paused again.

"I suppose it's safe to name her?" he asked.

"Name who?" I asked, in turn.

"Her," he said. "You're not going to dig her up, are you? You'll let her sleep?"

"If I knew who or where she was," I told him, "I would most certainly dig her up, for she couldn't possibly be any less co-operative than you have been."

He took that as a compliment. I could see it in the cunning of his smile as he turned his head to one side and looked up at me. A compliment and a victory. For it was proof the woman was safe; I would not have been so candid had I thought she were recoverable. Besides, nobody goes to Earth any more. It's a wasteland.

"She was worthy to be loved," he told me.

"I have no doubt she was," I assured him.

"No, that was her name."

"What, *Worthy-to-be-Loved?*"

He nodded. "I called her Amanda for short."

"I beg your pardon?"

"Amanda. It's from the Latin. It means –"

"Let me guess," I interrupted. "It means *worthy to be loved.*"

"Do you know Latin?" he asked, in apparent innocence.

"No one knows Latin," I told him. "Latin died with the plague, when the three percent of humankind that remained alive took ship for the stars. We departed with the barest of essentials: a few trillion gigabytes of scientific materials and a few dozen bodies like yours in cryogenic suspension, but virtually nothing of what used to be called 'the humanities' – literature, art, poetry, drama. You are the only person alive with a working knowledge of Latin, and who knows what other priceless treasures of human learning and accomplishment. We live in an age starved of beauty and truth, and you do nothing to ease our hunger. Don't you understand? We don't know who we are, old man, and you refuse to tell us!"

He shook his head. "I wouldn't say I had a working knowledge of Latin. I only took it in grade nine. I dropped it because I didn't want Old Man Deaver again. Deaf as a post, and his breath was like sewer gas."

I threw up my hands in frustration. "You've lost me."

"You seem to get lost quite often," he remarked.

135

One of several points of difference (he resumed) between Amanda and the antique ladies in the laundry room was that Amanda had no frilly things. On the contrary, Amanda's undergarments ran to the rudely functional and the barely adequate: brassieres with no snaps, panties so inconsequential they could be crumpled up and put in an egg cup, a slip or two to be worn unadorned beneath a cool and daring dress. Another point of difference was that Amanda was possessed of a sensual beauty that the two old ladies quite evidently had never enjoyed – nor even, perhaps, knew existed. They are not to be blamed. They grew up in darker times when the pleasures of the flesh were disguised as pathways to the devil. Darker times, indeed. I have often wished the present times were not so well lighted.

My building, known as the Craven Block, was owned and managed by two brothers, partners in property. The elder, Wilbur, was a genial, dapper gentleman, a low-key workaholic who loved his family but often confused them by his habit of alternating attentive generosity with benign neglect. The younger, Herman, was a bitter perfectionist, lean and bandy-legged. The fact that he had been born with the umbilical cord tightly wrapped about his already stiff little neck was generally regarded as a missed opportunity by those who had been forced to grow up with him.

It was a long process for Herman, growing up. He reached adulthood and adultery at about the same time, in his late forties. It was only then, his controlling parents finally dead, his brother happily absorbed in work and marriage and parenthood, his own marriage in a shambles of hard words and pain and apologies never uttered, it was only then he realized that it was possible to be confused and not know what to do about it – indeed, that confusion was the *condition* of not knowing what to do about it.

Herman fell in love.

Almost immediately, he fell into adultery.

Unfortunately, it didn't make him any less of an asshole.

Which explains why he showed up on his nephew's doorstep at ten o'clock one fine summer evening and ordered him to break up the party or find another place to live.

Now, Herman's nephew was Wilbur's son, Hilton, who happened to be my closest friend. Hilton's doorstep was two storeys above my own. The party consisted of six young men quietly celebrating Hilton's impending marriage. It was a stag, although none of us felt particularly ruminant. Except maybe Terrence. A sprinter by avocation, Terrence had recently bolted down the back steps in search of something to chew on at the Chinese lunch and grocery across the street, and inadvertently disturbed the laboured slumber of one Harry Harder, an emphysemic pensioner who lived in the apartment below.

Harry called Herman.

Herman got into his car, a conspicuous new Oldsmobile with lust of ownership gleaming from every millimetre of overpriced steel, and drove halfway across the city to confront his nephew with an ultimatum:

"Break up the party or find another place to live."

"Eh?"

"Our best tenant has complained!"

What made Harry their "best tenant" was no more than the union of circumstance and hyperbole, and everyone knew it but Herman. But a man who is utterly convinced of his own rightness cannot see a thing if he has not granted it permission to be seen. As he went home to his adulterous bed and Terrence and the others left, one by one, I could see in Hilton's aspect a growing recklessness of intention. "Deliberate recalcitrance," was what Herman might have called it. "Getting even," was what Hilton called it.

"I'm going to get a hammer," he said, "and I'm going to go over there and break every goddamn window in his goddamn car."

This ambition was coupled with a determination to become as drunk as possible within the limits of time and the supply of vodka, which, since the departure of the others, was excessive. But Hilton was a large young man, and powerful. He could have squeezed the life out of Herman without spilling his drink, and a dozen people would have thanked him for it. So the vodka was soon gone, and Hilton seemed none the worse, apart from a certain liberality of expression which, considering the circumstances, was not excessive. He wanted to rip the lungs out of Herman's chest – through his nostrils, mind you – and chop them up and feed them to the dogs. Alternatively, he wanted to fry up his uncle's testicles in a non-stick pan while Herman was still attached to them.

I thought the non-stick pan was a nice touch. "He fried his uncle's balls," I imagined myself testifying at the trial, "but it was in a non-stick pan."

Realistically, of course, there was the problem of getting Herman to sit still long enough to be thus abused, and in the end the only thing Hilton was really prepared to do was break every goddamn window in Herman's shiny new Oldsmobile.

But first he had to find a hammer.

"Is this the same hammer you had offered to Amanda?" I interrupted, for I was beginning to see a pattern.

"You're anticipating your tenses," he said. "I didn't know Amanda at the time. She wasn't living above Murphy's flat across the street. It wasn't Murphy's flat yet."

"So the first part of your story is in fact the second part of your story."

"It's probably the third or fourth part. It only matters if you subscribe to the theory that time is linear."

"And you don't?"

He shook his head. "Time is too complex to be circumscribed by human theory. In my own time the scientists were just coming round to that conclusion, but the poets had known it for centuries."

"And the historians?"

"Historians in every generation have created the past in their own image." He paused a moment, then grinned. "It's comforting to find that some things never change."

I nearly rose to the bait, but if I had learned anything in my dealings with him, it was that the best defence is attack.

"Why should I believe you?" I challenged him. "How do I know you're not making all this up as you go along?"

He looked wounded. "I wouldn't lie to you."

"Why should I believe that?"

"Because I'm the only person alive with a working knowledge of Latin," he said. *"Nunc dimittis servum tuum, Domine...."*

I think he was mocking me, but there was no way of knowing.

The Craven Block (he explained) had been erected in two stages, each with its own foundation. The first stage was a gracious two-storey structure of mottled brick facing 3rd Avenue. The roofs of the porches on the ground floor served as the floors of the balconies above, and in the summer you could reach out and pluck a leaf from one of the half-dozen dignified elms that graced that side of the building.

The second stage of construction was of a similar style but facing 25th Street, a much busier thoroughfare even in the 1920s, and so the builders had dispensed with the porches and balconies. No doubt the two structures had been attached with artifice and skill, but time and temperature had pulled them apart to the extent that you could, in places, thrust an open hand into the widening scar.

The flats themselves, excluding my own, were spacious two- and three-bedroom affairs with ample kitchens and formal dining rooms, and living rooms large enough to display the neo-Victorian monstrosities of furniture that were popular among the middle classes between the wars. Indeed, one of these had survived, an enormous chesterfield whose dark, vulturine curves occupied one corner of the laundry room, smelling mustily of all the ancient buttocks that had graced its cushions over the decades. Sometimes, coming in at night, I would find it troubling the periphery of my vision, and would turn on the light in the laundry room to reassure myself that no ghosts were sitting on it. Other times, I would find my heart inexplicably racing as my hands fumbled with the key. The dirt-floored corridor that led to the storage rooms on the other side of the building was suggestive enough in daylight with the sun casting shadows through cobwebs and dust-shrouded windows. But after sunset, who knew what dark creature might be roused to madness by my stumbling steps and jangling keys? Once inside my room, I would turn the lock with a sense of barely averted catastrophe, half expecting to hear a clawed hand scrabbling in frustrated hunger at the other side of the door.

Between the foundations of the first and second stages of construction there was a drop of two feet, and it was down here that Hilton led me in search of a hammer. A creaking plank door opened onto utter darkness and a smell of stagnant water. I thought first of swamps, then of rat-infested bilges.

"Where are you taking me?" I asked.

"Turn on the light," he said.

"There is no light."

"On the wall behind you."

"There is no wall."

There was a pause, then: "Turn on the fucking light."

I reached out blindly and struck several things, including Hilton, before I found the switch. I turned it on, but there wasn't much improvement. The single bulb hanging from a frayed cord in the ceiling revealed less than it concealed. An ancient boiler stood ankle deep in malodorous water. A pair of small, bloated corpses was immediately evident on the surface, and my imagination assured me there were larger ones, perhaps even humanoid ones, beyond the light's reach. Parged fieldstone formed the outer wall, and on the far side was a hesitant structure of uprights and warped boards that served to separate the boiler room from the rest of the basement. A battered door swung gently by one hinge, as if a nocturnal creature had recently fled.

Over there, Hilton assured me, there were more storage rooms, and a carpenter's shop, and a hammer. To cross the room, one had to cross the water. For this purpose some thoughtful soul had provided a single broad plank that sagged alarmingly as Hilton attempted to negotiate it. He came back to compose himself before trying again. His breathing, I noticed, was alarmingly heavy, and he seemed to be giving off a peculiar smell. To my expressions of concern, however, he responded with scorn.

At the second attempt he made it halfway across. Then he executed a demented pirouette, and the makeshift bridge bucked him off. He landed astride the plank, his pant legs soaking up the fetid liquid like wicks. He took a moment to recover his dignity, then waded the rest of the way as if that had been his intention all along. I followed more gingerly, gaining the far side as Hilton's broad shadow disappeared down a dim corridor.

I waited till a new set of shadows informed me that a light had been turned on somewhere ahead. I heard a crash, a distant curse. The dirt floor was soft beneath my feet, untrodden for years. I turned a corner and saw the light spilling from a narrow doorway and, stark against the opposite wall, a large and spectral creature deliberately striking a hammer into its fist. It was Hilton's shadow, though it was a heart-stopping moment before I realized it.

When I gained the doorway of the carpenter's shop, he favoured me with a look of grim satisfaction. I nodded once in the conspiracy of brotherhood, then watched him fall back against the wall and sink slowly to the floor, the hammer loose in his hand. Soon he was snoring. I took the hammer and placed it on the bench that ran along one wall of the narrow room. I turned out the light and squatted beside him, sharing his darkness and his pain as the creatures of night scuttled across the edges of consciousness.

I waited. He remained silent for a long time. I thought he had dozed off, but then he raised his head and gave me a little smile. "It's time for my walk."

"Is that it?" I asked.

"Of course not," he said, taking a cane in each hand. "That is never *it*."

"I think we should finish," I insisted.

"Bring the machine if you like," he said. "We can finish in the garden."

It was a year later, almost to the day (he continued, gesturing for me to follow him), that I made that same trip through subterranean shadows to find the hammer exactly where I had left it twelve months before. I took it across the street and up the stairs to Amanda's flat. She answered the door in a long, black dress. It was half dressing gown and half elegant evening attire – formally casual, if you know what I mean. Or casually formal. The curve of her leg, the gentle swell of her belly, the rise of her breasts beneath the sleek fabric distilled for me the essence of her grace. But it was her face that beguiled me most: the dark brows, the green eyes, the voluptuous lips. They say a man alone beneath a rising moon will cast his soul toward hell to spend one wild night in the faeries' dance. I would have gone that night, God help me. Willingly, I would have gone.

She took the hammer from me with a smile. She picked up a nail, gave it three sharp taps into the plaster wall, and hung a framed print of sun-drenched flowers and distant fields. Then she put the hammer down. She smiled again.

"Thank you," she said.

Whether he had finished or not, it became apparent after five minutes that he was not going to say anything more without being prompted. It was a game we had often played.

"What happened then?" I asked.

Again the little smile. "The rest of my life happened then."

"Of course, but —"

"I never left."

We walked in silence for a time. I wondered if he was being literal or metaphorical. "That was thirty centuries ago," I said to him. "You *have* left."

"Have I?"

He paused, leaning on two walking sticks at the edge of a bed of roses, the westering sun glancing across the folded blooms. I remembered what he had said earlier about a soft summer evening, a lean blue sky hung high with feathered clouds. The image was suddenly, achingly beautiful, and I found myself weeping there beside him. In a moment I realized that he was weeping, too, the tears running like rivulets down the deep furrows of his face. Then he began to speak, slowly, deliberately reciting from his 3,000-year-old memory:

He awoke at 4:00 possessed by demons, the streets deserted of all but taxis and the unburied dead. A train whistle measured the horizon — invisible distance — and in the conspiracy of darkness he faced his tormentor at last: the slips and curves of her woman's body, her lips an archer's bow half drawn, her dark breasts, her bottomless eyes. Mystical gender.

Do you remember the first time we made love? (he asked the street lamps and the fog): a basement room on a numbered street, the two ancient sisters in the flat upstairs arguing deafly over their breakfast, virgins both, and you a portrait of innocence in your nakedness. I thought then that if I could not possess you, could not contain you body and soul in the crucible of my faithless flesh, I would surely die.

How time must laugh at us. It is still four hours till daylight, but I can almost smell the coffee brewing on the stove, can almost hear the children's sleepy voices, can almost see you ascending and descending the stairs in your sloppy man's pyjamas on errands and non-errands and re-errands: the finite ritual of mortal minds and aging bodies.

But I still love you.

And I am still alive.

In the silence that followed, he lowered himself painfully to the ground, casting his walking sticks aside. At any other time I would have rebuked him, called an attendant with a wheelchair, covered him with blankets. But there was something so final about the way he arranged himself cross-legged on the path beside the roses, where he could smell their fragrance and contemplate their folds and colours, that my voice and hands were stilled.

I wondered what I would do with this sensation he had given me, these tears, this painful beauty. I wanted to die.

"Old man," I said, finally, "if this is your love, I don't want it. It hurts too much."

"If it doesn't hurt," he said, "it's not human."

He reached into his shirt pocket and took out a slip of paper. "I promised I would tell you one day what this means," he said, raising the middle finger of his right hand in the familiar gesture. I took the paper from him, then watched him die. There was nothing dramatic about it, nothing painful, just a quiet slipping away. He closed his eyes, and was still.

I opened the paper, and read it, and despite myself I started to laugh.

I can't be sure, but I think that's what he intended.

VANITIES

After careful consideration, Fergus concluded that there were three women he might have an affair with, could he but give himself permission. First there was Angela, who had shown more than a friendly interest in him since before they had even met. Often, during the sermon or as the ushers were moving up and down the aisles with their collection baskets, Fergus had looked up to find Angela's eyes on him, quickly averted, but not before a furtive smile of recognition and unseemly desire had flickered across her features. Their mutual attraction was manifest and fortified when they found themselves both elected to parish council, sitting across the table from one another in the church basement for three hours on the second Wednesday of each month, voting on motions and agreeing with one another on issues of little relevance to their everyday lives. Angela was the wife of one of the lectors, a systems analyst heavy with flesh and self-importance. She was conventionally pretty, mildly voluptuous, and he imagined she would be grateful for his attention, for surely she found little joy in her marriage bed.

Then there was Jane, a bitter, disappointed woman who had the office next to his. She was departmental assistant – *never* call her a secretary – and he a visiting professor. For him it was a two-year contract; for her it was a life sentence. Jane had spent her career under-valued and under-employed in the vain hope that if she did not behave as a woman in attitude, deportment and expectation she would eventually be granted the opportunities and privileges of a man. Alas, no amount of attitude could hide the fact that at thirty-nine she was still drop-dead gorgeous, with flowing black hair and a butt that begged to be ogled. She was unmarried, too, which reduced the sin in Fergus's mind to a single, rather than a double, act of adultery.

Finally there was Martha, the executive assistant to the broker who handled Fergus's personal investments. Martha was slim and red-haired, a combination that did not usually appeal to him, but her flesh was of such exquisite proportions that his prurience was aroused in spite of his natural inclinations. Martha's father was insane, a fact that somehow added to her appeal. The old man, she once confided as he was waiting for an appointment, lived as a hermit in a small town on the edge of the diocese, convinced that legions of black and Hispanic gang members from the inner cities of

America were on the march northward with intentions obnoxious to his peace. Martha was not beautiful in the conventional sense, but she was lovely: pleasant to look at and pleasant to be with. She was, Fergus thought, the quintessential Canadian woman – agreeable, polite, easily embarrassed. *Nice.*

These, then, were the three women he might give himself permission to love without exacting too large a payment from his conscience.

And yet...and yet...there was Colette, the dental assistant who was always so solicitous of his comfort when he lay helpless in the chair, his mouth propped open to the probes and drills of her employer. Colette was another redhead, and rebarbatively lean, but Fergus thought he might easily conquer this natural aversion for the sake of her face and its continual expression of tolerant amusement, as though they shared a private joke. Colette had no ambitions he could discern except to be who she was, and she was supremely content in her estate. Fergus admired her self-confidence.

So there were four, perhaps. But he was forgetting Maria, the dark Peruvian hostess in the restaurant where he often took his breakfast. Maria was truly beautiful, her voice a sensuous echo of her Spanish origins. She was small-breasted and a bit heavy in the belly, but her shapely buttocks seemed to defy gravity as she moved from table to table in her long dress slit to the thigh and offered menus and assurance that whoever she was serving was the most important person in her world at the moment. She no longer offered him a menu when she escorted him to his table overlooking the park, but instead offered to him the profoundly comforting phrase, "The usual?" Fergus would nod, secure in the knowledge that she and the cook and all the servers knew that "the usual" was scrambled eggs with sausages and hash browns and white toast and coffee.

There was Joy, too, another server in another restaurant – and another redhead! – who ran five miles daily and had the legs of an athlete and the buttocks of a goddess. Fergus often went for lunch just to admire her and exchange pleasantries. They got on well together, for Joy was working toward a degree in English literature and always picked up on Fergus's allusions and obscure literary jokes. She was a great admirer of George Eliot, which was reason enough, in Fergus's philosophy, to include her in that select group of women he would permit himself to make love to. For making love was far more than sex to Fergus; it was affection and friendship and mutual interests and something to talk about after the single, fleeting act that always left him feeling empty and obscurely disappointed. And, of course, children, the fairest fruit of a mature love.

So that brought the count to six, all women worthy of his attention. But he was forgetting Patricia, the buxom assistant to the dean at the small liberal arts college he sometimes had cause to visit on professional matters, and Alexandra, the mature student at the same college who had expressed an interest in working with him to learn the subtleties of the Shakespearian speech-act, and Ophelia the Valkyrie whose hair was a different colour every week but whose body remained relentlessly voluptuous. Ophelia never failed to give him a hug on meeting and parting, and Fergus could quite imagine himself lost in her embrace.

By final count, then, there were nine women that he might...but again, he was forgetting Jacqueline, six years his senior but with the supple flesh of a woman who had kept herself fit and never been tempted to bear children. Jacqueline was the managing editor of a literary journal, and she and Fergus often met on matters of mutual interest. She made no secret of her attraction to him, and a wild night of uncomplicated physical activity was definitely within the bounds of the possible, if not the probable.

And how could he forget Kate, whose need for affection was as obvious as the incandescent tresses of her golden hair and great maladroit child – the product of an unguarded moment eight years before – who followed her everywhere like a confused and overweight shadow.

Fergus made a list: Angela, Jane, Martha, Colette, Maria, Joy, Patricia, Alexandra, Ophelia, Jacqueline, and Kate. Eleven women – excluding, of course, the dozen or so he had managed to fall in love with before he met his wife. For love was a prerequisite for sex, as far as Fergus was concerned. It was not a religious or a societal stricture, but a matter of personal conviction. In fact, he suddenly realized, he had been fantasizing not so much about women he would like to have sex with as women with whom he might fall in love. For he could never tire of that heart-fluttering rush of hormones and adrenalin that came with the certain knowledge that here, at last, was one to be honoured above all others.

On an impulse, he struck Jane off the list. Last week he had seen her riding her bicycle across the university campus, sitting bolt upright as if the shaft that supported the seat did not conclude there but continued upward, replacing her spine with cold steel and rendering her incapable of all but the most minimal of lateral movement. One might have sex with a woman like that, Fergus reasoned; one could not love her.

For entirely different reasons, he then struck Angela off the list. In many ways she was dearer to his heart than the others, but the mere fact that he had met her in church complicated matters to the extent that he knew guilt would overcome love before love ever had a chance. And sex was out of the question. Contrary to the received wisdom of Western humanity, it is sex that complicates relationships, not love. Sex is demanding, importunate, unforgiving. If it is often casual to one of the participants, it is rarely casual to both. Love is the opposite. Love can survive sex, even revel in it, but sex cannot survive love without becoming subordinate to it, and sex *qua* sex will subordinate itself to nothing.

So much for philosophy, Fergus thought, striking Martha from the list. Lovely she might be, but sex would destroy their friendship as surely as fire consumed wood. If the match is never struck, though, the wood will last a lifetime.

The dental assistant and the Peruvian hostess were similarly struck from his list. He might regard them with the eyes of love, but the eyes cannot deceive the body, and in the end the body will have its way. If he were to have a physical relationship with either of them, he could never go to that dentist or that restaurant again – unless he were a brazen *conquistator-des-dames*, which he was not.

Joy would recognize that phrase unerringly as she leaned across him to serve his chicken burger and beer. "James Joyce," she would say, and launch into a narrative on the singular failure of the popular imagination to regard Joyce as anything more than an icon, someone to be admired but not read, ignoring both the humour and the tragedy in his work, especially the pornographic letters to his wife. "I mean, who could fail to see the essential humour in his self-deprecating love/lust? It's impossible to imagine that Joyce was unaware of, or did not exploit, the possibilities and the nuances of Nora's maiden name, Barnacle. Barnacles cling. They're hard on top and soft on the bottom, and anyone who has ever seen one in the flesh, so to speak, cannot help but mark the similarity in appearance between the soft underside of the barnacle and that portion of Nora's anatomy that Joyce wrote about, even worshipped. Why, even Stephen Dedalus...."

Fergus crossed Joy off his list.

Patricia and Alexandra were another matter, although the fact that they melded in his mind into a single entity would have been cause enough to strike them from his list. In his peripatetic mind they were types rather than individuals, a circumstance which even in the throes of unbridled desire he could not dismiss as unimportant.

He crossed them both off.

Ophelia was more problematic. A magnificent woman, statuesque, beautiful, extravagant in both flesh and feeling, relentlessly intelligent, Ophelia would never allow herself, even temporarily, the luxury of subservience. Whereas Fergus took great pleasure in cooking for those he loved, in serving them, Ophelia would rebel even at the thought of making a cup of tea for a man and placing it in his hand. He could make his own damn tea if he wanted it. What was she, his servant?

On second thoughts, Ophelia was not problematic at all. He crossed her off his list.

Resigned now, even eager, to reduce the list to zero, Fergus contemplated the last two names on it: Jacqueline and Kate.

Kate, though a brilliant conversationalist, spiritually inquisitive and obviously in need of affection, nevertheless had this great, futile daughter following her wherever she went. Fergus could imagine the look of surprise and shock as the child emerged from her womb: "What, *this*? From *me*?" She loved the child as best she could, but the thought of Fergus and Kate inadvertently producing such another was enough to give him pause.

He crossed Kate off his list.

That left only Jacqueline – the most difficult, perhaps, to extract from his desires because she was at once the most available and the most willing. She had made that clear enough. An amazing body she had for a woman of middle age. An impressive face, not beautiful, but filled with the humour and character that Fergus admired in a woman. A sense of humour. An intelligent grasp of the things that interested him. An easy conversationalist.

Would she be too demanding? Fergus doubted it, any more than he would be. Was she too old for him? No more than some of the others were too young for him. Would she bore him with literary talk? Likely not; at the end of the day she was probably as happy as he to leave the office behind.

Try as he might, he could not cross Jacqueline off his list. He was conscious at once of a great guilt and a great sorrow. It was as if he were now compelled to pursue his fantasy. It was no longer merely possible to have an affair with her, it was no longer merely probable; it was compulsory. He could have wept – and would have, were it not for a remote but insistent voice intruding on his consciousness.

"Wake up," it was saying. "Your public awaits."

He rose like a bubble from the depths of the sea, a burp from the abyss, a deep eructation from a creature so far beneath the air and the light it had no need of eyes. He became aware first of the tips of his fingers, then his toes. His palms itched, then his arches as the blood beneath the skin awakened and began to flow. He became aware of each individual part of himself as he ascended, from the physical extremities of hands and feet and legs and arms to the sturdy torso that support-ed them, the bowels that fed them and the heart that beat its blood to them, and finally to the crystal centre of thought and feeling, enlarging, expanding, gaining form and logic as the pressure of the depths receded and he was suddenly, gloriously conscious, gazing into the sad, gentle, and infinitely loving eyes of a woman who had long ago accepted the sentence of the biological judge who had decreed that she could never bear children.

"Jacqueline?" he said, tentatively, but with that heart-fluttering rush, almost tragic in its intensity, that came with the certain knowledge that here, at last, was one to be honoured above all others.

"Coffee's ready," she said. "And your eggs are getting cold."

Scrambled, he thought, with sausages and hash browns and white toast and coffee.

"Any dreams?" she asked as he came to the table.

"None to speak of. Why?"

"You were moaning in your sleep."

THE LANGUAGE
OF THE HEART

Sometimes when my father was reading to me he would stop, suddenly, and sit in silence as deep as Ireland, and the unshed tears were as plain on his face as if he had stood half the day by my mother's grave. When I was younger I accepted it, in the manner of a child rebuffed by silence but assured of love. I accepted it because he always went on reading after a time, and because he never failed to bless me as he tucked me in at night, and because he took me to Mass every Sunday at the chapel of the English saint, Thomas More, and afterwards we went for tea at Mrs. Laverty's, who had been a friend of a relation back in Belfast. I accepted it because I loved him, because he was a sure and steady man, and because he was my father.

But as I grew older I became less accepting, for it seemed through adolescent eyes that his pain was a memory kept alive for the sake of itself and the whisky that fed it. For he was not an abstemious man, my father. Often on a grey morning I would find the bottle emptier by half than it had been the night before. But he never disgraced himself nor made a spectacle, nor offered excuses nor asked forgiveness, so I considered it a matter between himself and his confessor — or his liver, whichever was the more demanding.

My own confessor urged me to obedience when he took me seriously at all. Which he rarely did, not being able to understand. It's a rare priest who knows what to say to a girl whose father has without warning become an elderly, unhandsome member of the opposite sex: a *man*, in fact, a sagging creature with mournful eyes and inexplicable flesh. I knew how much I owed to him, of course — everyone told me that — and I was not ungrateful. And always between us there was this bond of words, of spoken words and listened words as the dutiful father read to his idiot child.

"Ah, poor Thomas," they said — and I heard them, for I'm not deaf — "hard enough to lose a wife, but to be left with an idiot child..." and they shook their heads like old women, as often enough they were. And my father kept on reading to me, and I listened in grateful obedience, until one day he said something that took me by surprise.

"I'm afraid, Kathleen."

"Afraid of what, Da?"

We had been reading *The Canterbury Tales,* and he took the time to close the book and place it carefully on the table between us before he continued.

"Things speak to me so deeply...."

He had a flair for melodrama, my father.

"Is it Mother?" I asked.

He shook his head. "That wound is long healed."

I suppose it was something in the mood he had created, in the way he was looking at me and the way he was talking, that made me choose that moment to tell him what I'd known for years: "They say I killed her."

He was instantly furious. "*Who* says so?"

"The old women in the village. I hear them."

I had never told him before because I was afraid he would stop taking me into town with him if he knew. But I didn't know how much it would add to his pain until I saw the weight of it on him. They call me an idiot because I can't read and I can barely talk; even Da – who spent so much time listening to me and learning to understand what I said – sometimes didn't understand. But I can read a face well enough, and I know torment when I see it. If I had three wishes, I would spend them all on him, to atone for that moment.

"It's just talk," I said, as gently and as slowly as I could. Even so, I found my mind racing ahead of my lips, and I had to repeat myself. "It's just talk. They say if I hadn't been born, she'd still be alive. Be alive."

"Don't believe that, Kathleen. Don't you believe it."

What else was I to believe? I'd heard my father talking about it with Mrs. Laverty when they thought I wasn't listening, or couldn't understand. My mother had cancer, and refused treatment because it might kill the child within her. And so she gave me life as she sacrificed her own. My father blamed himself, but Mrs.

Laverty said he couldn't have known. Exactly what it was my father blamed himself for I don't know, and Mrs. Laverty didn't say what it was he couldn't have known.

"No," I said. "I don't believe it. I don't."

I poured him a cup of tea – there was always a pot on the table when we were reading – and put a drop of Bushmills in it to give him courage, for the whisky was always there as well. I waited for him to tell me what he was afraid of.

"You can't see the words, Kathleen. Is that what you tell me?"

Always the same question, as if he was asking it for the first time. I could never understand why it confused him so. I can't see the words. I can see the letters well enough, one at a time, and I know them A to z, and I can follow them through a word like a ferret in a rabbit hole, but when I draw back to look at it whole, the word isn't there any more. It's become something else. A mystery. My own name is a mystery when I look at it written down.

"If only I could write to you," he said.

"You *can*," I told him, "but you would have to read it to me, too."

He shook his head. "Not the same."

"Have someone else read it to me," I suggested. "Someone else."

He shook his head again. "Not the same."

"You'll have to tell me, then." I poured a drop more whisky into his cup. "Out loud. Like a man."

God knows how that came out so easily. *Like a*

man. What did I know about being a man? I knew little enough about being a woman. I suppose that's one of the things your mother teaches you. I remember one Sunday after Mass, Mrs. Laverty took me aside and told me about "the curse" and "riding a white horse." I couldn't see it, myself. What's to curse about riding a white horse? If only she'd said, "Listen, Kathleen, once a month you'll find yourself bleeding like a stuck pig. It's not fair, I know, but there's precious little you can do about it, so wear a sanitary napkin and replace it as often as necessary and put up with it till it's over." If only she'd said that instead of, "Ah, poor Thomas." What had Thomas to do with it, I'd like to know?

Nothing. Absolutely nothing. That's what I tried to tell the doctors, and the woman from the agency, and the people who kept poking and prodding me as if I were an animal at auction. "He did nothing! Nothing!" But I was just an idiot girl who couldn't read and was barely verbal, and it wasn't until they took me away that I realized none of them understood me.

But before that, when I said those three words – *like a man* – he looked at me with such a sorrow on his face that I had to reach out to him. He took my hand, gently at first, and rubbed it against his cheek. Like leather it was, but soft leather. He kissed me, and then he put such a grip on me – not painful, you understand, but firm, relentless – that I wondered if he would ever let go. And it was only then, idiot girl that I am, that I realized something was truly, desperately wrong, and somehow I had to make it easier for him to tell me.

I poured him another cup of tea, and put two sugars in it, and lots of milk so that it was rich and sweet and comforting. I didn't pour him any more whisky because there is no truth in whisky, no matter what the poets say. Even poor Thomas's idiot child knew that.

"Emma," he said – that's Mrs. Laverty – "Emma will look after you. I have her assurance."

What are you talking about, Da?

"If something happens to me, I mean."

What's going to happen to you, Da?

But he couldn't say anything more, not yet. So I took his rough hands in mine and patted them reassuringly, as if I were the parent and he the child.

"Nothing's going to happen to you," I reassured him. "Nothing to you."

He nodded, the way he did when the words wouldn't come, and finally he said, "Just tell the truth, Kathleen."

When have I done otherwise?

He nodded, and smiled. "Just tell the truth. Don't tell them what you think they want to hear, even if they threaten you, or try to trick you. Tell the truth."

How could I not tell the truth? How could he think I would lie?

You're frightening me, Da.

"You must be prepared, Kathleen."

"For what?"

"For what may come," and he picked up *The Canterbury Tales* and read on as if something had been settled.

Now, even an idiot child knows when she's being treated like an idiot. You start life with a soul as large as the sky, full of wonder and love. But gradually, as people enter and leave your life, as you pass from uncomfortable silences to pitying smiles, the sky grows dark, and the horizon comes so close you can reach out and touch it. It's then you realize you're at the edge of the world, and the world has grown so small that there's barely room in it for your hands and feet. Truly great souls can't bear being trapped in a human body, so they escape as soon as they can, like Thérèse of Lisieux, or even Joan of Arc. The rest of us must stay and watch the horizon come closer. The thing of it is, the people who laugh at you, the ones who dismiss you or treat you like some kind of pet – their souls are deformed, like our bodies, only they don't know it. I sometimes think we exist to warn them, to show them what can happen. But they don't see. I sometimes think they're bigger idiots than we are.

It was a week or so before my father stopped coming home. Mrs. Laverty came by to cook my supper, as I suppose she'd promised him, and she reassured me that he was probably held up in town, maybe the truck had broken down, nothing to worry about. Then she left, and I had to put myself to bed, unblessed, and stare into the empty darkness as if God did not exist.

My father didn't come home the next night, either, or the one after. Mrs. Laverty gave me scrambled eggs on toast, then good Irish stew with brown bread. I asked her where my father was, and she told me he must have gone away for a while. I asked her to read to me, but she said she didn't have the words. I told her she didn't have to have the words; the words were already there on the page. But she didn't understand, I couldn't make her understand, and finally she told me to read them myself if I was so smart.

It was another week before the woman from the agency came. I saw her car in the yard, a fast little red thing with headlights that flipped up like eyelids. When she got out of it – climbed out, more like; I could never have managed it myself – I thought she was beautiful. She was yellow-haired and red-lipped, with just a touch of eye shadow. She had a strong chin and a pleasant, trusting kind of smile, with even white teeth. She wore a dark blue suit with one of those short, short skirts that were just coming into style in the city; I'd seen them on the television at Mrs. Laverty's. I loved the sound her legs made, stroking themselves as she sat down and crossed them one over the other. I think she liked it, too. I've never worn nylons myself, so I could only imagine the feel of them against my skin.

She told me her name, but I've forgotten it now. She had a thin little attaché case that she held open on her lap. She told me she had just a few questions and I wasn't to be afraid. "Afraid of what?" I asked, and she answered with a smile that brought the horizon a little bit closer.

"Now," she began, "your full name is Kathleen Mary MacBride?"

I could not deny it.

"When were you born, Kathleen?"

"I don't know," I told her. "Don't...know."

In fact, I was born in nineteen hundred and forty-

166

nine in Belfast, Northern Ireland, where my mother is buried. I came to Canada with my father in nineteen hundred and fifty-three when Da's brother Edward, who had come right after the war – he couldn't go home, they said, not after fighting for the English – told him the social services were better if he was bent on raising the child by himself. Da wanted to get away from the North, anyway, and Edward had a farm here, so there was no question of Da being able to find work. But as for the date, I have no actual idea. We never celebrated birthdays, Da and me. I like to think it was on a spring morning when the air was thick with birdsong and the smell of growing things, but it might as easily have been autumn or winter, in the mist or in the rain. I've no clear idea what it's really like in Ireland. Da and Uncle Edward talked about it sometimes in a way that made me wonder why they'd ever left, but it was only half a story, if that; the other half was rain and bog and cold so deep it got into your bones. "Not like the dry cold, here, Kathleen," they'd say, but then when Edward was diagnosed he said he was going home, he didn't want to die in this country. But he did, for all that, and we had him cremated and Da spread the ashes in the back field. Mrs. Laverty said it was a shocking thing, not a Christian burial at all, and she refused to come to the ceremony. Not that there was much of a ceremony. There was just Da and me. We said the Our Father, and then he opened the urn and turned it upside down and the wind caught Uncle Edward and scattered him, maybe all the way back to Ireland. There can't be much of him in the back field, is all I can say.

I explained this to the woman with the red car and the attaché case, but she had some difficulty understanding me. She tried, I'll give her that. I could see it in her face, the muscles moving beneath the skin almost as if my stumbling vowels and crip-crip-crippled consonants were causing her physical pain. I told her that there are some things you know and some things you don't know, don't know, and birthdays were one of the things I didn't know. Finally she shook her head and said we'd go on to something else.

She gave me a pair of rag dolls and asked me to show her how they fit together. The one had a *thing* like my father's, and the other had great lumps on her chest as big as Mrs. Laverty's. I tried to fit the dolls together. Every which way I tried. I thought there must be some sort of secret to it. Then I thought that this might be one of the tricks my father had warned me about, so I put them down.

"Is that how the dolls fit together?" she asked.

The dolls don't fit together.

The woman showed me some pictures and asked me what they looked like, what they reminded me of. There were photographs and paintings, and some of them were just a bunch of lines and colours. She showed me one picture over and over, hiding it in the pile as if we were always coming to it for the first time. I suppose she thought I wouldn't notice. Idiot that I am, I did notice, and told her so. In retrospect, I think that almost set her against me.

"Are you happy, Kathleen?"

What could I say to that? *There is no happiness, and*

there ought not to be; but if there is a meaning and an object in life, that meaning and object is not our happiness, but something greater and more rational.

She looked stunned for a moment, then said, "I beg your pardon?"

I tried to tell her that there was a story by Anton Chekhov called "Gooseberries," and I had made my father read it to me over and over until I could bring the dialogue to mind as if I were reading it myself, and I thought she understood, but when she smiled and said, "I see," it was plain she didn't see at all.

"Now, Kathleen, where did you go to school?"

"I didn't." I shook my head. "No school. I didn't."

It's the contractions that trip me up. It is the contractions. I think if I didn't try to use them, if I did not, then I might not choke on the apostrophes and I might be able to make myself understood, but then it would take so much longer to say everything and I would sound even more of an idiot than I do now.

"Well, you're eighteen," she said. "There's no legal requirement..."

"No, no." I shook my head, and somehow I made her understand that I had never been to school. She worked hard at it, I could tell.

"What, never?"

I nodded, eager to make her understand more.

Unlearn'd, I know no schoolman's subtle art, No language, but the language of the heart.

"Alexander," I said. "Pope. Poet," I explained, but she paid no attention.

"You must have gone *somewhere*," she insisted.

Of course I'd been *somewhere*. I mean, you couldn't be *nowhere*, could you? But school was something we gave up on fairly early, Da and me. I remember Uncle Edward saying, "Just keep her home, Thomas. It's the best thing. We can teach her more between the pair of us than she'd ever learn at school."

Soon enough there wasn't the pair of them, there was only Da, but Edward was probably right. There was just the one teacher, and she had her hands full already without having to worry about Thomas MacBride's idiot child.

"They'll take her away." That was something else I remember Uncle Edward saying. "Let sleeping dogs lie."

So I stayed home, the sleeping dog, and Da read to me, and no one said anything, and no one came to take me away.

"But what do you *do* all day?" the woman asked.

I watch. I listen. I think.

"All day?"

Sometimes all night, too.

"Is that all you do?"

It's more than enough, believe me.

"But don't you have any interests?"

Haven't I been telling you, I have nothing but *interests.*

"Do you ever go out?"

Where would I go? How would I get there?

"You can walk, can't you?"

Not very well, and not very far.

It took us an hour or two, but that's what we said, more or less. Then I got up and walked to the door and back. At rest, it is true, and when I'm not trying to talk, I appear almost normal, but once I stand and begin to move, I look as if I'm riding a wheel whose axle is off-centre, my arms flailing to keep balance. I usually try to keep it from people if I can, but Da had told me to tell the truth, and I doubt this woman would have believed me if I hadn't shown her.

She sat there a moment, staring at me.

"You answered the door," she said. It was almost an accusation.

And I sat down again as soon as your back was turned.

"I would have noticed a limp like that."

"You didn't."

She closed her attaché case, her face as red as the car in the yard. "I don't believe it," she said, shaking her head. "You can't just..." but she couldn't finish the sentence. She seemed to be in the grip of some powerful emotion. Finally she just stood up and walked out. I watched her drive away.

On Sunday Mrs. Laverty came to take me to Mass, and no one seemed to notice that my father wasn't there. They didn't seem to notice I was there, either, even when I stumbled up to take the sacrament because the priest had forgotten to bring it to me in the pew.

The thing of it is, Mrs. Laverty lied to my father, or at least she told him a different truth than the one he chose to believe. "Emma will look after you," he'd said. "I have her assurance." But Emma wouldn't even read to me.

They have me in a wheelchair now, so that I can get about more easily. But there is no place to get about to, and nothing to do once you get there. I come to the workshop in the morning, where they have me doing useful things like stuffing envelopes. I have heard that I am "trainable," but I can't seem to get the knack of anything they want to train me for. We are all of us idiots here. Some of us can't talk, others can't listen. It's no great matter; there's nothing to listen to except the noises from the kitchen and the workshop, and at night the television.

My father told me to tell the truth. Sometimes I want to howl it like a curse. For *I* am the truth, it seems. Oh, not a very big truth, and certainly not an important one: just big enough to trouble him for eighteen years or so, just important enough to drive him away when he could no longer stand the sight of me. The silences, the sorrow, the whisky, the pain: those weren't memories, those were *me*. I was his truth.

But often, at night, I hear another truth, and I recite its names in the language of my heart: Eliot, Yeats, Chekhov, Pope, Chaucer and Shakespeare, Matthew and John, William Blake and Dylan Thomas, John of the Cross, and Moses and Ruth and Judith and Dickens and...and the list is so long that my muddled mind loses track of their names and I can remember only how the words made my heart sing when my father read them to me.

He didn't know how much I knew, how much I felt, how much I understood. None of them know. They keep us clean and fed and busy, and I should be grateful. And I am. I am.

But no one reads to me any more.

THE BIOLOGY OF PRIMATES

She drank tea in the afternoons, dark British tea, potent as tar, and lit thin cigarettes as long as her fingers. There was always a fresh one in her hand, as if they never diminished, and you couldn't tell that she actually smoked them unless you looked at the overflowing ashtray on the table beside her chair or listened to the deep masculine rasp of her voice. Mornings were ascetic, nicotine free, as she worked at her easel, hair tied back, a glass of water diminishing by slow degrees as she worked through the tortured visions that obsessed her: a single eye impaled upon an arrow, entitled, simply, "Agincourt"; a couple gazing on a placid rural scene, the woman's hands dripping blood, entitled "Pastoral"; a country house set amid stately elms, a murder or a rape – impossible to tell which – occurring behind french doors, entitled "Alison's Weekend."

Violence flowed from her brush like blood from a wound.

Lunch was a grilled cheese sandwich, invariably, fried white bread sopping up a dark pool of HP sauce on the edge of the plate. She was from the Midlands, said *cawn't* instead of *can't*, and read D. H. Lawrence with the devotion of a supplicant. She was lean but veinless, a natural blond with skin as smooth as her hair, silken, touchable, but unresponsive. Walking in the rain, she did not cover herself but strode on and onward like a person who had somewhere to go, occasionally looking back to see if something might be following. London was her livelihood and her passion, and she despised it. It had given her a reputation among the *cognoscenti*, a flat in Chelsea, and a desultory circle of lovers, of which I was the last. When I arrived at the flat in Lordship Place that afternoon, letting myself in with the key she had given me, I was not so much shocked as disappointed to find her lying in a pool of blood on the kitchen floor. The scene was laid out like one of her paintings, a tableau imagined or remembered, carefully posed: the white bread in the frying pan, cheese oozing out between the slices; the bottle of HP sauce on the counter; the pot of tea; the canisters on the shelf; the packet of cigarettes beside the ashtray; the body on the white-tiled floor; the inevitable and necessary blood.

I pulled out one of the stools she kept beneath the overhanging counter and eased myself onto it, placing my cane across my knees. Whoever killed her, I noted, had had the wit to turn off the gas; her lunch was cold in the pan, but the smell of seared butter still hung on the air. There was no hint of cigarette smoke; that would have come later, with the tea. She lay on her right side, her body curving inward, her left knee almost at her chin. Her arms were placed as she might have arranged them herself, with equal parts drama and pathos: one beneath and behind, flung outward with a violent grace, the other drawn inward as though she were about to suck on her thumb. It was a characteristic attitude of sleep. I had seen her thus in bed, often. Indeed, were it not for the fact that she was on the kitchen floor and not on her futon in the bedroom, and that there was a ragged oval of blood spreading outward from her solar plexus, I might have concluded that she was simply asleep. There was no horror in her face, no pain, no look of a fate long feared and suddenly come to pass. Rather, there was that same look of weary resignation I had seen so often when I had lain awake beside her, offering up to a feckless god the pain that kept me conscious for a moment or two of the oblivion that seemed to come to her so easily.

My right knee began to throb in the familiar pattern, the bones cracking audibly as I shifted the leg. That was nothing new, nor was the sudden arc of fire that coursed up my thigh. "Are you all right?" she used to ask when she saw the blood drain from my face. "It will pass," I replied, as it invariably did, in five minutes or an hour. I looked for the bottle of Glenfiddich she kept for me, the familiar green triangle of relief. It had never really eased the pain, but the prospect of pain is more bearable if one has before one the prospect of insensibility.

This, too, would pass. Then I would call the police.

Inspector Harley lived in Windsor and took the train into Victoria every morning. It was worth the expense, he opined, to be relieved of the anxieties of raising three sons in the cesspool that was London. His sister had emigrated to Canada twenty years before for much the same reason, only she had daughters instead of sons, which somehow made the farther move both more urgent and more reasonable.

These facts I gleaned in the first few minutes of our acquaintance, and on his first hearing my accent. He had heard of Calgary, he said. Oil. Gas. The Calgary Stampede. He seemed pleased by his knowledge.

"Are you a temporary resident?" he inquired conversationally as his colleagues photographed and fussed with the body on the floor.

"No," I replied.

He invited me to New Scotland Yard to make a statement, which would be duly recorded and placed in the file. *The file.* How quickly a human life is reduced to facts and words – or not even facts, necessarily. Simply words.

"We were lovers," I informed the WPC in Victoria Street as her fingers clicked across the keyboard. I felt a compulsion to expatiate: "I do not mean that we were in love. Far from it. But we seemed to fulfil a mutual need in one another. Our bodies fit together well enough, but that is not why we stayed together. Any other bodies would have fit just as well. The physical act is so fleeting, after all. It is over so quickly, and then there is a vacuum for shame and embarrassment and whatever notions of sin you were raised with to rush in and destroy what fugitive pleasures you've been allowed. And yet we return to the act, again and again, as if we had no choice, as if –"

"Please, sir," said the WPC, lifting her fingers from the keyboard, "just the facts."

"But there are no facts," I protested. "There are only impressions and memories, each one filtered through a human mind. Facts are for scientists."

"And the police," she said. "I appreciate your philosophy, sir, but this is not the time for it. If you would just describe the circumstances of your finding the body, I'll print it out and you can sign it and go home."

I envied her the simplicity of mind that would allow her to reduce the complexity of our actions to three simple constructs: print, sign, go home. But now she was gazing at me expectantly through her upper lashes, in the manner perfected by the late Princess of Wales. So I gave her the facts: "Alison worked every day from 8:00 a.m. until 1:00 o'clock, then stopped for lunch. I came at 2:00 most days, unless I was working myself, in which case I might not see her till evening. But today I wasn't working, so I came at the usual time and let myself in with my key. I found her as Inspector Harley found her. I did not touch her or move anything, except for the stool I pulled out to sit on. There were no signs of struggle, no evidence of forced entry. She was obviously dead, there was nothing I could do for her. After a moment I called the police. The rest you know."

The WPC remained with her fingers poised above the keyboard, waiting for me to continue. I waited with her. We waited together. Finally, she said, "Bit brief, isn't it?"

It was almost, I reflected, a compliment.

She took my address and telephone number, and I found they had formed part of my statement when she eventually handed it to me to sign. So had my "philosophy," as she called it, word for word. I wrote my name and handed the paper back.

"Inspector Harley will want to speak with you again, I expect."

I was offered a ride home, but I declined, taking instead a number eleven bus that crawled through Pimlico to the Kings Road in the congested London traffic. When it finally dropped me at the Old Town Hall, it was eight o'clock, dark, and cold. The street was noisy with people and cars, as London streets always are. I stopped at the off-license on the corner of Oakley Street for a half-bottle of whisky – my supper – and made my way painfully to my room.

Inspector Harley arrived the following morning and proceeded to destroy what peace was left me.

"You've been holding back on us" were his first words.

I acknowledged the statement without confirming or denying it, a skill I had perfected as a journalist.

"I've looked up your immigration records," he continued, "and your application for citizenship. You are *Doctor*, not *Mister*, James Gould."

"My doctorate is not in medicine," I told him. "It's in English literature."

"Now, that's interesting," said Inspector Harley. He was a brief chunk of a man, sturdy without being fat, but, oddly, without giving any impression of physical strength. You felt that he lived solely by his wits, which, judging by the expanse of skull exposed above a fringe of greying reddish hair, were considerable. He sat comfortably in my only chair, leaving me to the day bed which was still made up for sleep. "What is your area of study, exactly?"

"Elizabethan drama."

"Ah, Shakespeare."

"That is one name that comes to mind, certainly."

"I wonder why you left a successful career in Calgary for a life of obscurity in a bed-sit in Chelsea."

"There are at least two untested assumptions in that statement," I told him. "I am under no obligation to confirm or deny either of them."

Politeness is some people's armour against the world; discourtesy is mine. It often comes across as arrogance or condescension, I know, but I haven't the skill to refine the art to something less offensive. He took no offence, in any case.

"Quite right," he said. "A man's private life is his own affair. There's no reason you should have to share it with anyone. But your girlfriend's been murdered, don't you see, and that puts me in a bit of a quandary. Do I accept you as you are, an obviously intelligent, educated man who likes to keep himself to himself, or do I start probing into your personal life? My inclination is to accept you as you are. We might have a chat over a pint one evening and I might tell you about my boys and our life in Windsor, and only later realize that you hadn't said a thing about yourself. Under normal circumstances I'd probably shrug it off. But you see my position." He assumed an expression of benevolent regret. "I must find out who killed your girlfriend."

I had winced at his earlier use of the term. Now I found it intolerable. "She was not my *girlfriend*. I find the term demeaning. If you must describe our relationship, we were lovers."

"Do you know," he said, leaning forward as if he were sharing a secret, "that's the first bit of spark you've shown since the investigation began."

I recognized his interviewing technique: part good humour, part homespun philosophy, part reasoned argument — and all deception. His statements were phatic, meaningless, intended to establish a mood rather than impart information. None of his statements could be trusted, only his questions.

"You seem almost unmoved by her death," he said. "Most people are more demonstrative when they lose someone they love."

"I did not say I loved her. I said we were lovers. The difference can be profound. In any case, you have no access to my emotions, so you are in no position to judge how moved or unmoved I may be by Alison's death."

"I knew you were lovers," he said. "That was the first sliver of information you gave us." He took an untidily folded sheet of paper from an inner pocket and regarded it with interest for a moment before unfolding it on his lap. "'We were lovers,'" he quoted. "'I do not mean that we were in love. Far from it. But we seemed to fulfil a mutual need in one another.'" He looked up. "What do you mean by that?"

"When you have established a right to that information, I may give it to you."

"I'm afraid you don't appreciate the situation, Dr. Gould. It's the situation itself that gives me the right, don't you see. Your *lover*" – he gave the word a slight emphasis – "has been murdered. In the natural way of things, you are a suspect. I am a policeman. You perceive the implications of these facts, I'm sure. What you may not appreciate is that I am quite good at what I do, and I will get the information I need. How long it takes is up to you."

He sat back in the chair, positively seething with reasonableness. He already had the information he needed; what he wanted from me was confirmation.

"I killed a child," I said.

He started visibly. "You what?"

"I killed a child," I repeated. "That is why I left a successful career in Calgary for a life of obscurity in a bed-sitter in Chelsea. Call it penance, if you like."

"Well now" – his large face looked troubled – "it seems to me that we do things a bit differently over here. If a man kills a child in England, we're apt to put him away for a bit. We don't pack him off to Calgary. Are you telling me that if a man kills a child in Calgary they simply ship him off to London? For penance?"

"It's a bit more complex than that," I said.

"I imagine it is." He passed a hand over the dome of his scalp, patting down the hair that was no longer there. "Things usually are. I remember once I was waiting to give evidence, and his lordship was a bit miffed because he saw that I was reading in one of the back pews and didn't respond as quickly as I might have done when I was summoned. 'What are you reading, Harley?' he asked me, '*Biggles Adventure Omnibus? Billy Bunter?*' 'No, your lordship,' I replied. 'Nietzsche.'"

I supposed it was my turn to be surprised. I tried not to show it.

"Do you know what Nietzsche said, Dr. Gould? Nietzsche said that a man who despises himself" – he held up a forefinger to make the point – "nonetheless esteems himself as a self-despiser."

"So pride and self-loathing march hand-in-hand into Nietzsche's hell," I responded. "I'm not sure I would place much credence in the observations of a man who was institutionalized for beating a dead horse."

"Oh, I can sympathize with that, can't you?" He laughed a moment in genuine amusement. "But I think you'll find the horse wasn't actually dead, and all Nietzsche did was throw his arms around its neck. He couldn't stand the sight of the poor creature being flogged."

"Yes, well, they do say that Nietzsche doesn't need translating so much as decoding."

"I think you'll find that's Hegel they say that about, Dr. Gould." He smiled. "You'd be surprised how much reading you can get done in the back of a courtroom."

"The point is, Nietzsche was insane."

"Possibly."

He seemed to find something of great interest on the floor, for he fixed his gaze on it and there it stayed. I waited, as I had with the constable who took my statement. Inspector Harley waited. We waited together. I think we would have waited forever if the image of poor mad Nietzsche had not risen like a spectre between us, not to be banished except by speech. I was good at speech: verbal sparring, obfuscation, explanation. No matter what happened, I could always think of something to say. It was the key to my success.

"I was a sessional lecturer at the University of Calgary," I told him. "It paid slightly more than nothing, but it's a step on the way to a tenured position, and everyone has to go through it. I made ends meet as a part-time journalist – a commentator on the arts, a reviewer, that sort of thing. I started in print but I took to television quite naturally, and it soon became obvious that I would have to make a choice. Obvious to me, anyway. I could keep on lecturing at the university, writing abstruse articles on unread plays in the faint expectation that I might eventually get a tenured position and fall into a privileged life of the mind, or I could go into television full time and make a great deal of money right away.

"I was popular, you see. Very few people in Calgary ever knew me as an expert in Elizabethan drama, but close to half a million people across Alberta tuned in every week for *The Gould Report with Dr. James Gould.* My name was actually copyrighted as part of the title. I never called myself Dr. Gould, but the producers thought the PHD lent a certain credibility to the show, which was otherwise just pseudo-intellectual muckraking, as my former colleagues were eager to point out.

"I had a reputation for thoroughness, though. I had researchers and fact checkers. I wrote all my own copy, and I'd let another network scoop me if I thought I didn't have enough information to break the story. If a city councillor was getting kickbacks on a construction project, I documented it first and then reported it. If the councillor tried to bribe me to kill the story, I reported that, too. The format was half expository journalism and half reflection and analysis, with a short wrap-up at the end in which I told people what to think. Again, that's what the critics said. But enough people watched it to keep me on the air, and I had enough offers from other networks to keep my employers anxious. But Calgary was my home. I didn't want to leave."

Inspector Harley was leaning forward in the chair, all ears and shining skull. If I were he, I would have prompted me. But he seemed content to listen, even if I wasn't talking.

"The girl was admitted to hospital on a Thursday evening with superficial bruising to her chest and upper arms," I said.

He was entirely unsurprised by the change of subject.

"Her parents said she was having difficulty breathing," I continued. "The x-rays revealed a fractured rib, nothing serious in the ordinary way of things. They said she had fallen downstairs. She was a docile little thing, four years old but not especially bright, according to the attending physician, who bandaged her rib and kept her overnight for observation. The next morning he released her to her parents. That much was in the records.

"I had learned early on to record my telephone conversations, so when someone calling herself the duty nurse on the pædiatric ward called me that morning I got her on tape. She had been up with the girl most of the night, she said. The child couldn't sleep, she was afraid, she was crying, nothing unusual for children in hospital. They miss their parents. They miss their rooms and the familiar things children value: their toys, their beds, the light on in the hall. What was different about this little girl, the nurse said, was that she was the most articulate victim of systematic abuse she had ever encountered. 'She just needed a little coaxing,' the nurse told me, 'and then the whole story came out.' She gave me the girl's name and address and urged me to get over there with a camera crew. The girl wouldn't talk about it in front of a man, the nurse said, but she would talk to me because she had seen me on television.

"I couldn't act on the nurse's information alone, of course. It left too many questions unanswered. Why hadn't she called child protection? Why hadn't she called the police? And when I called the hospital to confirm her story, they had never heard of the nurse. Now, it's not unusual for people to conceal their identity from a journalist, so I tracked down the doctor. He was preparing for a weekend in Banff, but he took the time to reassure that me that he was trained to recognize the signs of child abuse and no child currently under his care was in any danger. He didn't even ask the name of my informant."

I glanced at the whisky bottle, empty from last night, and wished I had had the foresight to save a dram or two.

"The next time I saw the child," I said, "was Monday morning, in the mortuary. Her parents had beaten her to death over the weekend."

Inspector Harley rearranged his bulk in the chair.

"You never get used to it," he said, at length. "At least, I haven't. I used to think that if I had been in a certain place at a certain time, if I had listened a little more attentively or watched a little more closely, I could have prevented certain acts that resulted in tragedy. But the innocent will always suffer, Dr. Gould. The weak will always succumb to the strong. 'For ye have the poor always with you.' My Meg was fond of saying that, bless her soul. Read the Bible every night, the King James Version." He shook his head at remembered sorrows, then looked up. "What I mean to say, Doctor, is that you can't blame yourself for the death of that poor child."

"Gosh, no one's said that to me before. What a relief."

I thought for a moment that I had slipped under his guard and inflicted a wound – it had become a contest, of sorts – but his good humour appeared to be unassailable.

"I imagine you got a good story out of it," he said.

"But that's just it. I didn't. Even with the nurse and the doctor on tape, I had no story. The medical community closed ranks, the hospital administration threatened an injunction, and the police informed me that the tapes of my telephone conversations with the nurse and the doctor were inadmissible as evidence. The producers told me to drop it. When I pressed, they pressed harder. I hired a lawyer, and he advised me to drop it, too. Every door was closed against me. In retrospect I can only conclude that someone was extremely well-connected and extremely angry."

"Or extremely frightened," the inspector suggested.

"I've thought of that, too."

"So you shut your mouth and saved your job. Understandable, under the circumstances."

"It's a bit more complex than that," I said.

"What, again?"

I fetched my cane from beside the bed and pulled myself to my feet. The crack of bone against bone was audible. The familiar pain shot up my thigh, bone-deep from the knee to the hip socket.

"Are you all right?"

His concern was feigned, and a second too late. With sympathy, as with comedy, timing is everything.

"It would have been worse if I'd remained sitting," I told him. "But I really must go to the toilet."

"And after that," he said cheerfully, glancing first at the empty whisky bottle and then at his watch, "I expect you'll be wanting some breakfast. Or perhaps lunch."

"As a matter of fact —" I began.

"I know just the place," he interrupted. "A little caf' in South Kensington. They do a lovely prawn and salad sandwich."

I had been about to tell him that I couldn't look an egg in the face if it kissed me; a prawn sandwich seemed slightly less revolting. What I said was, "I can't possibly walk to Kensington."

"That's why Her Majesty has provided us with a vehicle." He gestured toward the door. "If it hasn't been clamped it will get us there in five minutes."

The inspector was optimistic. It was twenty minutes before he found a place to park, and another twenty before we reached the head of the queue. He ordered the sandwiches and black coffee, chatting amiably the while. All he required from me was an occasional affirmative, until we sat down. Or sat up, rather. We were perched on high stools at a counter overlooking Thurloe Square. A less congenial situation I would have found it difficult to imagine. My knee was throbbing insistently, the coffee was nothing like Starbucks, and the English have a rather different idea of "prawn and salad" than the rest of the civilized world. There were four prawns in mine – or shrimp, as they are more accurately called – and the salad consisted of a leaf of lettuce and a half-hearted scraping of carrot. The bread turned to mucilage as I chewed, and the blending of flavours, washed down with hot black liquid reeking of chicory, was reminiscent of a wad of newsprint that had a faint taste of the sea.

"Don't you like it?" Inspector Harley asked, his broad face at once solicitous and unbelieving.

"It's fine," I said – a truly Canadian response – as my tongue struggled to dislodge a glob of paste from my molars.

"It's not everyone's cup of tea," he allowed. "Meg used to make prawn sandwiches when we took the boys for a picnic in Windsor Great Park. I always think of them as a treat."

"For me, a treat is an hour's sleep without pain."

"Ah," he said, chewing thoughtfully.

"She was raped by five men when she was fifteen," I said. "Boys, really. A certified gang bang. She was drunk and stoned, and managed to convince herself that it was entirely her own fault. She shouldn't have drunk so much wine, she shouldn't have smoked so much hashish, she shouldn't have been dressed so provocatively, she shouldn't have gone out that night, she shouldn't have encouraged the fellow at the party. In fact, she shouldn't have been born. She only got what she deserved."

Again, Inspector Harley was entirely comfortable with the change of subject.

"After that, she said, it didn't matter who she went to bed with. She was promiscuous and indiscriminate, but as far as I know she died without ever having experienced an orgasm."

"My Meg," said the inspector, "used to say that orgasms were highly over-rated. The thing was to hold someone in your arms and love him and give him pleasure."

"Your Meg," I said, "was talking through her hat."

"I've often thought so." He acknowledged the truth of it with a rueful pursing of his lips. "Now tell me, Dr. Gould, what brought the two of you together?"

"Pain," I said. "Fear. Guilt. The mutual urge to self-destruction."

"Now, Dr. Gould," he said, wiping his lips on the square of tissue the management had provided for the purpose, "you're being a bit melodramatic. As a journalist, you must know that we're not so much interested in how you feel as in what you did."

"I didn't kill her, if that's what you mean."

"I'm glad to hear you say so." He crumpled the tissue and dropped it on his plate. "We would have come to it in time, inevitably. It's my job, don't you see. Sooner or later I would have had to ask, outright, 'Did you shoot Alison Vansart?' and you would have had to reply, one way or another. I'm just as glad to get it over with. I always find it embarrassing, having to put a man on the spot like that. So often it leads to" – he searched for a word – "unpleasantness."

"She wasn't shot, Inspector. She was stabbed."

"You could tell that, could you, just by looking at her?"

"Yes," I said, "I could."

"So," he said, "I'll ask you again: what brought the two of you together?"

I gave it some thought, just to throw him off. Let him think I was making it up. "It was art, I suppose. I met her at an opening in the Kings Road. I knew I was out of place the minute I entered the gallery. The room was positively seething with mobile telephones, and everyone reeked of The Body Shop. But I stayed because of the paintings. I felt I understood them. No, I *recognized* them. It was almost as if I had painted them myself. You'll probably accuse me of being melodramatic –"

"Not at all," he said, waving a hand dismissively. "Not at all."

"– but I recognized immediately what your Meg might have called a kindred soul."

"You think Meg would have said something like that, do you?"

"It seems likely."

"Interesting." He pointed to the uneaten half of sandwich on my plate. "Are you going to finish that?"

I told him to help himself.

"I only know two or three things any more," I continued, "and one of them is that a man who finds himself a misfit in a given congregation will cast around for other misfits. Opposites may attract magnetically, even romantically – though I have seen no evidence of it – but socially, like invariably attracts like. I found her standing in a corner, looking lost and uncomfortable. I introduced myself. At the end of the evening she took me to her flat in Lordship Place. We became lovers that night."

Inspector Harley finished his third half of sandwich and once again wiped his mouth on the tissue, which he had retrieved from his plate.

"Now, Dr. Gould," he said, "you have been very forthcoming, and I appreciate it. But it gets us no further ahead. A casual sexual encounter after a gallery opening doesn't really go very far in explaining how you happened to be on the spot to discover her body, or why it took you so long to report it to the police."

"I resent your characterization of our relationship," I said. "It was anything but casual."

"But you didn't love her." He looked puzzled. "You told me so yourself. Sex without love is casual by definition, I would have thought, no more than an episode in the biology of primates. Why, my Meg –"

"Stuff your Meg," I said.

It was time to change strategies, I thought, taking up my cane and beginning to ease myself off the stool. My leg was throbbing like a beating heart. Then suddenly I was up against the wall, the inspector's fists bunched at my collar. My cane clattered to the floor. A plate fell and smashed. People were staring, mostly in alarm, some in curiosity. The women at the service counter were talking excitedly in a language I did not understand.

"You pathetic, self-pitying *ponce!*" he hissed in my face. "Your *lover*, was she? You wouldn't know love if it came down from heaven and kicked you in the balls!"

I had not felt such raw emotion from a fellow creature since that evening in the parking garage near Broadcast Hill in Calgary five years ago. Just so had the big one held me when I dared to resist. I should have known better; I'd interviewed enough bullies to know what enraged them. But that was my punishment: not, as my attackers thought, for pursuing the story of the murdered child against strong advice and repeated warnings, but for allowing the child to be murdered in the first place. She was eighteen months in the grave, but I knew it with a certainty most men never experience, a certainty I have since imagined women feel when they bring forth a child and suddenly know beyond passion or reason that here at last is a reason to live. And a reason to die.

He eased his grip on my collar.

"You are stronger than you look," I said slowly.

"You're not the first person to have made that observation."

He picked up my cane and handed it to me, then, with a friendly nod to the other patrons, many of whom were plainly horrified by this unprovoked attack on a cripple, he left. I nodded in turn, and followed him out. There was nothing else I could do.

He steered deftly through the traffic, past the Victoria and Albert Museum and the soot-faced statue of John Henry Newman by the Brompton Oratory. I assumed that he was taking me to Victoria Street, to an anonymous interrogation room in New Scotland Yard where he would force the truth out of me.

"Why did you say it took me a long time to call the police?"

"Because it's true." He removed one hand from the steering wheel to gesture. "On your own evidence, you arrived at Alison Vansart's flat at 2:00 o'clock, but we didn't log your call until 4:00. That leaves two hours unaccounted for."

"Two *hours?*"

"Work it out for yourself, Dr. Gould. The math is fairly simple."

I tried to work it out, and couldn't. Two hours unaccounted for. Two hours in the presence of Alison's body. Surely not.

"I need a drink," I said.

"I anticipated that," and he pulled into a parking spot that seemed to have conjured itself out of thin air.

I had not been paying attention to where we were going, but I certainly recognized the buildings as we got out of the car: those great, defining edifices that every child of the Empire recognizes from history books and the biographies of famous men. We were well north of Victoria Street.

"I thought you were taking me to the Yard."

"The Yard." He laughed. "And I suppose you think of me as a Bobby."

"You need a helmet to be a Bobby," I said.

"So you were knee-capped in a parking garage," he said, placing a frothing pint of bitter in front of me.

I had not volunteered the information, and it was certainly not patent in my immigration papers or my application for citizenship.

"Attacked by a couple of goons who beat you sense-less and then put a bullet through your knee." He was watching my reaction. "Because you wouldn't leave well enough alone."

I could feel the blood drain from my face. "I was unaware it had been reported in the United Kingdom," I said.

"It wasn't." He was still gauging my reaction. "Or if it was, I didn't read it. It was described to me over the telephone this morning by Sergeant Shepley of the Calgary City Police."

THE BIOLOGY OF PRIMATES

"I don't remember him."

"No reason you should. He was responding to an anonymous tip, and you were unconscious when he got to you. The point is, James" – he used my Christian name deliberately – "you can huddle in a bed-sit in Chelsea for the rest of your life, but nothing will erase the shooting, the beating, or the death of that little girl."

"Thank you for those words of wisdom, Inspector." I drained my pint. "Do you take courses in triteness and tautology in the Metropolitan Police?"

He finished his pint, in turn. "Your round, I believe."

I wasn't sure how I could manage two pints and a cane simultaneously, but I hobbled gamely up to the bar. I returned with a thumb in one glass and a forefinger in the other, spilling beer behind me on the sawdust-strewn floor.

"I must apologize for my show of temper back there," he said, taking his glass. "Kierkegaard regarded marriage as the deepest form of revelation, you know. I can't help but agree with him."

"It's not a mistake I will make again," I told him.

He seemed satisfied with that. "Now perhaps you will tell me what brought you to London."

"I'm sure you have all the information you need already."

"You must let me be the judge of that, James. Any detail, however remote or unconnected it may seem, might turn out to be a critical piece of the puzzle. Surely you don't want to withhold information that might lead to the man who killed Alison Vansart."

195

"How do you know it's a man?"

"When I find a woman stabbed to death on her kitchen floor, experience tells me to look for a man as the culprit. Women don't do things like that." He made a dismissive gesture. "A bullet is distant, quick, impersonal. Almost humane. So is poison. But a man who stabs a woman, face to face, knows the dreadful price of death and is still willing to pay it."

My hand was shaking as I brought the glass to my lips, so that I had to put it down again, untasted.

"She was stabbed once through the heart," he said, "with a narrow blade, double edged. She probably felt very little pain, if that's any consolation."

It wasn't. And suddenly the image was overwhelming. I saw Alison on her knees, her hands held out beseechingly as the long blade entered her flesh, draining the life from her as if she were a vessel to be emptied — as, indeed, she was. I had not appreciated the truth of her until that moment. I put my head in my hands. I heard the inspector's voice beside me.

"You did love her, didn't you, James."

I nodded my head, wordless. I would have done anything for her.

Tactfully, but illogically, he changed the subject. "What do you work at, if you don't mind my asking?"

"I'm still a journalist, of sorts." I wiped the tears from my face, then wiped my hands, in turn, on my pant legs. "I write reviews for newspapers and literary magazines. That's what I was doing at Alison's opening. I had been commissioned to review it for the *Chelsea Journal*."

"I'm not familiar with that publication."

"It has a small circulation."

"Do you write for anything I might have heard of?"

"I use a pseudonym."

"Is that why you came to London? Surely there are newspapers and literary magazines in Canada."

"My grandmother was born in Glasgow," I told him, "so I could have my passport stamped UK GRANDPARENT. It allows me to work in this country without a visa and eventually apply for citizenship without having to jump through the bureaucratic hoops that immigrants are normally subjected to. That is the only reason I came to the United Kingdom. I came to London particularly because I judged I could live here and never meet anyone I had known before."

"May I see your cane?" he asked suddenly.

"My cane?" I gazed at him stupidly.

"Your walking stick." He pointed. "I want to see it."

It was an ordinary sort of thing, dark polished wood with a moulded plastic handle, a broad chromium ring where the handle met the shaft. I handed it to him, abstractedly, as if I had taken a step backward and was watching someone else do it. It hardly mattered what happened. He had seen that I did love Alison, despite my protests. But what was more important, and what he could not know, was that she loved me. I was the only man who had ever made love to her in her entire life, or so she said. And for the first time, I believed her. All the rest, as Inspector Harley might have put it, were just episodes in the biology of primates.

He weighed the cane in his hands, tested it for balance, sighted down the length of polished wood. Then holding the shaft in one hand he gave the handle a sharp twist and began to unscrew it. It moved easily, for the threads were finely machined, but he seemed surprised when the handle came off and that's all it was, a handle.

"I thought –" he began, and checked himself.

"What did you think?" I demanded, suddenly angry. "Did you think you would find a stiletto in my cane? My God, do you think *I* killed her?"

He gave me a long, thoughtful, almost a pitying look.

"I was almost certain of it," he said.

"But I loved her."

"I know, James." He screwed the cane back together. "I know."

CANIS REX

The dog barked continuously, apparently without pause for breath, certainly without pause for thought. A passing squirrel, a falling leaf, three hooded men entering the house next door and beating the owner to death with a shovel: the world went by indiscriminately, and the dog had only one response – barking: relentless, hoarse, and belligerent, like scrap iron falling on a hangover.

A mature, healthy dog, according to a voice Leona had heard on the radio, was the intellectual equivalent of a two-year-old human being. No great accomplishment, she'd thought. Can two-year-olds do calculus? Can they cook a meatloaf? Can they shut up when they're told?

These questions recurred as Leona lifted the jack-hammer to her basement wall and prepared to drown out the clamorous objections of the *canis ridiculis* that lived two doors down. Its name was Rex – "because he's king of the terriers," its master had explained to her one day as she was turning her compost in the alley. Terriers must be an inferior breed indeed, she reflected, if such as Rex were king. For Rex was without question the stupidest dog in south-west Calgary – an Airedale with an attitude and, as far as Leona was concerned, two balls too many.

"Give me three minutes with a sharp knife and a shot of Valium," she told her husband, a psychiatrist at the Children's Hospital, "and I'll soon take the wind out of his sails."

The advantage of Valium over a general anæsthetic, she explained, was that Rex would remain conscious throughout the procedure; he just wouldn't care – until the drug wore off.

Gordon was unhelpful. "I have to account for every millilitre I prescribe. I can hardly sign Rex into the hospital as a hatchet-faced child with two extra legs and tell people I'm going to cut his balls off."

"It might make an interesting case for you," said Leona, "a feral child, raised by wolves in the foothills."

"And what reason would I give for castrating him?"

"You wouldn't have to give a reason for castrating him. You'd only have to give a reason for shooting him up with Valium. *I'll* castrate him."

"Yes, well..." Gordon looked away distractedly. He didn't like the direction the conversation was taking.

"Shut up, you stupid animal!" It was the voice of Mrs. Nassiri next door. "Shut up or I'll have you butchered!"

The dog responded hoarsely, and at length.

The Nassiris' yard was separated from the dog's by a high board fence, sufficient for privacy but with a space along the bottom just wide enough for Rex to intrude with fang and snout when the fancy took him, which was often. Mrs. Nassiri sometimes tried to kick the beast, and Mr. Nassiri threw things, but Rex was always too fast for them.

"Did you know," Rex's master had said to Leona one afternoon, catching her in the alley as she was once again turning her compost, "that these dogs were dispatch carriers in wartime?"

"Oh, yes?" said Leona. A less subtle means of passing secret messages she could not imagine.

"Oh, yes," he confirmed.

His name was Theodore Longton Pishny-Crabbe — she'd seen it on the voters' list during the recent election — but his business cards just said Ted Crabbe.

"They've been used as police dogs, guard dogs, and hunters of course," he explained. "But I just keep Rex for company."

"Rex keeps us all company," Leona remarked.

"It's marvellous having an animal in your life if you don't have a permanent relationship." Pishny-Crabbe was British by birth, and his voice reclaimed a certain quality of expression when he became animated. "I've been married three times, you know, but none of my wives could adjust to the lifestyle. I told them, a real estate man has to be out at all hours. You have to know your market. You have to know your clients. You have to close the deal, because if you don't the other chap will jolly well close it for you. The competition is fierce, we're like gladiators out there, but I wouldn't have it any other way. My wives just couldn't understand." He shook his head sorrowfully.

"Rex understands, does he?"

Pishny-Crabbe gazed down at the dog with a mixture of fondness, pride and, Leona thought, fierce, almost sexual, loyalty. Rex responded by slobbering ingratiatingly into his master's hand and urinating onto Leona's compost heap. The dog rarely barked when he was with his master, but he dribbled like a leaking tap.

"Why," said Pishny-Crabbe, "Rex is so happy when I come home, it's as if I'd been away for weeks. No sour faces, no bad moods, no forgotten birthdays, no ruined dinners..."

No headaches, Leona thought wickedly. Aloud, she said, "Please don't let him do that."

Pishny-Crabbe laughed. "A dog has to do what a dog has to do."

"Yes, but he doesn't have to do it in my compost."

"My dear lady" – he gestured expansively – "it would be difficult for him *not* to do it in your compost."

It was true that Leona's enthusiasm for collecting organic waste had led to a somewhat larger heap of decaying vegetation than she had originally envisioned. Like the hole she was cutting in the basement wall, it had become something of an obsession. She collected her neighbours' trimmings and clippings as well as her own, making regular and increasingly far-flung forays down the alley with her wheelbarrow and garden fork. From some angles, Leona's compost looked like a distant mountain range. But she trusted the pile would shrink as the fibrous matter broke down, and she resented her neighbour's implied criticism.

Perhaps his balls will have to come off too, she thought as she turned away.

The three men who came to assassinate Mr. Nassiri later that month all fell into Leona's compost in their haste. They had parked their automobile on 17th Avenue, less than half a block to the north, and commenced to move at a rapid creep along the hedges and fences behind Gateway Drive, like hooded lobsters scuttling across the floors of silent seas. Scanning the high ground to the east, the curving alley to the south, the well-kept yards to the west, they were astonished by a sudden burst of machine gun fire and dove for cover. The lead assassin sent himself sprawling into a fetid mass of decomposing grass clippings, near-liquid vegetable matter, and aged sheep manure, the latter purchased at the spring sale of the Golden Acre Garden Centre on Macleod Trail two months before. His compatriots followed, in turn.

Leona, looking up from her labours, thought she might have seen a triad of dark figures plunging down behind the fence, although it was difficult to tell through her safety glasses and the cement dust, and when she turned off the jackhammer all she could hear was Rex's infernal barking. As he had only two modes, off and full volume, Leona was not to know that he was more than usually excited. The king of the terriers, in fact, had picked up not only the stench of rotting vegetation and manure, but the unmistakable odour of his own spoor mixed with it, as well as the fluids left behind by the twenty-three other dogs who had availed themselves of Leona's compost since. A light breeze from the north brought the odours within maddening reach as six befouled feet padded up the garden path, followed by Rex's snarling snout and snapping canines along the bottom of the fence.

"Hush!" said one.

"Quiet!" said another.

"Shut up!" commanded the third, not to the dog but to his companions, who should have known better than to give themselves away at such a critical juncture.

The assassins, as it happened, were descendants of the original *hashishiyun,* an exotic sect of eleventh-century Persians who, armed with the certainty of victory or paradise, habitually struck out from their mountain fortresses to slaughter the ungrateful and the unwashed. In nine centuries their faith had waned but little. Their armaments, on the other hand, had declined sharply. Indeed, these three had brought only one weapon, for they had no contacts in Canada and feared to bring more than a single small pistol over the border. It was for this reason they had chosen to enter the country from North Dakota at what they presumed would be an isolated frontier post on the edge of a sparsely populated state that abutted an even more sparsely populated province. They were surprised and chagrined to find a lively binational community straddling the border, and half a dozen customs agents on either side ready to dismantle their vehicle and probe their orifices in search of contraband.

Even with the Saskatchewan license plates they had purloined from a vehicle in a nearby parking lot, they were filled with apprehension as they approached the checkpoint.

Luckily, an enormous galleon of a car, listing like a wounded Spaniard, pulled in front of them as they held back. The dark-skinned occupants of the galleon were numerous and seemed in celebratory mood, shouting greetings to the assassins, waving to people on the street, and barely coming to a halt in North Portal before an immaculately clad Canada Customs agent waved them through. Swept along in the galleon's wake, the assassins, too, stopped just long enough to nod their uncomprehending affirmative as a clean-shaven, lantern-jawed young man – or perhaps it was a woman; it was so difficult to tell when they weren't veiled – leaned in the passenger's window to inquire if they, too, had come from the powwow at Mandan.

In reality, they had driven up through the Dakotas from Nebraska, Kansas, Oklahoma, and Texas where they had purchased their firearm, a Berretta. They had followed circuitous routes, stopping frequently in small towns to work for meagre wages as dishwashers or janitors to support their holy quest, and just as frequently for replacement parts and motor oil to keep their aging Buick on the road. Lewis and Clark and their indefatigable guide, the Shoshoni woman Sacajewea, had taken only slightly longer to reach the Pacific on foot. But here they were at last at the Medicine Line, and the crisply efficient androgyne in the paramilitary uniform barely acknowledged their existence before waving them through. And so, severely under-armed but filled with a bold purpose, the trio made their way north-west to a city called Moose Jaw ("What can it mean?" they asked one another), then west on the Trans Canada Highway to Calgary.

The next day, after an exhausting drive that in the Middle East would have taken them from Tehran to Tel Aviv and up the Fertile Crescent past Beirut, they found themselves in the modest bungalow on Gateway Drive that the former SAVAK agent shared with his wife and his Persian cat. It was mid-morning. The cat was asleep in a ray of sunlight in the master bedroom and Mrs. Nassiri was at the salon having the grey rinsed out of her luxuriant black hair. Mr. Nassiri, however, was tied to a chair in his kitchen, sweating freely at the point of a twenty-five calibre Berretta. He had been read the sentence of death, and it was about to be carried out.

Now SAVAK, as everyone knows, were the brutal secret police of the late Shah of Iran, Mohammed Reza Pahlavi, King of Kings. And Mr. Nassiri, as the three assassins knew, had once been devoted to the security of the Peacock Throne. Among a force of some 15,000 full-time agents and thousands more informers, there were those who gathered evidence and those who extracted it. Mr. Nassiri had been skilled among the latter. Eschewing such vulgar practices as whipping, beating, electric shock, and tying weights to the testicles, he had instead devoted his talents to pulling teeth and toenails, pruning digits joint by joint, and invading with broken glass or boiling water the tenderest orifices of those who did not confess their crimes in a timely manner.

Not surprisingly, SAVAK became a target for reprisals in Iran following the 1979 revolution. Sixty-one of its top-ranking officials were executed by the new Islamic republic between February and September of that year. Hundreds more were sent to prison. A goodly number were even stoned to death or spontaneously disembowelled by disgruntled neighbours when they attempted to take up civilian life. That still left thousands unpunished. The Ayatollah himself had called for "rivers of blood" to unseat the Pahlavi dynasty. The river had now been dammed, but there were those among the descendants of the *hashishiyun* who were not content to tread water in the reservoir, so to speak. Among them were the three men who finally made their way to Calgary in the penultimate decade of the second millennium. They had tracked the former SAVAK agent through Europe, picking up his trail first in Turkey, following it to Greece, then to Italy, north across the Alps to Germany, west through France and England, then over the Atlantic and across North America.

In New York City, ironically, they were welcomed as refugees from the brutal Khomeini régime. In Washington, DC, Mr. Nassiri was seen in conversation with a known agent of the Great Satan, and in Dallas he underwent plastic surgery, demonstrating final proof of his guilt, if any were needed. It was then, with his wife and his new nose, that he emigrated to Calgary, Alberta, Canada, where, feeling safe from pursuit at last, he set himself up as a security advisor to a local oil firm.

He did not need the money. He had fled Iran with enough cash to live five lifetimes in comfort, and his three grown children were safely ensconced in prestigious universities in Europe, where they could pursue advanced degrees to their hearts' delight. But Mr. Nassiri balked at the idea of inaction. If he could not employ his highly specialized skills in a nation constitutionally devoted to peace, order, and good government, at least he would not squander his twilight years playing whist and golf with others of his age, who had nothing more on their minds than the embroidered memories of a distant past and the present inconstancy of their bowels. He had only ever had two ambitions, wealth and anonymity, and as he settled into a modest life in a pleasant suburb of Canada's most vigorous city, he flattered himself that he had achieved both.

Make no mistake: Mr. Nassiri was guilty as charged. He deserved not only to die, but to die slowly and in great pain. Yet, for the assassins, the moment was not what it should have been. Weeks and months of hunting and planning had brought them to this pass, and what had they found? A monster? An infidel? A creature with burning eyes and retractable claws? No, he was only a little bald-headed man begging for mercy.

He would be shown as much mercy, they promised him, as he had shown his victims as an agent of SAVAK. This was not strictly true. They had no intention of torturing him or otherwise drawing out the affair. But they had been practising the line for weeks, with the odd effect that, when it was finally delivered, they spoke in unison. Mr. Nassiri might have been forgiven the sudden, idiotic hope that he was caught in the midst of some ghastly practical joke perpetrated by certain of his younger colleagues who had never, in his view, regarded their duties with sufficient seriousness. But the assassins, distressed and alarmed by the continual, savage barking of the dog on one side and the intermittent bursts of machine gun fire on the other, disappointed him. They were not to know that the machine gun fire was actually Leona triggering her jackhammer, or that Rex would have barked at the same pitch of frenzy if a squirrel had walked along the top of the fence. Furthermore, they were fastidious men, scrupulous in their ablutions, and they resented being covered with plant and animal waste at what should have been their moment of triumph.

To top things off, the Berretta jammed. Perhaps it had a faulty firing mechanism. Perhaps it was a consequence of being plunged into steaming compost. Whatever the cause, it was the last straw. Ahmed drew his pistol hand to his teeth and bit himself so hard that he drew blood. Ardashir, bellowing in sympathetic rage, drove his right fist so hard into his left palm that both were numb for days. Darius, who was of a more practical bent, ran outside and came back with the garden spade that Mrs. Nassiri had purchased at the spring sale of the Golden Acre Garden Centre on Macleod Trail two months before.

It proved fortunate for Rex, if not Mr. Nassiri. Comparing notes later, the assassins agreed that, had the pistol not jammed, the dog, too, would soon have surrendered its soul to justice. Indeed, as Ahmed was flinging the useless weapon away, Ardashir was restraining Darius from climbing the fence and beating Rex to death with the same shovel that had lately brought Mr. Nassiri to judgement. His rage was not so much against the dog as against relentless fate, the same fate that had forced Darius and Ardashir into exile one step ahead of the Shah's secret police years before, the fate that had turned their triumph to sorrow when they returned to Tehran following the revolution, the fate that had sent them wandering the globe nourished only by the hope of revenge. But revenge turned out to be as spiceless a meal as they had ever tasted. It did not bring back Darius's brothers or Ardashir's children. It did not compensate Ahmed for the thirty-four months he had spent in a SAVAK prison. It did not even bring the satisfaction of a job well done. It should have been an execution, clean and simple. Instead, it had turned into a travesty of blood and battery, and the three were dangerously close to panic as they fled back up the alley to 17th Avenue, where a policeman sitting in a patrol car happened to be measuring the speed of eastbound vehicles turning off Sarcee Trail. When the constable operating the radar unit saw three men erupt from the alley behind Gateway Drive and make for the rusted Buick with Saskatchewan plates he had recently ticketed for parking in a transit zone, his hand moved instinctively from the radar gun to the Glock on his belt.

Now, Calgary is a quintessentially Canadian city, a cosmopolitan mini-metropolis in which races, languages, and cultures co-exist in a society paradoxically united by its own diversity. Normally, a trio of men shouting excitedly to one another in Farsi as they ran out of a back alley in a suburban neighbourhood would have excited little comment. It was the balaclavas that gave them away – that and the fact that one of them was carrying a shovel that appeared to the constable's hawk-like eyes to have bits of blood and matted hair on it.

They did not surrender without a struggle. Indeed, they fought like weasels on amphetamines. But Constable Kowalski, an avid gardener in his spare time, was far more skilled with a shovel than were the assassins. Moreover, he topped each of them by a foot, and weighed as much as any two of them combined. He briskly disarmed them and, turning the tool to his own advantage, soon had them subdued, confused, and hand-cuffed to one another in the back seat of his patrol car.

A month later, the view from Leona's basement remained much the same. The hole in the wall was substantially larger, but still not quite large enough to accommodate the window she had bought for her pottery studio. She now owned the jackhammer, having paid out five times its worth in rental fees before the shop finally told her to keep it. Mr. Nassiri had been buried, his widow amply recompensed by his carefully managed stock portfolio. Clearly, the former SAVAK agent had been looking to the future. Equally clearly, the assassins had not. Their only plans beyond the execution of the SAVAK butcher had involved vague notions of escape from, or death at the hands of, the Western Imperialists. That Canadian justice would allow them neither was a circumstance they had not foreseen, and it vexed them. The Iranian government denied all knowledge of their actions. Gratuitously, so did the government of Libya, although Colonel Qadhafi clearly wished he had had something to do with it. The Palestinian leadership, while praising their motives, condemned their actions, or perhaps it was the other way around. Israel was silent on the issue, perhaps with reason, for it was the *Mossad*, with the CIA, that had guided the creation of the Shah's secret police in the first place.

Few mourned Mr. Nassiri, although most Calgarians were outraged and horrified by the manner of his death. Leona herself went on Valium for a time, and Pishny-Crabbe spent a feverish weekend cutting a club, a heart, a diamond, and a spade into his sloping front lawn and planting them with garish blossoms that quickly faded from neglect. In the rest of the city, opinion was fragmented. There were those who did not want to create an international incident. There were those who maintained that an international incident had already been created. There were those who held that the law had not been designed to cope with acts of international terrorism. There were those who pointed out that the Criminal Code was the Criminal Code, whether you were a citizen taking an axe to a fellow Canadian or a gaggle of foreigners taking a shovel to a recent immigrant. There were those who called for the reinstatement of the death penalty, but they would have done that in any case. The only thing everyone agreed on was that none of this would have happened if a myopic federal government half a continent away had not allowed a former SAVAK agent into the country in the first place. But when it became clear that it was an isolated incident committed on a foreigner by foreigners, that it had nothing to do with Calgary, *per se,* and that the perpetrators had been caught within minutes of the act, the debate lost its edge, and even the Canadian Civil Liberties Association found it difficult to get a sound-bite on the evening news.

Rex barked through it all. He barked at the ambulance that took Mr. Nassiri away. He barked at the forensics experts who came to collect and measure evidence. He barked at the police officers who came to take statements from Mrs. Nassiri and her neighbours. He barked at the federal agents who tried to take over the investigation. He barked at the limousine that came to collect Mrs. Nassiri for the funeral, and he barked at the mourners – four in all, including Leona and Gordon, an oil company vice-president, and an old lady named Emma Gladstone who lived down the block and lost no opportunity to advance the interests of the Liberal Party amongst her neighbours – who returned to the house after the interment for an exotic feast of Middle Eastern funeral meats. The Nassiri children had found themselves too pressured by the demands of academia to take time out from their studies to attend their father's funeral. Or perhaps they were too frightened by the prospect of public exposure as the sons of a former SAVAK agent. Whatever the truth of it, the house was up for sale within days. The widow was determined to return to the anonymity she had briefly enjoyed as the wife of an oil company executive, or at least to move away from the wretched dog next door.

"I cannot understand why she's giving her business to those multinational thugs," Pishny-Crabbe said to

Leona, his accent broadening as he pointed at the colourful FOR SALE sign on Mrs. Nassiri's front lawn. "My company is local. We have offices in Calgary, Red Deer, and Edmonton. We are Albertans serving Albertans. And I am her neighbour! Why would she list her property with anybody else?"

"I didn't see you at the funeral," Leona responded.

"I had an open-house in the north-east. I could scarcely leave my clients standing on the footpath, now could I?"

Perhaps not, she allowed, but the nasturtiums in his ace of diamonds could do with a bit of mulch and water.

"Ach!" he said, "I've no time for that. I have to show a house." He looked at his watch and made for his car. "We're like gladiators out there," he said over his shoulder. "But I wouldn't –"

"– have it any other way," Leona completed the sentence for him. Rex was already barking as his master drove away.

They say that pets eventually come to resemble their owners. Or perhaps owners subconsciously seek out pets that will grow to look like them. Whatever the truth of it, Leona had a sudden vision of Rex's hatchet face on Pishny-Crabbe's shoulders as he drove away, and she decided it was time she took matters into her own hands.

At the back of Pishny-Crabbe's yard was a wire-mesh gate that closed off a concrete slab on which he parked his RV, never used except for the occasional overnight boinking expedition to Banff with one or another emaciated creature from the escort service he patronized.

Behind this gate Rex was wont to prance and slaver whenever Leona trundled by with her wheelbarrow and fork. She sometimes slowed as she passed – not to see if she might induce a seizure or a heart attack as the creature jumped and writhed and scrabbled at the mesh, but rather, merely to observe what might happen. She had once seen Rex leap almost to the top of the gate, spin 180 degrees in mid-air, and land facing the opposite direction, confusing himself until Leona shouted, "Hey, stupid!" and raked the mesh with the tines of her fork.

Admittedly, she had occasionally teased the beast. Any animal as obnoxious as Rex, she reasoned, had no right *not* to be teased. But she had never offered him violence until that afternoon.

She began simply, filling a bucket with cold water from the outside faucet and carrying it down the alley. Mrs. Nassiri was in her garden, pruning the rose bushes and scowling as the dog offered advice from the next yard. Leona nodded companionably. The widow cocked an eyebrow.

Rex was on the spot, spinning and baying behind the wire-mesh gate. Judging her moment, Leona braced herself, lifted the bucket, and with surprising strength flung its contents full in the face of the terrier king.

It had no effect whatever. Rex continued to bark and bay and spin and snap – as if, Leona thought, its only desire was to chew her into chunks and then excrete her in half-digested piles throughout the yard, to be gathered up by Pishny-Crabbe's gardening service and sent to the landfill in green plastic garbage bags that would eventually burst in the summer heat, releasing deadly greenhouse gases into the atmosphere. She was determined to play no part in the creature's nefarious ambitions. She returned to her own yard with the empty bucket to think out her next move. Recalling the three assassins and their rich cultural heritage, she repaired to her kitchen and prepared a mixture of strong spices that included black pepper, cayenne pepper, coriander, cumin, powdered garlic, more cayenne pepper, and a handful of salt to enhance the flavour. With a full bowl of this potent mixture, she returned to the gate in the alley. Again judging her moment, she flung it through the fence directly into Rex's gaping mouth.

As she explained to the police later, she might as well have spent the time staring up a dead horse's arse.

The investigating officer looked up, but he did not smile. "May I remind you, Mrs. Keenan, that you are charged with a very serious offence."

"What," said Leona, "shooting a real estate agent?"

"Possession of a restricted firearm," he reminded her. "Unlawfully discharging a firearm within the city limits. Discharging a firearm with the intent to wound, maim, or kill. And creating a public nuisance."

"A public nuisance!" Leona was outraged. "Has that garden troll gone so far as to accuse *me* of being a public nuisance?"

"That garden troll," the officer responded, "has a serious flesh wound that will take months to heal, if not years, and several of your neighbours have complained about the growing pile of compost behind your fence, as well as the noise of a jackhammer that has been disturbing the peace for the past several months."

"You can't be serious," said Leona.

"Mr. Pishny-Crabbe intends to prosecute to the full extent of the law."

"What about the dog?"

The dog had not so much as paused to reflect on the diversity of flavours that had been presented to its palate, but licked its lips with a lolling tongue and continued barking as if Leona had thrown him a handful of mist. She kicked the fence in frustration, and Rex's frenzy ascended from the deranged to the homicidal. Leona stared. Surely something must happen to a creature deep within itself, she thought, when it lived at such a pitch. What was to prevent his lungs from collapsing, or his eyes from popping out, or his bowels from inverting themselves from internal pressure? Surely something would have to give eventually. But the longer she watched, the less it did. Indeed, the creature seemed to gain strength from its own dementia. It seemed almost to be finding footholds in the invisible air. Clearly, it would be only a matter of minutes before Rex mastered gravity, or even space and time, and leaped the fence to sink his powerful canines into the soft flesh of Leona's neck. She imagined the blood spurting from her carotid artery, the scream on her lips silenced by the brute savagery of the animal's attack.

For the first time, Leona was afraid of Rex. Her heart pounded. Her breath caught in her throat. She felt her legs trembling, not with weakness but with adrenalin as the fight or flight syndrome possessed her. Then, with fearful exhilaration, she was gone. She ran as she had never run before. She felt the earth turning beneath the thrust of her feet. She covered the distance to her own back gate like a cheetah on speed – or would have if she hadn't tripped on a protruding root. The cry on her lips was abruptly silenced as she plunged headlong into the fetid mass of her own compost heap.

Finding the pistol was an act of God.

It lay where Ahmed had flung it, a small dark thing, solid and useful. It fit into her hand as if by nature. She turned and aimed the thing – again, as if by nature – at the ravening beast that was bearing down on her.

She squeezed the trigger.

Now, perhaps Ahmed had been mistaken and the weapon had not really jammed. Perhaps he had merely failed to release the safety, an act subsequently accomplished by the casual turning of a garden fork in the compost. Or perhaps, as was Leona's experience of mechanical devices, it had in the fullness of time simply and inexplicably healed itself. Whatever the truth of it, the pistol discharged, and no one was more surprised than Leona to find Theodore Longton Pishny-Crabbe prostrate in the gravel of the alley, clutching his left buttock and writhing as if he had just been shot.

The second thing Leona became aware of, after Pishny-Crabbe, was the king of the terriers barking maniacally in the background. She turned to shoot him – enough, after all, was enough – only to find herself deftly disarmed.

"He's *mine!*" shouted Mrs. Nassiri, and Rex's last glimpse of life as he knew it was of a grimly professional Iranian woman falling to a sniper's squat, palming a .25

calibre Berretta and, with practised ease, squeezing off two rounds in rapid succession.

Rex went down, wounded but not slain, never to bark again.

Pishny-Crabbe, when it came to court, found that it was his word against Leona's and Mrs. Nassiri's. To each of their surprise, they attested, the pistol which had played a minor role in the recent revolutionary out-rage had turned up in the compost, and Leona had been examining it with curiosity when the firing mechanism engaged and sent a hollow-point .25-calibre slug into Pishny-Crabbe's left buttock.

The two additional bullets that found their way into Rex's throat were more difficult to explain. It was Mrs. Nassiri who proposed that Leona, in her alarm and inexperience with firearms, had caused the weapon to discharge twice more before she, Mrs. Nassiri, had been able to wrest it from her, Leona's, grasp. Leona did not dissent. Mrs. Nassiri further proposed that political assassins habitually loaded the magazine with conven-tional ammunition but kept a hollow-point slug in the chamber so as to make a bigger and bloodier show with the first round. This she knew from her own tragic experience in Iran, she said, and it explained why Pishny-Crabbe had lost the bulk of one buttock while the two subsequent rounds had merely passed through Rex's throat and not torn it out.

Had she made such a statement at the trial of Ahmed, Darius, or Ardashir she would have been immediately recognized for what she was: a member of one of the Shah's élite murder squads — although, in truth, Mrs. Nassiri herself had always preferred to load the dum-dum bullet third, for it lent a deadlier certainty to the shot if the first two failed. But the court did not know this, and after due consideration the judge accepted Mrs. Nassiri's explanation as rational, knowing little of such things himself.

It was when Mrs. Nassiri proposed that any normal dog would have fled at the first outbreak of violence, and that Rex thus had no one but himself to blame for his subsequent injuries, that Pishny-Crabbe protested. It was a vile calumny against the terrier king, he said. Rex would never flee in the face of danger. Why, dogs such as he had been used as dispatch carriers in time of war.

The judge allowed that, while this might well have been the case at one time, it was his understanding that the United States Marine Corps had since been training dolphins in a similar capacity, and the latter had proved more satisfactory in every respect.

You cannot, Pishny-Crabbe declared, expect the court to believe that a dolphin was capable of carrying a secret message through enemy lines, confounding the opposing forces and turning the tide of battle. To which the judge replied, looking about him as if to espy several other judges who had not been there before, that, as far as present knowledge would affirm, *he* was the court, and *he* could believe what seemed to him the truth – *viz.*, that dolphins were entirely superior in every way to dogs, and that, further, no dog, to his knowledge, had ever managed to attach an explosive device to the hull of an enemy vessel.

"And do you," Pishny-Crabbe demanded, "have a pet dolphin?"

"As a matter of fact, I do," the judge responded, for he had a one-percent interest in a marine-world amusement park that counted a number of dolphins amongst its assets. He could not dismiss the case outright, but he could find Leona guilty of much-reduced charges and sentence her to community work.

The truth was, on the day in question, Pishny-Crabbe had left his Day Planner behind, and it was only his iron grip on every minute of the 1,440 that were allotted to him each day that allowed him to lead the life he had chosen. In the split second between realization and despair, he had even considered continuing without it, for surely he would be held up to ridicule in the minds of his neighbours if he were seen to return moments after he had departed. But he might not be seen, he reasoned, if he returned via the back alley, particularly if he returned from the south rather than the north. It was the thought of the dog that gave him courage. Rex would be delighted to see him again so soon. Why, Rex would do anything he asked if only he could make himself understood.

But there was the rub: frequently he couldn't.

"Attack!" he bellowed as he saw Leona aiming the pistol. "Kill!"

No doubt Rex would have been pleased to sink his canines into Leona's yielding flesh, but he was confined behind a wire-mesh fence that even dementia could not overcome, and Pishny-Crabbe was turning to flee even as he issued the orders. The dog would die for him, he had no doubt; he was not so sure that he was willing to die for himself.

In the event, Rex never had the chance. Pishny-Crabbe had made a long detour up 17th Avenue and down Georgia Street to Grove Hill Road to gain access to the alley behind his own house. He was appalled to see Leona diving into her compost as he rounded the long curve of Gateway Drive in his silver-grey BMW. He later testified that he feared for her safety, and that was why he skidded to a halt and erupted from the car and ran at her, but in fact his first thought was that the woman was clearly insane and required subduing. It was only when she produced the gun, he claimed, that he began issuing orders to the dog.

This testimony was challenged by Mrs. Nassiri's lawyer, who made a good case for the possibility that Pishny-Crabbe was yelling at the dog as soon as he got out of the car. The issue was never settled, and it was with some prejudice that the judge subsequently heard how Pishny-Crabbe's buttock in its several pieces had taken flight over south-west Calgary.

Mrs. Nassiri paid the veterinarian's bill, which was considerable, but Pishny-Crabbe refused to receive the now-voiceless dog back into his home. Rex was renamed Buffy by a pair of ten-year-olds in the northeast, and submitted in silence to being dressed in ribbons and bows for the remainder of his natural life.

Pishny-Crabbe, though he had won a technical victory in court, was unable to face the humiliation of living amongst such people. He sold his house and moved to Edmonton, where he took a position with the same firm but in a reduced capacity.

Mrs. Nassiri, no longer having any reason to move, didn't. She would have been prevented in any case, for, like Leona, she had considerable community work to do in lieu of a prison sentence. Several years later she was deported to face trial in Iran when evidence came to light about her previous career. Mr. Nassiri would have been deported with her had he not already been beaten to death with a shovel.

The assassins were deported some years later to serve the remainder of their prison terms in Iran according to a humanitarian agreement negotiated between two now quite reasonable governments.

After she had finished her community work, Leona called in a well-muscled young man to finish the jack-hammering and install the window in her pottery studio. Once it was finally done she found herself overcome by an inexplicable apathy. She sold her wheel and her clay, and nine months later gave birth to Gordon Keenan II.

"If I'd known that was all it took," Gordon remarked one day as the baby bounced and gurgled on his knee, "I'd have done it myself years ago."

"I beg your pardon?" said Leona, on the verge of being appalled.

"I was just saying that if I'd known all we had to do to start a family was shoot a real estate agent, I'd have done it myself years ago. It was a joke, sweetheart."

"Ah," said Leona, and turned away as she started to cry.

CALLING FOR ANGELS

"*E*lizabeth?" *My God, you're lovely.* "Yes, you're in the right place, come in. This is Cheryl, and my name is Kieran. Yes, Kieran. It's Irish. Not that it matters, but most people ask. If you'll take a seat in that yellow chair on the far side of the room I'll put this INTERVIEWING, PLEASE DON'T ENTER sign on the outside of the door and we can get started.

"I imagine you've heard about this experiment from your classmates. You haven't? Good. The success of the experiment depends on the ignorance of the participants. I don't mean to suggest that you're ignorant, Elizabeth, just that you must be ignorant of the experiment in order to take part.

"Yes, that's a video camera, just like the ones they use on television. You're going to be a star.

"No, actually, all we're doing is examining some

aspects of speech anxiety. What that means, first of all, is that we want you just to sit there for a while. That shouldn't be too difficult. Then we'll ask you to stand in front of the camera and speak for four minutes on your views about capital punishment. Cheryl and I will act as your audience, so you can speak to us if you like," *or you can stare vacantly into space, as you're doing now. It makes no difference to me, and Cheryl never pays any attention anyway. She's only here because she thinks that if she scratches Dr. Wearg's back Dr. Wearg will scratch hers, all the way through graduate school. Who knows, she may be right.*

"We'll be rating some things as you speak, Elizabeth, and the video camera will be recording you. But only one other person will see the tape and it will be erased immediately afterward, so your confidentiality is assured," *although Cheryl and I sometimes review the tapes before we erase them if we feel the need of a good laugh.*

"There's nothing to be nervous about, Elizabeth. It's not an examination, and you'll have ample time to collect your thoughts before you get up to speak. When you're finished, I'll take you down the hall to Dr. Wearg, and he'll explain what it's all about. In the meantime we have this *participant release form* we'd like you to sign. It explains in a little more detail what we're doing and what's expected of you. Read it carefully, then if you agree to take part, fill in the date and sign it."

You know, Elizabeth, it amazes me just how obedient you people are. You're the sixty-third subject I've run in the past two weeks, and so far no one has refused to sign the release. Do you imagine your marks will suffer if you don't take part in this experiment? Do you imagine they'll improve if you do? I assure you neither Cheryl nor I, nor even Dr. Wearg, has any such power, although I suspect Dr. Wearg is not above suggesting that he has.

"Now just sit back and think about your views on capital punishment and I'll try to get this machine working." *It is so easy to lie in the service of science. We've disconnected the red light on top of the camera so you won't know when it's running. I'm supposed to fiddle around with it and pretend that I'm waiting for it to warm up while all the time it is inscribing your every sound and movement on its magnetic memory.*

Most people remain silent and relatively inanimate during this portion of the experiment. I see that, in this respect, you are no different than anyone else. But you move me strangely. Lovely I called you and lovely you are. But what does that mean? I would not call you beautiful, nor would I call you cute. Perhaps "striking" is the word I want. But no, that implies too much sophistication and you look too innocent to be sophisticated. Lovely, beautiful, cute, striking, innocent, sophisticated: we have reached a sorry pass when a student of psychology can produce only six words to describe a woman, and all of them are inadequate.

I see you are amused, Elizabeth. A brief smile plays about your lips. Do you sense my confusion? Then you must be sensitive indeed, for I am standing behind a screen, watching you in the monitor. You don't even know the monitor is on, do you? I find it curious that no one has yet verbalized a suspicion that the camera is running during this portion of the experiment. It's pointing at you, Elizabeth. It's humming. Does that suggest nothing to you?

Ah, I see your mind is elsewhere. You're watching Cheryl. I imagine Cheryl is adjusting a strap or a seam, or perhaps she's brought out her pocket mirror. Very self-conscious is our Cheryl — or self-aware, as she prefers to call it. And not without cause. Cheryl's is the most remarkable body in the department. At least, her behaviour is appropriate to the assumption. Psychologists, you see, think that because they can explain their feelings it's all right to have them, and Cheryl is a bit of an exhibitionist. Many of her male colleagues have taken a keen interest in her work. I fear they are no more subtle than she. But I see that four minutes have elapsed.

"Okay, Elizabeth, now I have to administer something called the STATE TRAIT ANXIETY INVENTORY, though this is only the STATE portion; Dr. Wearg will be giving you the TRAIT portion later. It's fairly straightforward. There's only one page. On the left are a number of statements people use to describe their feelings, and on the right are four possible responses, ranging from NOT AT ALL to VERY MUCH SO. All you have to do is read each statement and fill in the appropriate response. Let's take the first statement as an example. 'I feel calm.' Now, if you find yourself on the verge of sleep you will, of course, fill in the circle under VERY MUCH SO."

Ah, Elizabeth, your laughter is like an embrace.

"On the other hand, if you're afraid you'll throw up at any moment, then NOT AT ALL is the appropriate response…"

Mistake. Mistake. Inappropriate verbal suggestion.

"…and so on with the other statements. Remember, it's not a test. There are no right or wrong answers. We just want you to indicate how you're feeling now, at this minute," *just as if you were an ordinary human being taking stock of your emotions instead of one of a hundred gullible students Dr. Wearg has coërced into giving four-minute speeches on their views about capital punishment.*

"Finished? Good. Now, if you'll stand in this area here I'll get a fix on you with the camera and Cheryl will tell you when you can start," *for you can't just plunge into it as you would a shimmering lake on a hot day with your exquisite body carefully exposed in the briefest of leaf-green bikinis. No, Elizabeth, these things are carefully orchestrated. Your speech will be divided into eight thirty-second segments. During each segment Cheryl and I will be rating you according to certain recognizable behavioural patterns which you may or may not exhibit. So the beginning of your speech must be co-ordinated with the flashing of that little green light on the wall behind you. Every thirty seconds the light flashes on, then Cheryl and I look down and mark the appropriate columns on the mimeographed sheets of paper before us. During this first segment, for instance, I am going to put an X in the column marked* SWAYS, *another in* FACE MUSCLES TENSE, *and a third under* VOICE QUIVERS. *However, I see a complete lack of behaviour which might fall into the category of* ARMS RIGID *or* FACE DEADPAN. KNEES TREMBLE *might be applicable, but you're swaying too much for me to tell, and one thing Dr. Wearg drummed into us was that we can take nothing for granted. Your behaviour must be overt and clearly recognizable before we can mark it down, like the* EXTRANEOUS ARM AND HAND MOVEMENT *you're exhibiting now. It's a pity there is no category called* BRASSIERE CLEARLY

ABSENT BENEATH THE THIN KNIT FABRIC OF AN
EARTH-BROWN JERSEY, *or* JEANS FIT LIKE A DRIVER'S
GLOVE, *for I would surely mark those columns.*

*But I see you have finished your speech, and that's too bad
because you still have two minutes left and there is no column marked* FIDGETS AS THOUGH SHE WERE WEARING A
HAIR SHIRT.

"We prefer that you stay up there for the full four
minutes, Elizabeth," *otherwise our results will be invalid
and your participation will have been for naught.*

"I'm sorry, Elizabeth, you cannot open the floor to
questions." *Cheryl and I are allowed neither to ask nor to
answer. "Don't give them any feedback," Dr. Wearg said,
and he trained us to be wonderfully vague, to neither support nor impede.*

Is that a STAMMER *I hear? Pull yourself together,
Elizabeth. You are mistaken if you think either of us is
remotely interested in what you're saying, although you have
made some rather remarkable leaps in logic and I suspect
your position would be considerably less assured if you or
someone you loved were facing the noose.*

"All right, Elizabeth, you can sit down now and fill
out another STATE TRAIT ANXIETY INVENTORY. It's the
same as the one you filled out before, only it's four minutes later, and again I must emphasize that you indicate
how you're feeling at this minute." *While you're doing
that I'll rewind the tape and Cheryl and I will add up our
marks and compare them by number and placement to see if
there is any consistency in our observations. There always is,
of course, because Cheryl cheats. She doesn't watch the sub-
jects, she watches me. Where I make an* X, *Cheryl makes an*

X. *This is known as inter-rater reliability: Cheryl relies on me for her data and I rely on Cheryl for raw material for my fantasies. But she's crafty, our Cheryl. Sly. She varies her results enough to allay any suspicions Dr. Wearg might have, but not enough to substantively affect the statistical significance of our inter-rater reliability.*

"Finished? Good. We'll take your tape down the hall to Dr. Wearg's office and he'll go over it with you. In fact, an hour from now you'll know more about the experiment than I do," *for Dr. Wearg has seen fit to withhold certain information from his raters lest it adversely affect their rating. As if it could possibly make any difference at this stage of the game. To Cheryl, you see, that's all it is: a game. And she plays it rather well. Good at games, is our Cheryl.*

You're not unlike her in that respect, Elizabeth, though I have not yet discerned the rules of your game, nor why you chose me for the ceremony. Was it by chance we met in the cafeteria the following day? There was such a welcome in your recognition, in your body language and your eyes. I see nothing now but those wide green eyes staring up at me through the half-light cast by stars and the street lamp outside your bedroom window, your eyes embracing me, pleading with me to be gentle, to be masterful, to be loving, to be kind. You invoked all the clichés. You wanted the earth to move, the heavens to blaze, the angels to descend and lay their hands upon your breasts. But it wasn't like that, was it, Elizabeth? It never is the first time, or the second, or even the third. You're lucky if it's like that once in a lifetime. Expecting pleasure, we cling too tightly to our desire and receive pain instead. For the pleasure of the act can never sate the hunger that precedes it, nor ease the emptiness that follows. It's a cruel joke. Calling for angels, we receive instead fierce Macha, the crow goddess, who delights to dance among the slain.

But you get used to it, Elizabeth. You grow numb. The numbness spreads. As the years progress, you will find that it hurts less and less each time.

THE CASE OF
JULIANNE CORELLI

Julianne was in the kitchen washing the cat when her mother came in to say that the archbishop had called and would be over directly. The cat was glad of the respite.

"I hope he doesn't stink," said Julianne.

"If he does," said her mother, who had bathed twice herself that day, "you're not to say anything."

The child did not reply, but dried her hands, then carefully folded the towel and replaced it on the rack beside the sink.

"What's an archbishop?" she asked

"You know Father Rowan."

"Yes," she said guardedly. The reeking cleric had been an almost daily visitor since the funeral.

"The archbishop is Father Rowan's boss."

"I thought the bishop was Father Rowan's boss."

"He is, dear, but the bishop has a boss, too. The archbishop is a bigger boss."

"Like the pope?"

"The pope is the archbishop's boss."

"Does he stink, too?"

"I don't know, child." Julianne's mother rolled her eyes. "I sincerely hope not."

The cat, who had retreated to a corner to groom itself, caught a speculative gaze in the eye of its young mistress and fled.

"The poor creature," said Julianne's mother.

"But he smells so, Mummy."

"It's a cat's business to smell, dear. It's one of the things they do."

"You can wash a cat," said Julianne.

"But you can't wash an archbishop. Kindly keep that in mind when His Eminence arrives."

His Eminence, when he arrived, was a man of ample tonnage and obvious appetites, exquisitely dressed and immaculately coifed. He settled himself heavily in the most comfortable chair in the living room and graciously allowed Julianne's mother to serve him tea and scones with her home-made raspberry jam.

The archbishop ate heartily, but carefully, so as not to soil his black vest and trousers. He spoke of the unseasonable coolness of the weather. It was mid-July already, but his sister's garden was at least a month behind.

Julianne's mother ate sparingly, and sipped her tea as her own mother had taught her, the fragrant liquid receding in minimal increments. She had brought out the Royal Albert for the archbishop, and a mug for Julianne. But Julianne wasn't thirsty, she said. She poured the archbishop a second cup of tea, trying to conceal the fact that she was holding her breath. She watched him help himself to another scone and spread it liberally with jam.

"Just like my mother used to make," he said with deep satisfaction.

"He's lying," Julianne whispered to the messy little cleric who had accompanied His Eminence. The cleric, who had been introduced as Father Harkins, raised one fleecy eyebrow.

"He's just making conversation," he whispered back. "It's not meant to be true or not true."

Julianne accepted the explanation with a shrug. The archbishop affected not to have heard, as perhaps he hadn't. Julianne stayed well away from him as she helped her mother clear away the tea things.

"You're a pretty little girl," the archbishop said when mother and child had returned to the living room.

"I know," said Julianne. Enough people had condescended to tell her so that it seemed pointless to contradict him.

"Julianne!" said her mother.

The archbishop waved a tolerant hand. "How old are you?" he asked.

"Eight."

"Do you remember what happened?"

"I'm only eight," said Julianne reasonably. "At my age, there's not much to forget."

"Precocious as well as pretty," said the archbishop to

the child's mother. The child's mother smiled uncomfortably and said nothing.

"I mean," said the archbishop, "do you remember what happened at the funeral?"

"I smelled flowers," said Julianne. "A woman smiled at me."

"A woman," said the archbishop, casting a meaningful glance at Father Harkins, who had produced a notebook from an inside pocket and was writing in it with a pencil. "What kind of woman?"

"How many kinds of women are there?" Julianne asked.

"Well," said the archbishop, leaning forward as if to impart a confidence, "there are mothers and daughters, sisters, aunts, old women, young women…"

"She smelled of flowers," Julianne said.

"Yes, child, but what did she look like, this woman?"

"She was beautiful, like Mummy." The child was leaning against Father Harkins, toying with a fold of his jacket. "You don't smell like flowers," she said.

"I imagine not," said the priest. "I imagine I smell like old books and cracker crumbs."

"No, you don't. You smell like…" She gazed at the ceiling, considering. "You smell like Saturday morning when I don't have to go to school."

"I'll take that as a compliment."

Julianne was pleased at his response. She forced herself to look across the room at the archbishop, who was not pleased. He was not even smiling.

"Can you tell me anything else about this woman?" said the archbishop, shifting his bulk in the chair. "Did she touch you? Did she say anything?"

"She didn't need to touch me," said the child. "And she didn't need to say anything."

The archbishop shifted again, a quick, impatient movement. He was unused to children, and tried to conceal his frustration. He failed. Father Harkins gave a slight cough. The archbishop gave him a poisonous look.

"Julianne, it is *extremely* important that you answer my questions."

Julianne retreated into the folds of Father Harkins' jacket, which seemed several sizes too large. "Do I have to?" she asked.

Her mother intervened. "Just do your best, dear."

"But my best is never good enough," the child complained. "Daddy's always asking questions, and you and Father Rowan and the doctors and the police, but no matter what I say you keep asking more questions." Abruptly, she turned to Father Harkins. "Do you want to see my dollies?"

The priest put a hand on her shoulder. "Perhaps we're asking the wrong questions," he suggested.

A look of gratitude suffused the child's features, and relief, even joy...and then, inexplicably, dread. Her eyes rolled upward in their sockets. She began to speak in a strange and compelling voice. Even the cat seemed to be listening as she chronicled a horror no child should have to witness.

Men were marching, she said. The sun glinted on their bayonets. There was fire and blood. The air was filled with smoke, stinging people's eyes and filling their lungs. The village was on fire. People were running toward the river, trying to escape, but they were shot down as they ran. The river was red with blood. There was a little boy with no face, a woman with no arms. Bodies floated like logs on the water. Children were running along the shore, calling to their parents. Soldiers lifted them on their bayonets and tossed them into the flow. The women screamed. The children cried. And there was laughter...such terrible laughter...and a smell in the air....

"No!" she cried. "No, no, *no!*"

Her body stiffened and she screamed. Father Harkins caught her as she keeled over. He picked her up and carried her to the couch where her mother had been sitting. He placed her gently on the cushions. Her mother fetched a blanket and spread it over her. There was no sound but the rise and fall of her breathing, which grew fainter as she lapsed into natural sleep. The priest resumed his seat. The archbishop ran a pale hand across his brow.

"She'll sleep for twenty minutes or so," her mother said, "and wake up with no memory of it."

"Thank God for that," said the priest.

"Thank God, indeed," said the archbishop, and turned to Julianne's mother. "Does this happen often?"

"Often enough to give me nightmares, if not her."

"Please, Mrs. Corelli, I need specific instances to report to Rome."

"What has Rome got to do with it?"

The archbishop's eyebrows scurried up his forehead. As well ask, what has faith got to do with salvation?

"What I think was the intention behind Mrs.

Corelli's query," Father Harkins interjected, "is the fact
that Julianne is in many ways an extraordinary little girl,
but we must keep in mind that she is, after all, only a
little girl."

Julianne's mother heaved a small sigh of gratitude.
Life had been difficult enough since the funeral without
all the outside interference. To meet someone who
showed some sensitivity to her daughter's dilemma was
cause to give thanks.

"Yes, well..." said the archbishop, accepting for the
moment his subordinate's judgement and blundering
into a concomitant area of interest: "I understand your
husband is no longer living with you, Mrs. Corelli."

Father Harkins winced at the bluntness of his shep-
herd's statement, but obediently recorded it in his notebook. He was nothing if not obedient, and he had been
told to take down every word.

"That is correct," said Julianne's mother stiffly.

"Do you mind telling me why this should be the
case?"

She minded very much. "It should *not* be the case."

"And yet it is," the archbishop persisted.

Mrs. Corelli heaved another sigh, this one of defeat.
"It has to do with the way he smells," she said.

The priest looked up brightly. "Do you know," he
said, "a woman once accosted Samuel Johnson, who was
not as fastidious as he might have been, and said, 'Dr.
Johnson, you smell.' 'No, Madame,' Dr. Johnson
replied, '*you* smell. *I* stink'."

Julianne's mother laughed out loud.

"Thank you, Wilfred, for that historical anecdote,"

the archbishop said, and shifted his gaze to Mrs. Corelli in the expectation that she would respond in a manner appropriate to a laywoman addressing an archbishop. He was not immediately disappointed.

"It is true that my husband no longer lives with us," she said, but the words came haltingly. It was not easy to reveal the details of a personal crisis to a stranger, however high the authority he invoked. "It is neither his choice nor mine. Nor Julianne's, if it comes to that. She loves her father dearly, as do I. But since the funeral, her sense of smell has become acute. More than acute, almost super-natural. The fact is, Your Eminence, Julianne cannot stand to be in the same room with her father for more than a few minutes. Apparently he smells. Or stinks," she said, with a nod to Father Harkins. "I have to bathe four or five times a day myself simply to remain tolerable to her, and she's constantly washing the poor cat."

"She didn't seem to object to my odour," said the archbishop.

Mrs. Corelli said nothing, but glanced at her daughter, unconscious on the couch. The archbishop could draw what conclusions he might.

"Yes, well," the archbishop blustered, "she practically cuddled up to Father Harkins."

Mrs. Corelli still said nothing.

"Yes, well," said the archbishop again. "Perhaps, while the child is unconscious, we might review the details of the case."

"The *case?* We're talking about my daughter!"

"You must forgive us," the priest interjected. "His Eminence meant no offence, I assure you."

"I am perfectly capable of making my own apologies, Wilf. *If* I consider it appropriate." To Mrs. Corelli, he said, "May I continue?"

"While my daughter is asleep," Mrs. Corelli replied, "I will try to answer any questions you have."

"Perhaps we might start with the death, then."

Father Harkins lifted one knee over the other and balanced his notebook on it. An effeminate gesture, Julianne's mother thought. As if to reinforce the observation, the priest tossed a stray lock of hair off his forehead.

"The death," she said, composing herself with difficulty.

"Yes," she said.

"Julianne was killed on April fourth," she said. "She disappeared on her way home from school. Her body was discovered the next day in a clump of trees on the edge of a golf course south of the city. She had been raped and strangled. As the cause of death was indisputable, her father and I saw no reason her body should be subjected to the further indignity of an autopsy, so we forbade it."

"You forbade it?" The archbishop raised an eyebrow. "Surely, in the case of violent death, an autopsy is mandatory."

Mrs. Corelli nodded. "According to the law, yes. But the law is..." She searched for words.

"The law is an ass?" Father Harkins suggested, quoting another of his favourite authors.

"What I was going to say is that the law is not absolute, especially if your husband happens to be a senior medical officer in the health region."

The archbishop, who knew to a nicety the extent of his own influence, nodded sagely. Though he wondered why the name had not registered before. It wasn't as if it were a common name. Dr. Stefano Corelli, Chief Medical Officer of the Meewasin Valley Health Authority. A prominent Catholic layman, active in the diocese, close friend and staunch supporter of the local bishop.

"A terrible thing," he said, "to lose a child. But to lose a child in such a manner...." Words failed him. "I can only imagine what you went through...."

On the contrary, Julianne's mother thought, you cannot imagine any such thing. Goethe said there was no act he could not imagine himself committing, and took that as a measure of his own greatness. Pitiful man. Let him give birth, she thought, just once....

"Forgive me for dwelling on it, Mrs. Corelli, but you say Julianne was raped. I suppose there is no doubt of that?"

She bit her lower lip. "None."

"So, technically" – the archbishop rearranged himself in the chair – "technically, then, she is no longer a virgin."

"She's eight years old, Your Eminence. Of course she's still a virgin."

"But technically," the archbishop persisted.

"Technically," said Mrs. Corelli, "she is as innocent in God's eyes now as she was then. If you want to take it up with anybody, take it up with the Almighty!"

"Quite so, quite so," said the archbishop, retreating back over the line he had unwittingly crossed. "Perhaps we could skip to the funeral now."

"There isn't much to skip," said Mrs. Corelli. "Immediately the body was released, we arranged for burial. There was to be no embalming, no makeup, no false undertaker's smiles placed on our daughter's face. My husband and I consider such practices unnatural – indeed, abhorrent. So there was nothing to prevent us from proceeding immediately. Father Rowan, our parish priest, was prepared to celebrate the Resurrection Mass as early as April sixth."

The archbishop cast a meaningful glance at Father Harkins. "The third day," he muttered.

"But we decided on the seventh, to allow time for her grandparents to fly up from Arizona. On the day, the church was full to bursting. I remember being surprised by that. I hadn't thought we had so many friends. But with Steve's colleagues and my friends from college – I'm taking a degree in comparative literature – they added up. And I suppose when a child is murdered we are all diminished, and even the secular must find some way of sharing the sorrow. Not that it made a great deal of difference in the end, for, as you know, Julianne sat bolt upright in her coffin and demanded to know why everyone was crying."

There was a long silence. Father Harkins gazed complacently out the window. Julianne's mother gazed at Father Harkins, wondering if he was gay. The archbishop stared at the floor, wondering if it would be wiser to reveal or conceal the scepticism he felt.

They all looked up as Julianne stirred, moaned gently, turned over...and began to rise from the couch. The folds of the blanket resolved themselves into a curtain, or a shroud, as the small body was lifted up by invisible hands. Soundlessly she ascended, supported by nothing but air and light, until she was hovering like the sunrise, weightless and glorious, suffused with the brilliance of the morning. A smell of flowers filled the room, a fragrance as sweet and natural as a baby's breath.

The archbishop stared, open-mouthed. He cast a furtive glance at the child's mother, then at his assistant, as if to assure himself that he was not hallucinating. Clearly, he was not. Julianne's mother was bathed in the same light, her face a mixture of consternation and awe. As for Harkins, the priest looked for all the world as if he, too, might levitate at any moment. It was too much for a rational man to take in. He ran a finger around the inside of his collar, which seemed suddenly too small for the flesh it encircled.

Julianne stirred, shifted beneath the hovering blanket, and descended once again to the couch. Her breast rose in a great, shuddering sigh. Then she was still.

"Does *that* happen often?" Father Harkins inquired.

Julianne's mother took a deep breath and exhaled slowly. "Mercifully, no."

"I...I had heard..." said the archbishop, in a voice as small as an echo. "I had heard that a murdered child rose from her coffin and beseeched her mourners to stop mourning. I had heard that she forgave her murderer, though she could not name him. I heard it. Everyone heard it. Many even claimed to have witnessed it. But I confess, Mrs. Corelli, I did not believe it until this moment."

Julianne's mother tried to smile, and failed. The

archbishop shook his head ponderously, at once confused and appalled by his doubts.

Julianne awoke, wide-eyed. For reasons that neither of them could explain, then or later, Father Harkins was instantly at her side. She looked up at him, smiling delightedly.

"You are a messy person," she said.

"Why, bless you," he said, and laughed out loud. "Shall I tell you a secret?"

"If you whisper," she said, casting suspicious glances at her mother and the archbishop.

He leaned close and whispered, "I can't help it."

Julianne giggled, an entirely childish sound. "Would you like to see my dollies now?"

"I would love to see your dollies," he said, and found himself being led away, the child's hand in his. She stopped at the chair where the archbishop sat, no longer a participant but a distant spectator. She was breathing through her mouth, but she knew that would only work for a few minutes. People always smelt the worst right after she woke up. She could smell her mother and the priest. She could even smell the cat in its corner, but that was a simple, animal, washable smell. The archbishop was different.

"I'm sorry," she said, "but you'll have to leave."

"Julianne!" said her mother, but the archbishop raised a hand to silence her.

"It's quite all right, Mrs. Corelli." He rose, ponderously, and prepared to depart, the weight of revelation heavy on his shoulders. "What she smells, I'm afraid, is the stench of human sin."

He wondered what the child's father had done to warrant her gentle condemnation. He shook his head, glanced at the priest. "I'll wait for you in the car, Wilfred."

Julianne thought her heart would break. "You don't smell as bad as when you came in," she said brightly, hoping to cheer him up. Not surprisingly, it didn't. It wasn't true, in any case.

"Shall I tell you a secret?" Julianne asked earnestly once the archbishop was gone.

"If you like," said Father Harkins.

She lowered her voice to a whisper. "That man doesn't believe in God."

Julianne's father was allowed to return to his family in mid-September, two months after the archbishop's visit. He was a grateful man and happy to be home, but still a trifle puzzled that he had been obliged to leave in the first place. Whether he stank less or Julianne's rhinal acuity had abated with time he neither knew nor cared. A battery of medical tests had demonstrated to his own satisfaction that his body odour was no more offensive than anybody else's, and a good deal less offensive than some. He agreed to bathe every morning, and again when he returned from work. It was a small price to pay, he thought, for a normal family life, though how normal life could be with a child like Julianne remained to be seen.

Coincidentally, Julianne's murderer was apprehended that same month. The child recognized him immediately when he came to the door, though he seemed to have aged a dozen years in the six months since he had committed the act. Forgiveness was what he came for and forgiveness was what he received – from Julianne, if not from her mother.

Mrs. Corelli had grown used to strangers in the house, though she had also grown to despise them. People came to ask for blessings, which Julianne bestowed with impatience, or withheld as the mood took her. People came to be cured of various ailments, usually unsuccessfully. "It won't work," she would tell them, but they beseeched her to try anyway. People came to touch and to gawk. People came to argue and denounce. People came to turn her away from the papist heresy. People came to enlist her aid in various causes. To petitioners and critics alike she was uniformly candid, even rude sometimes, but she was only a little girl, after all, and there wasn't much she could do about the state of the world.

When her murderer came to ask forgiveness, however, that was something she *could* do. Unfortunately for the felon, Julianne's mother was privy to every word they said. She was never far from her daughter when people were in the house, and she often enlisted the aid of friends and relatives, and sometimes even a security service, so that Julianne would never be alone with a stranger. When it became apparent who the bent, underfed caricature of a man was, she called the police. He gave himself up gratefully, and went away to face a battery of charges that would keep him behind bars for the remainder of his natural life.

Julianne's visions continued, usually in the most inappropriate places – at school, at church, in a restaurant with her parents – so that Dr. and Mrs. Corelli grew afraid of taking her anywhere lest she embarrass them publicly and shock everyone within hearing and sight. For they were invariably images of violence: people running, people shooting, people stabbing and being stabbed, images of blood and fire, of bodies bloated and bursting, of corpses heaped in disarray, of children weeping. The capacity of the strong to inflict mayhem on the weak never ceased to appall her imagination, though mercifully she never gained the art of remembering what she had seen after she woke up.

It was Wilfred Harkins who suggested that Julianne's visions were the result and the purpose of everything that had happened to her. She was to bear witness, he wrote in a brief but fascinating article in the diocesan newspaper, whenever and wherever the spirit moved her. She was to shock people, revolt them. She was to send them from the room in hysterics. She was to reduce them to tears, jolt them out of their complacency. And once in a hundred times, perhaps, she was to move someone to *act* on what she had shown them in her innocent agony.

"If you want to know the truth," he concluded, quoting a Greek proverb, "ask a child or a fool."

If this required a certain sacrifice from her parents in terms of public embarrassment and social ostracism, he suggested to them in a subsequent visit, they might possibly be willing to make it, considering the circumstances. Their child had been restored to them, after all. It was not much God was asking in return.

"Only our social lives, my professional reputation, and our standing in the community," Dr. Corelli remarked dryly. But they promised to take the priest's words under advisement.

The archbishop duly made his report to Rome. It was the product of sober second thought, he told himself. He made mention of Julianne's "visions," if such they were, but pointed out that any child with access to a television could have pieced together similar tales of horror simply by watching the evening news. The failure of the appropriate authorities to perform an autopsy on the allegedly murdered child's body was sufficient in itself to cast suspicion on the affair. Her parents' further refusal to have the body embalmed, the archbishop feared, pointed to a degree of collusion on their part, although it could never be proved. The testimony of Carl Rowan, the parish priest, was suspect, as were the subsequent declarations of witnesses to the so-called resurrection. In circumstances fraught with emotion – and what circumstances could be more fraught than the funeral of a murdered child? – people are easily deceived, as often as not by their own unacknowledged yearning to live in a world that is substantially kinder and more just than the one they must, in fact, inhabit. As to Julianne herself, the archbishop had interviewed the child personally, and, aside from a regrettable tendency toward emotionalism, which was surely explicable by the circumstances in which she found herself, she seemed a perfectly ordinary eight-year-old girl.

In short, he concluded, the case of Julianne Corelli, whether one of hysteria or of deliberate deception, required no further action from Rome.

STRANGE TRIBE

And if you gaze for long into the abyss,
the abyss gazes also into you.
– Nietzsche

Billy Greyeyes told me he had seen a white moose at the narrows, with antlers as big as trees, but when he got it in his sights it vanished like smoke. A week later Annie Bear gave birth to a male child with six fingers on each hand, and all that day a dark cloud hovered over the south shore of the lake. The next afternoon the loons were calling, and everywhere the small forest creatures were going to ground. The brief night passed in silence, without a breath of wind. In the morning, when Joel Natoweyes told me he had found the tracks of a cloven-hoofed animal where the white men had been camping near the mouth of the bay, it was confirmation rather than surprise. My blood turned to ice.

It was high summer in the north. The sun had risen at 4:30, and it still lacked four hours till noon as I accompanied Joel to the white men's camp. We paused to watch a float plane taking off from the lake, with its reassuring twentieth-century roar. When it disappeared over the tree line we remained standing, Joel and I, with our backs to the trees, and listened to the mechanical hum until it was no more than a sympathetic vibration in our ears. It was then that the silence of the forest pressed in upon us, and we could not resist looking over our shoulders, as if we expected something to emerge from that ancient calm.

I had lately been troubled by dreams, receiving strange and awful visitations in the night.

"It's too soon," I said.

"For what?"

"To be frightened."

What I meant was, "It's too soon to be immediately afraid for your personal safety." It was never too soon to be frightened.

There were two tents in the camp, each big enough for two. Two canoes had been carried up past the water line and turned over, paddles and life-jackets stowed beneath. The fishing tackle laid out beside the tents plainly told what they had been doing there.

"They had fish last night," said Joel, and I was conscious of a sudden, idiotic hope: if, against all wisdom, they had left food lying out, it was just possible that a bear or a pack of wolves had come into the camp and scared them off. There was no sign of firearms. They had nothing but knives to protect themselves. And hadn't

I seen wolf tracks by the shore? Perhaps they were even now summoning the courage to return, laughing bravely and assuring themselves that they had followed the only wise course.

"They cleaned them up the shore and brought the fillets back here to cook." Joel indicated location and activity with brief nods of his head. "The heads and guts are still there on the rocks."

My heart sank. It had been, after all, an idiotic hope.

"That's not right," I said.

"Scavengers should have taken them by now," he agreed.

"Are those wolf tracks by the shore?"

"Dogs," said Joel, scanning the ground. "They came early this morning – three...no, four of them. Here they are coming in" – he pointed to the tracks in the soft earth – "and here they are going out."

"Anything else?"

"They left a hell of a lot faster than they came." He looked abashed for a moment, then he said, "Sorry, Father."

I had asked him not to call me that – "Call no one your father on earth," it says in the Scriptures – but it seemed a trivial thing in this deserted campsite, as trivial as his thoughtless profanity. Hell was a state, not a place, and it remained unchanged by what people chose to call it. The word itself had been a regular feature of all but the most genteel vocabularies for a generation or more. Still, I was touched by Joel's delicacy – or intended delicacy – of expression.

"Something frightened them," I said, "and they

cleared out. Pity it didn't frighten the men who were camping here. Until it was too late, I mean."

"At least one of those men," said Joel, "was a woman."

I looked at him in mild surprise. "You can't tell that from their tracks, surely."

"Women have narrower feet," he said, "and they take shorter steps." His lips curved upward in his familiar smile. "But it's easier when you see a box of sanitary napkins in one of the tents."

I'd missed that. My chosen career has left me ignorant of such matters.

"Could a menstruating woman have had that effect on dogs?"

The look he gave me could only be described as respectful scorn.

"Maybe when something's wrong, unnatural, it has a smell to it," he said. "But the blood is a natural part of being female. Dogs do it, too. Bears, wolves. It might have made them curious, but it wouldn't have frightened them."

"Could that have been what attracted them in the first place?"

He laughed aloud, a reassuring sound. "Not unless she'd made a circuit of the camp rubbing herself against the trees."

I supposed it had been a silly question. As for the smell, I could detect nothing unnatural in the trees or on the water. Still, something was dreadfully wrong.

As if to punctuate the thought, there came a heart-rending wail from deep in the forest. A cry of anguish rather than fear. I shuddered from the crown of my scalp to the back of my heels. There was no room for doubt any more.

Still, it was a human cry, and I found cause for hope in that.

Joel crossed himself, an automatic gesture. I followed somewhat tardily. Neither of us betrayed the slightest inclination to follow that sound into the forest. It was fear that prevented us, not cowardice. We needed more information.

"Tell me what you read on the ground," I said.

"Does it really matter?" he asked.

"Yes," I replied. "It really matters."

He inspected the area, no doubt glad to apply his remarkable and wholly logical skills to a situation that had become utterly illogical.

"They ate," Joel said. "Two fish, northern pike. At least, there are only two heads up the shore. They threw the bones in the fire. The dishes are clean. They knew the danger of leaving food out. Afterward they sat by the fire – an hour, maybe two, long enough to let the night draw down. One of them was restless; see, his prints are unclear, he kept moving his feet. Another one just sat there and let his footprints sink into the earth. He was wearing boots, too. New ones. The treads are hardly worn. The woman, she was wearing moccasins, like you, Father. No treads, no seams. The other one was a woman, too. She sat with her legs stretched out, her feet close to the fire. Probably slept in her socks, like Maria."

He paused, and I thought of his Maria, slack-bellied after eight children but with the very Spirit's light in her eyes. I'd given her communion that morning, put God on her tongue, and felt myself unworthy.

"Then, this morning...." he began.

"The dogs," I said.

He nodded. "The dogs came because they smelled human, and human means food. But this time it meant something else, and they ran."

"Did they know it yet, the humans?"

"They got up, the three of them –"

"I thought there were four of them," I interrupted.

"Not any more." He shook his head, an emphatic negative, and the grim, unholy logic of it came home to me.

The scientific method gives us one way of thinking, one way of knowing. This the modern world has embraced because it comforts us and requires no sacrifice. Ghosts, demons, and the myriad creatures of nightmare do not exist because they cannot be explained by observation and experimentation. One might gaze into the abyss and postulate its origin, but one is not required to leap into it. A fine and rational faith. Religious faith follows a different logic that seems no logic at all, and offers us another way of knowing. It gives us rules and reasons and it comforts the credulous with certainty. But this was faith of a different order. This was faith as old as the rocks, as old as the water and the sky. It was the faith of the living earth, and the laws it conceived were designed to kill the weak and the faithless. Maria had once remarked to me that I preached more on goodness than on rightness, and that the two were not necessarily the same.

Was it right, then, that her husband and I should now be confronting an evil as old as legend? It certainly wasn't good.

"They built up the fire," Joel said. "One of them went down to the shore for water." He paused. "Then it came out of the tent."

"And they ran."

He nodded in confirmation. "You can see where they went into the forest here, and here.... The undergrowth is trampled, branches broken. They'll be easy to track."

"And the creature followed?"

"Maybe it looked normal from the knees up." He nodded again. "It was the feet that scared them, the split hooves."

"Will anything else change?" I asked, recalling unlikely tales of shape-shifters and werewolves from childhood Saturdays at the movies – recalling, too, the shape of fears that had been haunting my sleep these nights past. Of course it was impossible that any living creature could so transform itself. Flesh was not so imaginative, nor bone so malleable. Yet here was the impossible, begging to be disproved.

"I don't know," he said, gazing into the forest. "We should speak with the elders."

"Yours or mine?"

"Both."

I expected nothing from my bishop, and that was what I got. An urban bureaucrat, he had been offered our vast northern diocese at the tender age of thirty-nine owing solely to his administrative ability. He had accepted the see for fear he would not be offered another, and now awaited transfer with ill-concealed impatience. He asked me first if I needed a holiday, then he offered to send up the diocesan exorcist. I reminded him that I *was* the diocesan exorcist. A thunderstorm south of the narrows precluded further conversation over the radio phone. Nature cut us off, saving me the trouble.

The Cree elders were little better. Those who believed us recognized the beast as a visitation from the spirit world and a sign that something was wrong in the fabric of creation: the cloth had been torn and something had slipped through. It happened from time to time. But there was nothing to be done. Traditionally, the cannibal creature had to be hunted and killed by its own clan, but this creature's human name was not known. Even if it were, it was unlikely on the evidence we had gathered that any member of its family could be brought north in time to stop it, much less be persuaded to kill it. For the condition was not permanent, although a person once possessed will change and change again until old age or justice ended its depredations.

I notified the local detachment of the RCMP, and just before noon Joel and I were accompanied by a reluctant constable to the camp at the mouth of the bay. Grant MacIsaac was a traditional Catholic with a superstitious awe of the church and, consequently, of my own humble office. I had never had cause to be grateful for that heresy, but the constable would never have come had I not invoked the authority of my priesthood. Even so, he saw no evidence that a crime had been committed.

I nodded to Joel, and Joel proceeded to tell him the story he had seen written in the earth around the campfire. Still, the constable saw no reason to involve the police. The dog tracks, the human tracks, the moose tracks – for such they obviously were – were evidence of nothing more than the presence of dogs, humans, and a moose.

"Does it not strike you as odd," I asked, "that a moose should be walking about on its hind legs?"

"No odder than a priest walking about in moccasins," he retorted with a furtive glance at my footwear, and another at Joel's. "Who said it was walking on its hind legs, anyway?"

"Whatever made these tracks," said Joel, "was walking on two legs, not four."

The constable looked from one to the other of us in patent disbelief, then shook his head and began to walk away.

"*These* two legs," he said over his shoulder, "are taking me home to my dinner."

"What if they haven't returned by nightfall?" I called after him.

He stopped, turned. "Then I'll *think* about starting some inquiries."

"He'll regret this," I said to Joel. "Oh, that's not a threat, it's a prediction. His scrupulosity won't allow him to forget that he treated a priest of the church with anything less than respect. He's in for a session with his confessor. I, unfortunately, am his confessor."

At another time, Joel might have laughed. Like the constable, he held the church in some awe. At the same time, he was unable to take entirely seriously a God who gave him eight children and the means to support, at most, four. He laughed often, but now he laughed not at all.

"What do we do?" he asked.

"We go after it."

"But the elders —"

"I know," I interrupted. "The elders said there was nothing to be done. Unfortunately, I am not a Cree elder, I am a priest of the Roman Catholic church, and my duty is clear. I must find this ravaged soul and put it to rest. You needn't come, Joel. I can't force you. But I'd be the worst kind of liar if I told you that I didn't want you with me."

He hesitated only a moment. "When do we leave?"

"As soon as we can make ready." I took out the vial of holy water I had brought and made a circuit of the camp, sprinkling it liberally in all directions. I could almost hear it sizzling as it hit the ground where the creature had walked.

I have said that faith gives us certainty, but at the end of the day the only certainty is doubt. Were I asked to define humankind, I would say not that we are tool-makers, monument builders, jesters, or chroniclers, but that we are the doubting animal. And so it was with doubt that we set out that afternoon — doubt and Joel's Remington. I didn't know if the beast was killable by such means, but the weapon offered a certain comfort, as did the crucifix at my breast and the vial of chrism I carried in a plastic bag in my pocket.

As Joel had said, they were easy to track. They had plunged headlong into the forest, careless of branches and undergrowth. One of them had fallen and almost immediately been attacked. The signs were clear: trampled undergrowth, broken branches, a splash of blood. But the man had escaped somehow, and propelled by fear had overtaken his companions. The signs of that were clear, too: a scrap of cloth on an overhanging branch, a scrape of skin where a smaller, weaker creature had been thrust against the jagged bark of a spruce tree.

Still, it was an hour before we found her.

She was propped against a stump, staring ahead with open eyes, unable to see in death what she had been unable to believe in life. Her throat was cut – or rather, chewed – and her belly ripped apart. The creature had taken the organ meats, had not eaten them but taken them, rended them, chewed them and spat them out. The woman's breasts were layered with scraps of her own liver and heart, the space about her trampled and dark with blood. The cloven prints were unmistakable in the moss.

"Merciful God," said Joel, and crossed himself.

I took the vial of chrism from my pocket and knelt and signed the cross on the woman's forehead. "Through this holy anointing and God's loving mercy, may you by the grace of the Holy Spirit be freed from your sins. May God save you and in divine goodness raise you up. In the name of the Father, and of the Son, and of the Holy Spirit."

"Amen," said Joel.

It was all I could do. Perhaps it was enough.

"We can't just leave her here," I said.

"She'll be safe from scavengers for a time," said Joel. "Not even crows will eat this flesh until the stink of evil has gone from it."

"Did she resist, can you tell?"

"Oh, yes. She fought with all her heart."

I did not ask him how he knew, but I found it comforting. My own heart quietened with the knowledge. But as we pushed on through the forest I heard the crows begin to gather behind us. Joel turned and cocked his head to listen, then returned to the trail.

Brother crow is a great respecter of evil, I thought, but he cares not a whit for sanctity. Behind us nature was taking its course, and that was right. Not good, perhaps, but right.

The creature's ravaging of the woman had taken time, and given the other two a chance to get well ahead. Their panic must have diminished, for the human body cannot indefinitely support life at such a pitch. It must stop from time to time, if only to recover the resources for flight.

We came to a place where one of them had tried to climb a tree, and another where they had stopped to fashion weapons but had not the strength or the competence to complete the task: branches half ripped from trees still clung by their tendons to their trunks, sharpened sticks lay abandoned on the forest floor. By the evidence, they had only a pocket knife – at best, two pocket knives – between them. The futility of defence must have seemed only too obvious: a sharpened stick that broke in human hands would break again and more easily beneath the onslaught of the creature that pursued them.

Always they resorted once again to flight.

Where they stopped, we stopped, and they stopped often, their path chosen for them by rock and water as often as they chose the path themselves. And wherever they stopped I could feel their horror and smell their fear. I could imagine them returning to reason, that most human of gifts, as their bodies gave out: thinking this way and that, where to hide, how to fight, where to make a stand, then giving in to terror once again as they saw in their memories' eyes the hideous vision of a human body walking on goat's feet.

Joel lost the trail only once. We waded downstream and then up again along a narrow tributary. Plainly, he was puzzled.

"Do you have anything plastic?" he asked me. "Clear plastic."

I took the vial of chrism from my pocket and handed him the bag I had wrapped it in to keep it from staining my clothes. He laid it on the surface of the water and looked through it to the stream bed, where footsteps became visible, heading upstream. When he pulled up the bag again, they were gone. It was not long before he found where they had plunged once again into the forest. He returned the bag to me; he would never have tossed it aside. I stooped to drink, gagged, and spat the water out. It tasted foul.

The boreal forest does not cool as a deciduous forest cools. Rather, it seems to heat from beneath: while the inverted umbrellas of pine and spruce and the ragged limbs of tamarack soak up the sunlight and reflect it back to heaven, the solid rock of the Precambrian shield, which is rarely more than a foot beneath the surface of the soil, hour by hour surrenders the accumulated heat of æons to sustain the frail life forms that thrive in its bright and maddening season.

In winter the rocks withdraw their warmth to the centre of the earth. The waters freeze. Plants and insects die, and many animals, while others turn colour and grow the miraculous fur that has allowed humankind to survive here for millennia. But man and beast must walk in careful balance, for it is a mortal symbiosis and there is not much, sometimes, to distinguish the hunter from the hunted.

We did not stop as the day advanced, but pressed along the revealed path, increasing our speed as the sun began its long, slow descent to the west. We no longer talked, but saved our breath to feed our blood, for Joel perceived a need for urgency as he scanned the terrain ahead.

The insects were intolerable, yet they had to be tolerated, their legless buzzing and their mindless assaults. Indeed, the slap of a hand on human flesh became almost reassuring, as did the steady padding of our feet on the forest floor, repetitive, repetitive, almost running now. In a realm of incessant birdsong, of nameless rustlings and gruntings, of quick movements on the edge of sight and strange cries in the distance, the sounds of human passage had become solitary and unique. Even the deliberate, ponderous activity of porcupine and beaver were stilled. There was nothing to hear but the sounds we made ourselves.

A pair of loons called above the forest. I looked up and saw the points of four swift wings glinting in the sunlight, sudden as a breath. The loon is a creature of twilight, more canny than fox or fowl, a fish-eater, master of wind and water alike. Legend says that when the forest has become fodder for the beast, the loons are the last to leave.

Swiftly we ran, and swiftly the beast ran before us.

An elder had once told me – half in jest, I think – that the wolf is my spirit guide. I would have been grateful for brother wolf's keen ears, his loping, tireless gait, and his thick coat to protect me from the brambles that clutched as I moved upright through the forest.

I was grateful for Joel, for the persistence of his courage. Though the path of flight was clear in the earth below and the trees above, the trampled moss and the broken branches, I required a leader. When we came to a rock outcropping where the path divided, where terror or reason had driven them apart, it was my companion's strength that kept me from turning back.

"It stops here," said Joel, puzzled.

"They split up," I said, for such was obvious even to me.

"It stops here," he repeated, scanning the ground. "The trail stops here. The path divides, but the creature did not follow...either of them."

"That's impossible," I said, scanning the ground in turn.

"I know," he said, then paused, and cast his eyes slowly upward.

"I have heard," he said, "that it can fly."

"That's absurd!" Fear was whetting my temper. "If the creature could fly it would have overtaken them long ago."

"If you believe that," he said, "then you misunderstand the nature of the hunt."

But I did not misunderstand. Rather, I remembered, and I cried out in pain. I remembered shadows moving on the path before me, images at once defined and destroyed by light: a swift leg caught in a breath of moonlight, the turn of a thigh as it vanished among the leaves, muted laughter, long hair brushing my cheek. I remembered images of temptation and desire, of writhing torsos and glistening thighs, and faces looking in from the edge of the fire. I remembered terrible beauty and terrible corruption and the fearful darkness in which I had awakened night after night, bathed in sweat, not the hot sweat of the healing lodge but the cold, desperate sweat of a man who has seen what he was not meant to see. And always there was a distant, savage music on the air, and the stench of branded flesh.

The images left no trace of nightmare. There was no narrative, no hook for an analyst to hang some significance on. There was just fear and darkness and a sense of deep, unquenchable desire, all drowned again in sleeping and re-awaking, all swept aside in the automatic gestures of a celibate who is not permitted such thoughts. A man who knows not woman is no less a man for that, but no less open to temptation, either. A man who believes that celibacy will keep him pure and holy must also believe that sexual union with a woman is impure and unholy – and a man who believes that is lost. He will forgive himself extraordinary faults for that one sacrifice and commit treason against his own intent.

With memory came certainty: the creature's sole purpose in pursuing its companions was to draw us – to draw me – into the forest behind it. I had invited it, and now it sought me in the only way it knew how. I knew it like a blow to the solar plexus: hard, sharp, breath-taking, incapable of misapprehension.

"I have awaited you, holy man," said a voice deep as nightmare, dry as fire. "I have awaited you with hunger."

She stood – for woman she was, naked and volup-tuous. She stood and displayed herself to me, another woman's blood dried and flaking on her chin and breasts and belly.

"Holy man," she repeated, mockingly, and I shook my head in violent negation.

She whispered the words again, the soft wind of her breath shaping the curves of her lips.

Holy man.

The ancients of the desert used to invite the devil to their prayers that they might do battle, but I was no such brazen soul. I could say nothing. I could not even pray. I could only stare and wonder. She was terrible and beautiful and she was all that I desired: the curve of her belly and the thrust of her thigh, the full breasts lifted high by the arch of her back, the dark soft places of her body waiting to be explored. I wanted her more than I had ever craved sanctity or peace or even the love of God, for she was tangible, touchable, and within my grasp. And eager. Already I could feel her flesh against my flesh, feel her body rising to my lips and hands. It was the tribal dance, religious ecstasy transformed in the mystical flesh. I would ravage her, and afterward lay my head on those soft breasts and sleep myself beyond the claims of faith or vow.

She saw me strong in my desire, ungovernable as the blood that fed my flesh, and she smiled, her parted lips revealing teeth like razors.

Later I realized it was her only mistake, that smile, the attempt to appear human after all. For in that smile I saw the woman we had left behind us in the forest, bathed in her own blood and now being eaten by crows. I hesitated, just for a second. I put a hand over my heart, as if that were enough to protect it from those terrible teeth. It was a gesture, nothing more. Something to plead my case. *I did resist, at the end. Yes, I resisted.* But even as the thought of resistance entered my mind I felt my strength running out of me like water. I could almost feel it draining into the earth and air.

The creature watched, briefly puzzled.

"Is this what you want, then?" she asked, and before my unbelieving eyes she was transformed into a young man, a beautiful young man, strongly muscled and triumphantly male.

I staggered, sought handholds in the air. The creature saw my weakness and snarled. It was not my weakness she wanted, but my strength.

"Where..." I began, and paused to take breath. "Where is Joel?"

"I will kill you," she said. "I will eat your living heart and spit the blood in your face."

"Where...is...Joel?"

"I have already killed him." The creature pointed, and I saw my friend and guide impaled on a branch above the forest floor, his limbs hanging from his torso like the arms and legs of a rag doll. "He awaits my pleasure."

I did not believe her, mother of lies. I was seeing what she wanted me to see. And she wanted me to see her smile again, to see that her teeth were as sharp as they had been, the lips as voluptuous. She could not own me. She could not command me and make me like herself. But she could destroy me, and take pleasure in doing it. I could see the excitement of anticipation and hunger coursing through her muscles like blood, veins throbbing beneath the skin. I could almost hear the heart pumping in her chest.

"But no," she said, and stopped. She laughed in deep pleasure.

"I shall kill you as a wolf," she said, drawing close so that I should smell the blood and corruption on her breath. "I shall eat you as your own spirit guide, you witless human creature."

The creature must have sensed my relief — if one is to be eaten, after all, it is better a wolf do it than a cannibal — for it hesitated a moment, a fleet look of fear in its briefly human eyes. But the changing was upon it already. The eyes turned feral and dark, the brows about them thick with sprouting fur, the head changing shape, lowering, growing smaller. The air was electric with supernatural energy as the thing descended to all fours, as hands and feet turned to paws, as its belly was pulled up between its hind legs and its chest expanded between its forelegs. A she-wolf it was, for the creature had returned to its natural sex in the metamorphosis, a she-wolf with a growl as deep as legend. But it did not attack. Rather, it held back, casting about, head lowered, testing my scent. It feinted and retreated, made to attack and then thought better of it. It was clearly confused, as though the body were receiving commands to which the brain could not quite give assent.

Finally, it turned and fled into the forest.

And Joel climbed down from his tree.

As a rule, Joel took communion twice a year, Easter and Christmas, and barely came to church more often than that, except for the baptisms and confirmations and the other inescapable rites of passage – including marriage, now – of his expanding brood. So I was surprised to see him later that week at the end of the short line of communicants at early Mass.

He took the wafer with unusual reverence, it seemed to me – no, not reverence, *gratitude* – and turned to face the crucifix before walking slowly back to sit with Maria.

After the dismissal, I found him waiting on the porch. We waited together until everyone had left, then longer in silence as he turned his thoughts to words.

"I've never killed a man," he said, finally. "But I've

killed a lot of animals. I've skinned a lot of animals."

We waited again as he remembered and I imagined all those lives, all those skins.

"Hunters usually want a trophy," he said, with some distaste. I knew he disliked the idea of hunting just for sport, though he would never deny the sport in hunting. But economic necessity had made him a guide for others. "It's usually the head."

I nodded, but still didn't say anything. He wasn't finished.

"A moose has got a brain no bigger than my fist." He made a fist. "A wolf's is even smaller. I've always wondered how something so small could be so important, how that one little organ can control so much flesh and bone, so many actions and thoughts. You can hardly call them thoughts, though, can you? It's instinct. They don't have to think about how to stalk an animal, how to kill it, how to couple with their mate, or how to escape from a hunter. It's all instinct. We catch them because we're smarter than them, usually." He hesitated. "Maybe...maybe the beast could change itself into a wolf, but then it couldn't change back."

Finally it was my turn to speak.

"You mean, it wasn't smart enough any more?"

"Maybe."

I thought for a moment.

"That's absurd," I told him.

"Yes," he agreed, "it is."

I thought for another moment.

"God is good," I said, as if that explained everything, or even *some*thing.

Joel shook his head. "God is *right*," he said. "As for good, maybe that's just something we made up."

I looked past the portico of the church to the forest, which started a stone's throw from where I stood and continued east and west to two oceans and north to the barren lands. I thought, for a moment, of a strange tribe damned for the remainder of natural life to that vast and trackless land, killing, eating raw flesh, dying violently at the hands of nature or others like themselves. How many legends might spring from such a hapless fate – tales of evil spirits, of cries in the night, of faces on the edge of the fire, of creatures almost human in their ferocity and greed?

I shook my head. It was too much to think about.

I breathed deeply in the clean northern air, acutely conscious of being alive, of being a priest, of being who I am. I went back into the church. I glanced up at the tortured man hanging eternally on his cross. Had that *really* been necessary to redeem miserable mankind? I wondered.

I shook my head again.

God is indeed good, I thought.

I was not yet ready to concede that he was right.

SHADOW BOXING

"The creature had the head of a rat and the body of a man, a well-built man with broad shoulders and a narrow waist. It wore a double-breasted suit, grey with gold buttons, the shoulders padded. Its face was expressionless. 'What are you?' I asked. It didn't answer. It came toward me. I watched it as if I were a camera moving in. Smaller and smaller parts of it grew larger and larger until there was nothing but a single staring eye, black as ebony. Still it came closer, until our lenses fused. Then I fell through...."

"You fell through?"

"I fell through its eye and tumbled into nothingness."

There was a long silence. Finally, Dr. Hillary said, "How long have you kept this from me?"

"Weeks." Joseph shrugged. "Months, maybe."

The doctor shifted in his chair, a sure sign of annoyance. "You of all people should appreciate the importance of dreams."

"Of course."

"Can you think of any reason why this particular dream should be significant?"

Joseph thought a moment. "It was the day I learned that my nephew was a Satanist."

Hillary frowned. It was unprofessional to register disapproval in front of the patient, but in this case the psychiatrist's views were well known – as, indeed, were the patient's.

"By 'Satanist' I presume you mean a priest of the Universal Brotherhood."

"Call them what you like," Joseph said. "They worship Satan and they practice human sacrifice."

"Only on the aged and the infirm, or on those who request it. And with the blessing of the state, I might add. It is a simple ritual. They inflict no pain."

"How comforting," said Joseph. "And of course you approve, Doctor. Your views are well known."

"I neither approve nor disapprove," said the psychiatrist. "I am not a religious person."

"You don't have to be a religious person to disapprove of devil worship or human sacrifice."

"Satan is just a word, more theory than reality, and harmless enough if it brings people comfort." They had been over this ground a hundred times before. "Are you close, you and your nephew?"

"He's my brother's child. They left the capital years ago. I hardly know him."

"Yet you are afraid of him."

"I am afraid *for* him – and for his children, and my sister's children, and their husbands and wives, and their children."

"How on earth does it affect them?"

"Evil is insidious."

"That is rather an antiquated notion for an educated man."

"I believe," Joseph began…but you had to be careful what you said about what you believed. You couldn't always tell what was real and what was shadow. "I believe, Doctor, that there is something on the other side that we trifle with at our peril."

"The other side of what?"

"Of life. Of death."

"But you are a rational man."

"That is why I believe it." Dr. Hillary frowned again, then tried to mask the expression when he found Joseph gazing at him with a not unfriendly interest. The psychiatrist was irritated. Did the fool not realize how lucky he was to have been assigned to him rather than one of the behaviour modification crowd with their implements and chemicals?

Indeed, Joseph knew it, and he knew better than to make overtures of friendship. But still he looked, and his compassion, if involuntary, was intractable. Suddenly he smiled. It was a calculated affront. A face devoid of judgement or discrimination, he knew, a face without opinion or even prejudice, is a face with no more intelligence than a rock. The doctor's frown had given much away.

"Our time is up," Hillary said shortly.

He said it every week. One of these days, Joseph thought, he was going to be right.

He rose and held out his hand boldly. The doctor's displeasure showed yet again. The smile had been bad enough, but this gesture of manly goodwill was entirely inappropriate. Their relationship, nonetheless, might be prejudiced by the doctor's refusal to accept it. Reluctantly, he offered his own hand in return.

Joseph left, imagining the doctor washing those limp, damp appendages at the stainless steel sink in the corner of his office, and laughed. Even so, he washed his own hands in the first public lavatory he came to.

He was spending the summer in the hills, driving down to the capital each day for his shift at the factory and driving back in darkness to his camp above the river. He was lucky to get four or five hours sleep in a night, so busy was he with breaking the law. And once a week, at the court's insistence, he drove in for his visit to Dr. Hillary. It had been the tribunal's opinion, widely publicized, that Joseph was not-quite-harmlessly mad, but that a weekly visit, at the state's expense, to the celebrated psychiatrist should deburr the rough edges of his psychosis enough to make him fit company for his fellow citizens. Dr. Hillary, of course, knew that Joseph was not mad, but he dared not know, or let on that he knew, the extent of his sanity.

"You don't have to stay, you know," Hillary had told him once in an unguarded moment. "You could go north, to the barren lands, be a free man."

"The barren lands," said Joseph, imagining endless

vistas of rock and snow, with only the occasional burnt-out husk of a building to remind him of the great cleansing. "The borders are watched."

"More to keep undesirables out than to keep them in," the doctor remarked. "With your connections, I'm sure you could find a way. Plenty of your kind left in the barren lands, I'm told."

Joseph shrugged. "These lands seem more barren to me, somehow."

So he stayed. And so they sparred, once a week, like shadow boxers who cannot decide which of them is real and which is shadow. Sometimes it was amusing. Sometimes it was almost enjoyable. It was always a challenge. The danger was in thinking it might be beautiful. It was not. However graceful the feints and parries, however clever the attack or the defence, it was not beautiful, nor ever could be.

And Joseph returned each night to his camp above the river, where he could see the lights of the capital stretching from horizon to horizon, and could almost feel the throbbing of a million hearts.

There will be wars and rumours of wars. There will be famines and earthquakes. People will betray one another and hate one another. Love will grow cold. But anyone who stands firm to the end will be saved.

"Stand firm," he said, to the city and to the night. "Stand firm!" he shouted, and the words came back at him from the echoing hills: *firm...firm...firm....*

Everything seemed different since the dream, from the way a door opened or a candle burned to the way the cars approached him on the highway, swooping down the overpass like vengeful angels drunk with speed and power. And the beast, the great dark beast that followed him through the night.

"Stand firm!" he shouted again, and the words came echoing back: *firm...firm...firm....*

"You never give up, do you?" said a voice behind him.

Joseph turned to greet the young woman who had spoken. Ragged clothes and unkempt hair could conceal neither her gender nor her beauty. Joseph ached at the sight of her, she looked so like her mother at that age: strong, healthy, joyously female, with a glow of pure life about her that made him want to weep at his own inadequacy.

"I can't think what you mean, Annie."

"Even when no one is listening, you have to preach."

"You were listening."

She smiled. "How did it go today, Uncle?"

"Nothing changes. 'Are you still breaking the law?' he asks. 'Flagrantly,' I reply. He tells me to stop. I say I can't. Then we spend fifty minutes analyzing my psychoses. We shadow box. Nothing changes."

"Come and sit by the fire. Mother's awake. She's been asking for you."

He followed Annie along the winding track, defined more by shadow than by light, that led down to the sheltered place away from the wind and the prying eyes of those who sought him, for good or ill. He followed her, unsettled by the rise and fall of her woman's buttocks, the swing of her hips, the overt *femaleness* of her. According to the fashion of the age, she was modest, even prudish. Sixteen years old and still a virgin.

Unheard of. Still, Joseph could have wished she were not so unequivocally sexual.

"A group arrived after you left this morning," she said over her shoulder. "Women mostly, a few children. They'd been walking all night."

"Did they bring food?"

"They offered what they had."

"Which wasn't enough," Joseph interpreted.

"No, but we have extra from –"

"Child," he interrupted her, "you know we would have to feed them even if we didn't have extra."

"Of course, Uncle, but all they want –"

"I know what they want," he interrupted again. "Is it safe?"

"They showed the proper signs," she nodded. "Are you ready?"

"I'm never ready."

"But you will do it?"

"I will do it."

A faint breeze brought the sweet poplar smoke to his nostrils before he saw the fire. There was still some distance to go. He wondered if he should tell her about the beast. There was nothing she could do, of course, and she was so young. But he valued her wisdom.

"I would like..." he began. She did not prompt him, which had the effect of prompting him despite himself. "I would like your opinion, Annie."

"You don't have to ask for my opinion," she said lightly. "You know I'll give it anyway."

"Every night when I turn off the highway, I feel a presence of some kind."

She slowed, but did not turn. "A presence?"

"As if something were following me, a great dark beast loping along beside me in the ditch."

"Does it have a species?"

"Feline, I think."

"A panther," she suggested. "Perhaps it's your spirit animal."

"Perhaps." Drawing abreast of her as the path widened, her face came out of shadow and looked at him clearly. She was so like her mother, he thought again. So beautiful....

"Or it could be your cousin."

She frowned. "Is it malevolent?"

"No, but neither is it benevolent. It's just there, a dark presence loping along beside me in the ditch."

"Male or female?"

"Does it matter?"

"If it's your spirit animal it's probably male."

"I don't get that sense from it."

She was agitated. Perhaps he should not have told her. He tried to change the subject: "Has your mother had much pain today?"

"Where does it leave you?" she demanded.

"What?"

"This animal," she said, "this creature that lopes along beside you. You said it picks you up as you turn off the highway...."

"No, I didn't. If anything, I pick it up. As to where it leaves me, I couldn't say. It's nothing that definite. It's a presence. I don't actually see anything. I sense it."

"Okay, when do you stop sensing it?"

"I suppose" – he thought a moment – "I suppose it's by the first lookout."

"So it doesn't follow you into camp?"

"Not so far as I know," he said.

"So it can't be just a shadow," she said.

It had been a mistake to tell her. He had been hoping, he realized, that she would tease him with it, rob the creature of its significance. He should have known better.

"I must say" – he deliberately lightened his tone – "I didn't expect you to take it so seriously. I just thought it might amuse you."

She gave him a sharp look. "You don't expect me to believe that."

"Well, it's not the first time I've been accused of seeing things that aren't there. As you know, the state thinks I'm quite mad."

"So do I, sometimes."

She glared at him a moment, then something inside her seemed to give way all at once, to accept defeat, although no battle had been joined. Her shoulders, her whole body, seemed to sag.

"There have been more mutilations," she said. "In the east pasture this time. The usual thing, cows and horses, no obvious cause of death, genitals surgically removed. I just thought maybe, if this beast of yours was real...." She let the sentence trail off.

"I'm afraid the mutilations will turn out to have an all-too-human explanation," said Joseph gently. "The sects are growing daily."

She nodded. "I'll post more guards in the east pasture."

"Do we have more guards to post?"

281

"I wasn't speaking literally," she said, leading him into the clearing where there were some fifty people awaiting him – a hundred if you counted their shadows – mostly women and children, as Annie had said. As one, they looked up, at first in fear, then he raised his hand in the sign they all recognized, and their apprehension gave way to hope.

He prepared to break the law, as he did every day, sometimes twice, occasionally even three times, depending on the need. It was an odd sort of law, he thought, that only he could break, an odd sort of law that took him into the capital once a week to spar with the celebrated psychiatrist. Shadow boxing, indeed. Which of them was the shadow?

But he saw the people were assembled, saw his sister, Annie's mother, being brought out from the tent where she lay dying. Was he really the last one, as they believed? It was impossible to say. He put on the clothing, ragged and patched after so many uses, that made him visibly different from the others. He arranged the items on the table before him – "the visible means of invisible treason," the court had called them – and bent to press his lips to the table itself. Rising, he saw his shadow fall across the vessels. He looked about him, at his sister and her daughter, their friends, the group that had arrived that day, unknown faces, hidden intentions. Any one of them might be a spy, an agent of the state or of the Brotherhood. He preferred to think, instead, that one of them might be an angel.

He opened his arms as if in welcome, and said, "Let us begin our celebration in the name of the Father, and of the Son, and of the Holy Spirit...."

COYOTE

It was a filthy night. The wind had been gusting from the northwest all day, and in the evening it brought rain, a spattering at first that swept the dust from the sky and streaked the windows black, and then a howling downpour that forced its way between the cracks of sills and panes to soak the walls and puddle on the floor. The dogs retreated to the farther room, cowards all, whining like pups as shrieks of lightning assailed their singular sins like the priests of hell demanding confession and repentance. I opened the door of the woodstove in order to gaze at the flames, and wrapped myself in a blanket with a hot rum toddy and a candle beside me – the lights had been the first to fail – and between the claps of thunder I read Montaigne's essay on the power of the imagination. But words, whole paragraphs, escaped me as heaven bat-

283

tered at my shelter. When I had finished my drink I made another, then another, the kettle simmering on the woodstove, until I could no longer separate anxiety from curiosity. I put my book aside, blew out the candle and stood by the window to see what God might reveal to me between the strobes of lightning and the violent darkness.

There was a coyote, limping and sodden, skulking across the yard.

There was a stag by the edge of the wood, transfixed in the furious light.

There was a fox, grinning and fearless, hunting through the storm.

There was a cross, a sudden vision struck by lightning in the cemetery across the field; I could almost hear the dead bones rattling in their graves.

There was an old man wrapped in a blanket, labouring up the drive.

I blinked and looked again, but he was lost in shadow. I saw the trees bending and swaying, a darker darkness against the ravaged sky. I sensed the space around me stretching and contracting as wind and rain defined their kingdoms. I felt the shell of wood and glass that protected me shudder in resistance.

There he was again, fifty paces closer, braids flying in the wind like snakes on the Medusa. I was conscious of a momentary fear, then simple curiosity as the knock came at the door.

I was greeted by a face as deep as legend. He spoke in a language I did not know. When it became apparent that I was lost in his tongue, he switched to mine.

"My name is Lonethunder," he said simply. "I have had a dream."

"Good for you," I replied.

He would say no more until I had invited him in. I could hardly blame him. The wind was threatening to sweep us both into the darkness. I gestured a brief welcome. He responded with a mixture of gratitude and satisfaction, as though I had passed the first of several tests in which he had taken a personal interest. He handed me his saturated blanket and went directly to the stove, shedding jacket and shirt on the way. In the glow of the fire I watched as he proceeded to strip off his boots, jeans, socks, undershirt, and finally a tattered pair of jockey shorts that might have been mistaken for a piece of netting. Naked and brown, his skin hanging like limp leather on once-powerful muscles, he raised his arms and warmed himself, turning in a slow circle to expose each part of his body to the warmth.

"Ah," he said, "God is good."

"If you say so."

I relit the candle and lifted the kettle and made us a couple of rum toddies, mixing the strong dark liquor with hot water and sugar and a squeeze of lemon juice. The old man drank his greedily and held out his glass for another.

"Would you like a robe?" I asked.

He nodded. "And another hot rum toddy."

I brought him my housecoat and his second drink.

"There was a coyote and a fox and a stag in the yard," he said, slipping his arms into the woollen sleeves and wrapping the belt around his ample belly. "Coyote is a trickster; he never is what he appears. Fox is sly, but not smart like Coyote; he lives by instinct, not by wit. Stag is noble and proud, and frequently eaten. Which would you rather be?"

"Coyote," I said. It seemed obvious.

"Why?"

"Because Fox survives by instinct alone, and Stag seems a bit of a dork."

He smiled. "Now, why do you think your woman left you?"

"Because she prefers dorks to coyotes?" It did not occur to me to wonder how he knew.

He smiled again. "Humour is the beginning of wisdom."

He turned to face the stove and opened wide the housecoat to expose his flesh to the flames. The rainwater dripped from his braids and puddled on the floor. I was glad he was facing away from me, that sagging flesh, *memento mori*. I was still young enough, or so I flattered myself, to rebuild my life. But here was a life that was nearly over.

"One of your own medicine men said that life was a brief interval between two great mysteries," he said, turning to face me. "Do not pity me, Coyote. I am embarking, not departing."

If it was strange to hear the words of Carl Jung on the lips of my visitor, it was stranger still to hear nothing from the dogs. Normally their territorial instincts would have overcome any wrath from heaven, and they would have greeted the arrival of a stranger with barks and howls to rival the pounding of the rain and the thundering discontent of the lightning. But they were quiet, not even whining.

"They sleep," said the old man, again plucking the thought from my mind. "They know who I am. More important, they know who they are, and they are content."

Suddenly it was all too much: the dogs, the storm, the unlikely concatenation of wild creatures in the yard, and the even more unlikely old man who had materialized out of nowhere. It was the rum. Josie had always complained that I drank too much, and here was proof: without even noticing, I had become too drunk to separate reason from fancy. I was pissed on solitude and hot rum toddies, willing to accept irrational experience as part of the normal fabric of life. I put down my glass and picked up my book and sat in my chair by the stove and began to read:

> A strong imagination creates the event, say the scholars. I am one of those who are very much influenced by the imagination. Everyone feels its impact, but some are overthrown by it....

I looked up. The old man was still there, wringing out his braids.

"What did you say your name was?"

"Lonethunder."

"Apt," I said, as the windows shuddered in their panes. I couldn't believe the dogs were sleeping through this. "You said you'd had a dream."

"We will eat first."

He was taking a good deal for granted, I thought. But on the instant I was conscious of a gnawing in my belly, as if I hadn't eaten all day. In fact, I realized, I hadn't.

"We will take meat together," said Lonethunder.

I wasn't sure about meat, but I knew there was some broccoli in the fridge, a bag of carrots, and I always had bread and cheese. Maybe there was still a chicken in the freezer, but I couldn't hope to thaw one in time to eat it tonight.

"Venison," said the old man.

"I'm afraid I —"

"You will find a well-cured haunch on the doorstep."

"Why on earth" — I was ravenous at the thought of it — "didn't you bring it in?"

He shrugged, an eloquent gesture of shoulder and brow. "I wasn't sure of my welcome."

A furred creature fled snarling into the storm as I threw open the door. A fox or a coyote, I couldn't tell. The important thing was that it had only managed to take a couple of bites. I picked up the haunch of meat and brought it inside, cradling it in my arms as if it were a child. It was a deep and lustrous wine colour, with the faintest streaks of white running through the flesh.

"A knife," Lonethunder commanded. "A frying pan. Wild mint, if you have it. A bit of salt."

I surrendered the meat reluctantly and went into the kitchen. Of course I had no wild mint, but I brought him oregano and thyme, dill weed, sweet basil, and rosemary. He sniffed each judiciously, selected the rosemary, and sent me back to the kitchen for butter and a whetstone. Luckily, I had both. He directed me to stoke the fire while he sharpened the knife.

He cut thin scallops from the joint and fried them in butter, sprinkling them lightly with herbs and salt. The aroma was maddening, but still the dogs did not wake. When finally he speared one of the pieces of meat and held it out to me, I took it in my bare hands and bit into it, careless of the heat and the juices running down my chin. It was heaven. It was comfort and ease. It was an unspoken prayer answered by a savage god. Stag had died for this, I thought, and I was more grateful than Stag would ever know.

Lonethunder ate as I did, taking the sizzling meat in his hands and downing it wolfishly. We were throw-backs, the pair of us. We were no better than animals, rending the flesh from a fellow being and devouring it like primitive carnivores. We ate with the raw lust of hunger, and it was a glorious thing.

We sated ourselves, and then the dogs finally awoke. Barney came in first, the golden retriever who had to my knowledge never retrieved anything more useful than a stick. Close on his heels was the mongrel Xerxes, half the size, whom I had saved from an ignominious death at the hands of the SPCA. Last, as usual, came Napoleon, Josie's single-minded Cairn terrier who, when push came to shove, had refused to get into the car with his mistress and so had been left behind. They had all been "fixed," as the euphemism has it. If dogs could talk, I have no doubt they would have spent long hours discussing the circumstances under which each had sacrificed his balls to the greater good.

Thinking such thoughts as the dogs came in, I was beset by an obscure anxiety that the old man would know, somehow, and disapprove. However, he simply gathered them around him on the floor and cut pieces from the still-ample joint and fed it to them raw. They were remarkably civil about it. Only once did the ever-ravenous Xerxes manage to snatch a chunk of meat that had been meant for Barney, and he was rewarded by missing his turn the next time round.

When he was finally cutting the last slivers of flesh from the bone, the old man looked up at the ceiling and cocked his head to one side. "The storm is passing," he said. "We have been spared."

"This time," I said.

He nodded sagely. "You are learning, Coyote."

I wasn't sure that I appreciated the appellation. Coyote is a trickster. He never is what he appears. I thought of the coyote I had seen earlier crossing the yard, limping and sodden, the very image of defeat. What had he really been up to?

"You said you'd had a dream," I said.

"It can wait," he said, and without another word he lay down among the dogs and went to sleep.

The storm passed, as Lonethunder said it would, and I awoke to a world as fresh and clean as Eden. The air was pure, the clarity of the light almost painful. Even the destruction of nature – the broken limbs, the flattened grass, the upturned pails and garden furniture – seemed somehow right, as if they pointed to a separate, a deeper meaning of things. The dogs followed me out to the yard as I made my morning recognizance. The geese in the pond at the bottom of the garden honked a discordant greeting, and Xerxes went after them, as he always did, baying like the noble hound he obviously wasn't, stopping at the water's edge, afraid of getting his feet wet. Napoleon followed, yapping instructions at Xerxes or the geese, I was never sure which. Barney, who was above such things, or perhaps simply too stupid to recognize an essential function of his genes, trotted contentedly at my side. The single cross that surmounted the plot of ancient graves across the field seemed to shine in the morning light.

"Ah yes," said Lonethunder, who had materialized at my side, "the *mooniyas* trinity."

I supposed it was his function to be enigmatic, mine to be credulous.

"The Father, the Son, and the Holy Spirit?" I inquired.

"No," he said. "The cross, the clock, and the dollar. Many have forsaken the cross for the clock and the dollar. Few have forsaken the dollar for the cross, and even fewer have forsaken the clock."

As if to punctuate his statement, the bells from the nearby monastery began to toll, summoning the brothers to morning prayer. There had been a time when I might have joined them, but I had found that no amount of prayer could compensate for a failed marriage, too many debts, and not enough rum.

"Do you want some breakfast?" I asked, thinking what a happy marriage might be made between a cup of coffee and a tot of Captain Morgan.

"Let us first visit the dead," he said, and he struck across the field toward the graveyard. I followed, having nothing better to do at the moment, and the dogs followed because they never had anything better to do. It wasn't long before Napoleon's little legs were floundering in the mud, and I picked him up and carried him, an action he invariably regarded as proof of his superiority, which he made no attempt to conceal from his fellows. The smaller the dog, I reflected, the larger the ego. I wondered if there might be some faint correlation between humans and dogs in that regard.

Lonethunder plodded ahead, the rich wet earth squishing up between his bare toes. He was still wearing my housecoat, a comfortable woollen thing that Josie had made me in the first year of our marriage. I had not worn it myself for ages.

"This one," he said, pointing to a modest headstone worn by time and weather, "was alive when my grandmother died, and this one" – he pointed to another – "might have known my father. You are blessed to live so near those who have gone before."

I hated to disappoint him, but none of these were kin to me. They were of a different past entirely. Indeed, twice in the past century my ancestors had shed blood to prevent such as these from taking over the world.

"You are wrong," he said, with that annoying facility he had for reading my mind. "These were conquerors of a different sort. They sought not this world but the next."

I raised my head at a familiar sound. A crow was struggling up from the distant wood, crying like a child.

It was wounded and in pain, or so it appeared. I raised my eyes higher and saw the hawk circling against the sun, assured of its prey. But the crow lived by wit, and as the higher creature gathered its wings and dove for the kill, the darker bird suddenly regained the full power of flight and gracefully swept out of the way. And suddenly there were two crows in the air, dodging and feinting to confuse the hawk, drawing the predator away from the fledglings in the nest. I had witnessed the scene a hundred times. There were always crows in the distant wood. There were always hawks in the sky. But there were always more crows than hawks, and it amazed me how easily the hawks were duped.

"Brother Crow," said Lonethunder, "will throw his siblings out of the nest to assure his own survival, and a year later he will risk his life to protect a fledgling like himself who would murder his brothers and sisters. I have often wondered why God does not leave them all to the hawks."

"But there would be no crows then," I said.

"Exactly," he replied, "and Stag would rot where he died, and Gopher and Squirrel would multiply beyond imagining, and you would be slaughtering the songbirds to shut up their din."

"Is there a point to this?" I asked, for I was growing weary of his ponderous wisdom.

He thought a moment. "There was a time," he said, "when the buffalo outnumbered the crows and the hawks, the gophers and the squirrels, the songbirds, the stags and the does, the coyotes and the foxes. There was enough for all, and more than enough. Then they were gone. In a single generation." He shook his head sadly. "Have you ever wondered at how easily you defeated us? I can tell you in a single word: buffalo."

"And I can tell you in another: sheep."

"Sheep?"

I nodded. "My family fled the Highland Clearances in 1814, the Year of the Burning, when the lairds decided there was more profit to be got from sheep than from crofters, and they burned our cottages even as they evicted us. The few who did not die of poverty and disease have spent a long time wondering at how easily we were defeated."

He gave me a searching look. "This still touches you, Coyote."

I shrugged. "It was a long time ago."

"I will tell you my dream," he said, casting his eyes over the gravestones and the single cross. "It is a fitting place."

I put Napoleon down in the furrows to fend for himself a while. He seemed anxious to murder a butterfly that had been troubling the graves.

"I prayed for guidance in the winter of my years," the old man said, "and the spirits took me to a village by a stream. There were eighteen tipis, and women, and many children. There were a few old men, but the young men were away at the hunt. The women were preparing for their return. The knives were sharpened and the fire pits were ready. Hides stuffed full with saskatoon berries were gathered for making pemmican, along with wild mint and onions and all the other things God had placed on the earth for our use. There were dogs and horses, too, though of course the men had taken the best of the horses to the hunt. Overhanging all was an air of waiting, of expectancy...

"And of sorrow, too, for in one of the tipis a young man had been left behind who was dying of the fever. The spirits took me to his side, and I saw that there were sores on his body and blood in his mouth. A woman was bathing him with cool water from the stream, but still he burned. His eyes were dead already. His spirit was just waiting for a propitious moment to depart.

"And I was it, apparently. I was the moment. For as I hovered over him in my dream, his eyes suddenly came alive again, they shone like the moon, and he looked directly at me and said, 'Carry me home, Lonethunder.' Then he was gone, and I was gone, and I awoke with a great sorrow in my heart, for I had asked for guidance and the spirits had given me pain instead.

"The men returned without meat, for the buffalo were gone, and they packed up the village and moved toward the sunset, where the medicine man told them the buffalo still flourished. He was wrong, of course. It was no more than a wishful dream. But the woman who had been bathing the young man stayed behind to mourn him a while, and then she left with her baby, his daughter, in another direction, leaving her tipi where it stood, with the body of her husband inside, laid out in his graveclothes, for she had not the strength to honour him as she should.

"It was then I awoke for the second time, and I knew what I had to do."

He had begun walking back toward the house. I hurried to catch up, leaving little Napoleon to flounder in the mud behind us.

"Which was?" I asked.

"Why, to find him, of course, and carry him home."

"But you don't even know who he was."

"He was my grandfather," said Lonethunder. He stopped. "And the woman" – he looked at me directly – "the woman who was bathing him was your great, great grandmother."

"That's impossible!"

He laughed, a great thundering roar that gave meaning to his name. "I told you, Coyote never is what he appears."

"It's impossible," I repeated. "I've traced my family back ten generations. There are parish records – births, deaths, marriages. We arrived in Canada in 1820, in Montreal. A generation later we were settled in Ontario. But no one ventured further west than that until my parents came to Saskatchewan in 1955. I remember my grandfather speaking Gaelic, for Christ's sake, and my father still had a few words of it when he died."

"I can imagine a few births and deaths, even marriages, that might not have been recorded in your parish records," said Lonethunder, and he began to walk again. "I can imagine a younger son looking for adventure, going west with a trading party, taking a country wife, perhaps, as was the custom, and leaving a fair-haired child behind when he returned to his version of civilization. It is a common story, but one that would not be told, I think, in the drawing rooms of Ontario. I can even imagine that child, nurtured on stories of his great *mooniyas* father, setting out to find him when he was grown, and eventually being accepted, if not welcomed, by a family whose conscience would not allow them to do otherwise. That is a less common story, but one more worth the telling, I think."

"Do you have any proof of this?" I demanded.

"Proof?" He shook his head. "*Mooniyas* always looks for proof. Is it not enough that you are here, and I am here? If your tribe had had bits of paper scrawled with words, would it have prevented the chiefs from turning you out and setting fire to your homes? No, Coyote, all the proof you need is in your heart."

We had reached the house again – me, the old man, and the dogs, even little Napoleon who had somehow navigated the furrows and the stubble and the mud to arrive, short-legged and breathless and not a little put out, at my feet. The old man paused at the door. He pointed to the pond at the bottom of the garden where the geese were nesting.

"That is the water," he said, "that your great, great grandmother drew to soothe her husband's fever. That is the field" – pointing to the graveyard – "where the hunters returned empty handed. And that is the wood" – pointing again – "where the women gathered fuel for the fire pits.

"I have come," he said, "to carry my grandfather home."

We broke our fast with bread and cheese and strong black coffee. The bread I had made myself two days before. The cheese was ordinary Canadian cheddar from the Co-op. Lonethunder ate little, preferring to portion out his breakfast in bits and scraps to the hovering dogs.

"You'll make them fat," I scolded him.

He shrugged. "Perhaps that is their fate."

I was remembering my grandparents, stalwart middle-class Ontario Tories, white as any WASP, but with a critical difference: they were Catholic, and they clung to the outdated notion that religion was a commitment of the heart, not the social class, and so in many subtle ways in the society of southern Ontario they were outcasts, no better than the Irish or the Italians. At least, that was how it had been explained to me. But I remembered, too, a dark-haired aunt – not my aunt, my father's – a woman with high cheek bones and a gaze as searing as an eagle's. A throwback, she called herself, a Pictish woman from the hollow hills. One never knew when those ancient genes might spring forth again to embarrass a respectable family.

It was a joke, of course...or perhaps not quite a joke. And perhaps the throwback was not twenty generations, but only two....

I needed a drink. I took my coffee to the kitchen and spiked it liberally with Captain Morgan. Lonethunder, damn him, caught me in the act.

"Are you so ashamed of us," he asked, "that you would dull your wits with alcohol rather than talk with me about your family?"

"You're going to have to stop materializing out of nowhere," I told him. "It's quite unnerving."

"You haven't answered my question."

I took a defiant quaff of my coffee-and-rum. "How would you feel," I demanded, "if you'd spent your whole life as an Indian and suddenly one night an ancient Scotsman showed up and told you that your name was MacDonald?"

"But it is," he said.

I choked briefly. "I...I beg your pardon?"

"My family name is MacDonald. My father was called Angus. He was proud of it."

"So where does Lonethunder come from?"

"That is the name that was given to me by an elder when I reached manhood. As yours," he added meaningfully, "was given to you last night, Coyote. My name is Lonethunder, but when my pension cheque arrives at the end of every month, it is made out to Dermott MacDonald."

I knew there was not enough rum in the world to get me out of this, and I emptied my mug into the sink. "What you're telling me, then, is that I'm an Indian."

"No more than I am *mooniyas*, Coyote. But if you cut us open, you'll find that we all look the same inside."

"Pah!" To the best of my knowledge it was the first and only time I have uttered the word. "I have to let the ducks out."

The ducks were a minor source of income. They kept the insects down in the yard, and I sold them live in the fall on the understanding that what happened to them after they left the yard was no concern of mine. I had no trouble killing chickens – there is nothing like the sight of a hen making off with her sister's recently severed head to spur one on to further decapitations – but I had been growing increasingly uncomfortable about the ducks, whom I found quite companionable in their way. It seemed unfair to gain their trust and friendship only to sell them into certain death a few months down the road. Ironically, or perhaps prophetically, I had always given them names, like Angus and Dermott.

It was Dermott who led the procession down to the pond as I let them out of their night-time shelter, and he waddled like a self-satisfied English butler at the head of a column of half-grown footmen and house-maids on their way to the servants' hall for tea. On the instant, I decided that none of these would die by my volition this year, and I was immediately conscious of a profound and unexpected sense of relief.

Once again Lonethunder materialized at my side.

"Little clowns," he observed.

"I find them rather endearing."

"The best clowns are, Coyote." He gazed around the yard, taking in the details. "The fire pits were over there." He pointed. "If you dig deep enough you will find ashes that are ten thousand years old, and the bones of buffalo that died before Moses led his people out of Egypt. The stream that feeds your duck pond" – again he pointed – "followed the same course for fifty thousand years until you dammed it to build the road and reduced it to a trickle through a culvert."

"*I* didn't dam it."

"Until *we* dammed it," he corrected himself. "We leave our footprints upon the earth, however carefully we tread."

I followed his gaze across the yard. Josie's footprints, I realized, were everywhere: the herb garden by the kitchen, the rock garden by the pond, the vegetable garden, the flower garden, the paths from bed to bush and back again. She had spent her time here in a futile attempt to impose herself on the landscape, to tame it, to bend it to her will. I remembered her labouring through the long summer days, that fabulous body sweating freely in a halter top and the briefest of cut-off jeans, digging, planting, watering, nurturing, moving and rearranging, only to awake the next morning and find that the deer had eaten her seedlings, the rabbits had destroyed the lettuce, the moles and the voles had undermined the roots of her most delicate plants, and a billion insects had feasted on the leaves and flesh of her ambitions as if she had sown a hundred varieties of vegetables and flowers solely for their enjoyment. She was not a woman to be easily defeated, but a mere twenty seasons in this place had accomplished what thirty years of vigorous defiance had been unable to do before that. Interpreting her discontent in terms of her husband, therefore, she left him – not because she preferred dorks to coyotes, but because she could not admit that mere nature had got the better of her.

In her last year with me, I remembered, she claimed to have discovered a circle cut into the earth, with rocks buried at the four points of the compass. It took a considerable exercise of the imagination for me to differentiate the shallow circularity from the surrounding yard, even when she paced it out, walking the circumference as if she had laid out the circle herself in a previous life. The shape became marginally more apparent when she mowed the grass, but it still seemed little more than an idea. Even so, she found a significance to it that I failed to appreciate, and immediately set about transforming it according to her own vision. It was when the space refused to be transformed, when it became apparent that nothing but the wild prairie grasses would grow there, that she finally gave up and left.

"Lonethunder," I said, "I know where your grandfather died."

He nodded. "I have been waiting for you to show me."

I took him to Josie's circle at the edge of the yard. It was overgrown again, fecund with the same deep-rooted grasses that had flourished there since the last Ice Age. I showed him the stones that Josie had unearthed at the four points of the compass, and the others she had brought to try to complete the circle. I tried to find the flower beds she had laboriously laid out and planted, the lilies and anemones, the ornamental grasses, the gladioli and the tulips, the early blooming and the late dying, but there was no trace of them. She had envisioned a broad disc of riotous colour, with blossoms overtaking and supplanting one another in a continuous cycle from the first thaw in the spring to the first frost in the fall. But nature had resisted her. The earth itself had resisted her, and now there was no trace of her at all. For the first time I felt the magnitude of her defeat, and for the first time in two years I did not blame her for leaving.

The old man paced the circumference purposefully, as Josie had done. He halved the circle beneath his feet, then quartered it, alternately staring at the ground and at the sky. He shaded his eyes to watch the sun, then turned to see where his shadow fell. The trampled grass recovered and he trampled it again, his bare brown feet crushing stalk and stem against the moist earth. Finally he stopped and turned to me.

"What brought you here, Coyote?"

It was a question I had often asked myself, but I was no closer to an answer now than I had ever been. I shrugged, an ineffectual gesture. "Josie always said she wanted to live in the country."

He shook his head. "She brought you here because it was where you belonged, and she left you here for the same reason. I think we had the same dream, she and I, but she was not old enough to understand it." He made a self-deprecating gesture. "I have only now fully understood it myself."

I caught a movement in the corner of my eye. There was a coyote at the edge of the wood, a grinning face among the trees, watching. I wondered if it was the same coyote I had seen crossing the yard last night, limping and defeated, at the height of the storm.

"One of your medicine men taught that there was no path to God," said Lonethunder, speaking quietly, almost to himself. "Rather, there is an abyss, and you must close your eyes and leap into it."

I recognized the words of Francis of Assisi, the gentle lunatic who had exchanged privilege and reason for a life of abject poverty in the service of a voice only he could hear. Why should I be surprised? Had not the old man quoted Carl Jung the night before?

"I have leapt," he said, "and I have arrived."

There was a look of wonder on his face, mingled with an anguish I found painful to look at. He fell to his knees. I should have been frightened, I suppose, when the coyote broke from the wood and loped up to the old man's side. At the very least, I should have been surprised by this blatant violation of the natural order of things. Instead I was grateful, for the old man told me to leave him.

And so I left.

No doubt there were procedures to follow, laws to observe, authorities to notify. But no one was watching, so I simply dug the grave and laid him in it. Coyote watched from a safe distance – we did not yet trust one another – and when I was finished, he loped away.

ACKNOWLEDGEMENT

The introductory essay, "Cruise Control," appeared in a slightly different version in the spring 2002 issue of *In Medias Res*, a literary journal published at St. Thomas More College, University of Saskatchewan.

ABOUT THE AUTHOR

Donald Ward is a writer, editor, and designer. He is married to Colleen Fitzgerald and they have two daughters, Brigid and Caitlin. They live in Muenster, Saskatchewan, within earshot of the bells of St. Peter's Abbey.

HEROIC FANTASY VS.

neon dreams

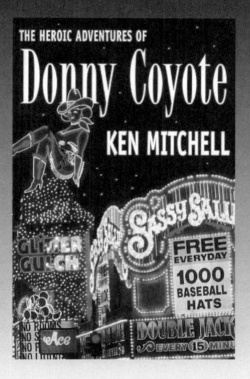

THE HEROIC ADVENTURES OF DONNY COYOTE

by Ken Mitchell

ISBN: 1-55050-263-8

A Superhero Story for Our Times

COTEAU BOOKS
WWW.COTEAUBOOKS.COM

Stories of heroic proportions are at Coteau Books